A SAM ACQUILLO HAMPTONS MYSTERY

Chris
Knopf

COP
JOB

The Permanent Press
Sag Harbor, NY 11963

Copyright © 2015 by Chris Knopf

For information, address:
The Permanent Press
4170 Noyac Road
Sag Harbor, NY 11963
www.thepermanentpress.com

Library of Congress Cataloging-in-Publication Data

Knopf, Chris—
    Cop job / Chris Knopf.
        pages ; cm. — (A Sam Acquillo Hamptons mystery)
    ISBN 978-1-57962-393-7
        1. Acquillo, Sam (Fictitious character)—Fiction. I. Title.

PS3611.N66C67 2015
813'.6—dc23   2015020499

Printed in the United States of America

CHAPTER ONE

I got there just in time to see the crane hoist Alfie Aldergreen out of Hawk Pond. He was still strapped in his motorized wheelchair. Grey green salt water poured off his rigid body and cascaded over the chair's tubular chrome framing. His head was twisted back and his eyes were closed, thank God, though his tongue, a swollen purple mass, protruded through his lips, which were partly chewed away.

Dead bodies are never pretty.

The scene was lit like a night game at Yankee Stadium. Cops in uniforms and political people from the town milled around. Few had official functions to perform, but all tried hard to look as if they did. I saw Joe Sullivan in the middle of it all, a Southampton Town detective upon whose broad shoulders the burden of sorting through this dreary affair had already settled.

I was called there by Jackie Swaitkowski, a lawyer who worked for a philanthropic law firm specializing in hard-luck cases like Alfie's. I saw her standing near the crane, wearing a summer suit with a hem an inch or two above the entirely professional, clutching herself around the middle in a rigid pose of shock and sorrow.

When I tried to go to her, a patrol cop stopped me by shoving the end of a nightstick in my chest.

"Step back," he said. "This is a secured area."

I looked down at the stick.

"I'm here with attorney Swaitkowski," I said.

I looked over his shoulder and the cop followed my gaze. As luck would have it, Joe Sullivan and Jackie were deep in conversation. The cop dropped the stick and I brushed by, making a little more body contact than was probably necessary.

"Oh, Sam," said Jackie, as I approached.

I let her put her arms around me, and even gave her a slight squeeze. Sullivan just stood there and waited.

"What the hell happened?" I asked him.

"Your friend Hodges was fishing off the breakwater. When the tide went out, he saw the top of Alfie's head. It was almost sunset before he realized what it was."

"Any ideas?" I asked.

"Not yet," he said. "Jackie?"

She looked down at the ground and shook her head.

"He's been very agitated lately. Paranoid. More than usual," she said, looking up at me.

We were all aware of Alfie's mood swings. A regular presence along Main Street in Southampton Village, year-round, Alfie was known to have conversations with himself, or people no one else could see. He was usually happily engaged, often playing a very credible alto saxophone, though sometimes his face was lit with fear, and he'd stop passersby to warn them of impending catastrophe.

I'd spent a fair amount of time with the guy, sitting next to his chair on a park bench drinking coffee I'd bought for the two of us. One time I had to talk down an angry shopkeeper who thought Alfie had stolen some of her merchandise, when in fact one of his invisible companions had made it a gift. That's when I introduced him to Jackie, whose free legal services became a regular necessity.

"Not like suicidal or anything?" I asked.

Jackie looked around the area where we stood—a parking lot serving a boat launch adjacent to the harbor's breakwater.

"How far are we from the Village?" she asked. "Eight, ten miles? How would he even get here?"

"There were no wheelchair tracks leading up to the breakwater," said Sullivan, nodding toward a gravel-covered area cordoned off with yellow tape. "He'd have to fly to get there himself."

"Any other tracks?" I asked.

"Trucks, trailers, footprints everywhere. Nothing you could take an impression of. Not in gravel. We'll be back in the daylight for a closer look, but I wouldn't get your hopes up."

Alfie had a one-room apartment behind a small, freestanding art gallery a block from the center of Southampton Village. The gallery space changed hands every season, but the owner, Jimmy Watruss, let Alfie rent the back area for a small percentage of his disability check. Like Alfie, Jimmy was a veteran attached to a mechanized unit during the Iraq War. The only thing Alfie told me about his service was when the wizard Gandalf joined up with his platoon. Apparently his fellow soldiers demurred when he set out across the desert to challenge the rising threat of Mordor.

Back stateside, the army shrinks set him up with a drug regimen, and after a few months of observation, sent him into the civilian world. The first thing Alfie did was buy an old Fiat S1955 Ducati motorcycle, which he drove into a bridge abutment trying to avoid a volcano that had suddenly erupted on the New Jersey Turnpike.

The VA put most of him back together, but there was no saving the bottom half of his spinal cord.

Alfie wore his DCU—short for desert camouflage uniform— every day, though he'd never let people draw him into a conversation about the war. I don't know how he ended up living in Southampton. I never asked, and even if I had, he probably wouldn't have remembered. I did get to see his apartment once, when the batteries in his chair ran out and I volunteered to push him back home. The room was spare and immaculately clean, his uniforms and modest belongings neatly stored in portable, olive drab metal closets.

PAUL HODGES, who lived aboard an old forty-eight-foot Gulf-stream motor sailor in the Hawk Pond Marina, emerged from a cluster of men watching the crane. I waved him over. In his late sixties, Hodges's arms were still strung with ropey muscles, the legacy of long years in commercial fishing and construction and slinging questionable sustenance at his restaurant in Sag Harbor. Never an attractive man, age had been unkind to his grey puffs of curly hair and his face, which you might mistake for a less attractive version of Ernest Borgnine's.

"That poor son of a bitch sure didn't catch his share of luck," he said. Despite myself, my eyes were drawn to where Alfie sat in his DCUs, slumped over in his chair, his long brown hair stuck in sodden, forlorn strands across his face. He was guarded by two of Sullivan's men so no one could touch the body before the medical examiner arrived. Not that anyone wanted to.

"I feel bad about this," said Hodges. "There he was the whole time I'm fishing. I thought his hair was seaweed. Sorry," he added, looking over at Jackie.

"You ever see him motoring around the marina?" Sullivan asked.

Hodges shook his head. "Never seen him anywhere but the Village. Never really knew the guy. Not like these two," he added, using his thumb to point at Jackie and me.

"Was he on his meds?" Sullivan asked Jackie.

"I don't know. I'm his lawyer, not his caseworker. But I know who is. Esther Ferguson."

Sullivan looked at his notebook and wrote down her name. "I know Esther," he said. "Tough cookie."

Tough as in a cross between Joe Frazier and a rabid badger. She didn't like me, which placed her within a fairly crowded field. Her beef was my occasional intervention on behalf of Alfie, which offended her social worker prerogatives. I was offended that she didn't always do as good a job looking after her clients as she did upholding her exclusive right to their care.

So we were even.

"Alfie was murdered. That's the gist of it," I said.

"I could make a case for it being an accident, or suicide," said Sullivan. "But why?"

Sullivan had been a plainclothesman for about five years. Before that he was a patrol cop assigned to North Sea, the wooded, watery territory just north of Southampton Village. I lived in North Sea in a cottage off the Little Peconic Bay—when I wasn't staying on the *Carpe Mañana*, which was berthed next to Hodges's in the Hawk Pond marina.

A Smart Car pulled into the parking lot and I knew the medical examiner had arrived, based entirely on the weirdness of the vehicle.

Carlo Vendetti was a cheerful scarecrow of a guy with long, slippery black hair stuck out of his baseball cap, disguising the fact that the rest of his head was as bald as a baby's ass. You'd say he had a weak chin, if he actually had a chin. With a beak-like nose and black-rimmed glasses, Carlo was a right geek if there ever was one. That was okay with me. I got along fine with geeks.

"Sam the Man," he said, as he approached our little group. "Detective," he said to Sullivan. "And the most stunning defense attorney in the Eastern United States," he said to Jackie, taking her hand by the fingers and giving her knuckles a light kiss, much to her dismay.

"Hi, Carlo," she said, gently extracting her hand.

I didn't disagree with Carlo on Jackie's looks, I just never thought of her in that way. Too much of a tomboy, too frenetic and churned up with Catholic guilt and attention deficit disorder for my taste. I liked her better in the steady hands of her boyfriend, a guy about the size of a sequoia with the equanimity and forbearance to match.

"Come with me, doctor," said Sullivan, placing a guiding hand on the ME's back. "Let me introduce you to Alfie Aldergreen."

Hodges tagged along. I waited until they were all out of earshot, then asked Jackie, "What do you think?"

She pushed a wad of kinky reddish blonde hair back off her face, a gesture signaling equal parts confusion and distress.

"First I thought, 'Who'd want to kill a harmless, crazy guy in a wheelchair?'" she said. "But, of course, people like him get killed all the time just for being harmless and crazy."

"Did he say anything unusual last time you talked to him?" I asked.

"Like I told you, he was really worked up. He said a secret organization was out to get him. You know he was paranoid, but not that big on conspiracy theories. More focused on individuals. Conan the Barbarian comes to mind. Most would think crazy is crazy, but these folks have their themes. They usually don't deviate."

I'd spent enough time with Alfie to know that was true. His main thing was imaginary people, either inside his head or hanging around nearby. If you spent enough time with him, you could almost believe they were actually there.

"So no ideas," I said.

She shook her head, hard enough to cause the brushed-away hair to fall back into her face. She swept it back.

"Nothing. Zilch. In a big city you might think sicko sadists preying on the disabled. But we don't have that sort of thing around here, do we?" she asked, hopefulness in her voice.

"We might," I said. "Who knows."

"There's a cheerful thought."

I pulled her over to where officialdom circled Alfie's dead body. Carlo Vendetti had Alfie's shirt open and was feeling around his inert chest, looking inside his mouth, and probing his lower abdomen. I noticed Alfie's hands were wrinkled like an old lady's and there were red ligature marks on his forearms, just above where they'd been duct taped to the chair.

"I'll know a lot more when I get him on the table," Vendetti said to me, as if I had some official standing. "But since the water's still pretty cold for July, the body's in decent shape. There're no apparent wounds or contusions, no external bleeding, though there's salt water in his nose and mouth."

"How do you know that?" asked Sullivan.

"I can smell it," said Carlo, holding up a gloved hand. Everyone fought to keep the cringing under control. "Plus his skin is blue, indicating oxygen starvation, and his limbs are secured with duct tape."

"So?" Jackie asked.

"So he drowned. Correct that, he *was* drowned, intentionally. Not conclusive until we do the lab work, but you asked."

An ambulance came shortly after that, and Carlo directed Sullivan and his men on how to get Alfie out of his chair and onto a gurney. The chair went into the back of a police SUV as evidence and the paramedics got in the front seat of the ambulance, since there was no need for life support.

I hung around until the area was clear of all but a single patrol car left to secure the crime scene, then dragged Jackie over to my boat where we could have a few drinks in the cockpit with Hodges and settle our nerves for the tough night's sleep ahead.

"Why do I get the most upset when bad things happen to people with the least intrinsic value to society?" Jackie asked, looking down into a plastic cup full of red wine.

"I'd tell you if I knew what intrinsic meant," said Hodges.

I swirled around my own cup, giving the ice cubes a chance to chill the vodka to the proper temperature.

"We've got to let Sullivan get to Esther before we do," I said to Jackie, "but that's where I'd start. I'd also go see

Jimmy Watruss. He'll talk to me. I've done a lot of carpentry
work for him over the years."

"So he likes you?" Jackie asked.

"Didn't say that. Just said he'd talk to me."

"I'll be fishing," said Hodges. "In the Little Peconic."

IT WASN'T all that late when I got back to my cottage. My dog,
Eddie, was sitting on the lawn waiting for me, recognizing as
he always did the sound of my old Pontiac rumbling up the
street. As soon as I turned into the driveway, he jogged over
to the parking area so he could try to climb into my lap when
I opened the door. He never made it all the way in, and I
never made it out without a small struggle. It didn't matter
that we repeated this ritual several times a day. For him, at
least, it was endlessly engaging.

"Such a pain in the ass," I said, gently shoving him back
onto the grass, where he bounded off toward the cottage for
the next stage in the process. I followed.

Amanda Anselma met me out on the lawn, which wasn't a
surprise. She often drifted over to my cottage from next door
and let herself in when I wasn't around. Eddie didn't mind,
since she was a reliable source of Big Dog biscuits, a reward
he officially didn't qualify for, being more of a midsized dog.

She also fed him aged Brie and fresh grapes, biscotti and
prosciutto, albeit in small doses, so maybe that had something to do with it as well.

"I hope everything's okay," she said, as I slipped my right
arm around her and pulled her into me.

"It's not," I said, kissing her full on the lips. "I hope you
weren't worried."

"I always worry. Everything could be fine, but why waste
the emotion?"

"Somebody murdered Alfie Aldergreen," I said. "Dumped
him in his chair off the breakwater on Hawk Pond. Hodges
found him."

She pulled away from me so she could put her hand over her heart.

"That's horrible. Who did it?"

"No idea."

"I'm so sorry," she said. "I know how hard you tried to look after him."

"Sort of," I said. "Others did a lot more than me. Like Jackie. She's got that look on her face."

"The avenging angel?" she asked.

"Something like that."

We all went out to the sun porch, which was in its summer mode—storm windows off the screens, ceiling fan engaged, cool drinks in slippery wet glasses on the side tables. The Little Peconic Bay sending in the musical lap of tiny bay waves, the southwesterly breeze rippling the lawn, Eddie panting and slurping water from his bowl in the corner of the room.

"So what are you going to do?" Amanda asked.

"Find the bastards."

"Of course you are."

She chose that moment to thrust a slender, naked leg out from the silk robe she'd chosen to wear for the trip across our adjoining lawns. I got the not overly subtle message.

We hurried through the rest of our drinks and took it from there.

NOT LONG after that, the phone rang. It was Jackie.

"How often do you listen to your voice mail messages?" she asked.

"I never listen to my voice mail messages," I said, once I was awake enough to talk.

"Me neither. Most of the time. But I saw the little light on the answering machine and thought, what the hell."

"And?"

"It's Alfie. Two days ago," she said.

I listened to some clunking sounds as Jackie put her cell phone within proximity of the answering machine.

"Jackie, Jesus Christ, they're going to kill me," said the tinny, yet unmistakable voice of Alfie Aldergreen, clearly agitated. "I mean, after all these battles with the forces of eternal darkness, I get wasted by some cop job? What the hell is up with that?"

CHAPTER TWO

I once worked as an executive for a multinational industrial corporation where I was in charge of about a thousand people, mostly technicians and engineers. Now I'm a cabinetmaker working for a builder in Southampton, New York. I like this job better, though it doesn't pay as well.

The corporation is gone, sectioned off to eager bidders after it succumbed to an ugly financial scandal. I'm still here. So there you go.

I'm fifty-nine years old. It's not a bad age, though I wish I were more like thirty-nine. That's a better age, though I'd rather be thirty-nine without all the drama and trouble that went along with that time of my life.

I have no idea how old Eddie is, since I rescued him from the pound, though he seems like the same dog that first jumped into my car, tail sweeping the air in a gentle wave, mouth an eager grin.

We live together in an easy alliance. I feed him, give him shelter and complete freedom, and he lets me. I also hit golf balls off the breakwater above the pebble beach for him to retrieve, which he never tires of doing. Probably why both of us are more limber and lively than our ages should allow.

Remarkably enough, it's been about twelve years since I lost my job, and subsequently my wife, the big house, and all that money. I've recouped a bit since then, but not a day goes by that I don't miss things about my old life, while thanking God that it's gone forever. This is the kind of cognitive dissonance I specialize in, which will likely be the case to the end of days.

Amanda inherited the house next door, along with a lot of other houses, which she spends her days fixing up and selling. I help her out occasionally, though we know it's better for us to keep our homes and jobs separate. We still manage to visit each other a lot, facilitated by the convenient proximity.

Amanda turned forty-six the week before Alfie was killed. We celebrated by ignoring the birthday and getting drunk out in the Adirondack chairs we keep at the edge of our common breakwater. It takes a lot to get us drunk these days, but we gave it our all, and the fact that we woke up that morning still on the lawn was proof of success.

We did it all over again the night Alfie died. Whether we were in the mood for more denial or a new routine was settling in, it was hard to tell.

I was first up, and used the time to look at Amanda's beautiful Italian face, framed perfectly by an indomitable head of thick, auburn hair, seeing her brilliant green eyes flash open, uncomprehending at first, but then light up with gentle good humor.

"We passed out again," she said.

"We did."

"Who got the blankets?"

"I don't remember," I said.

"Does it matter?"

"No."

More than anything, this was the musical score accompanying my life. I liked how it sounded, though I didn't know exactly where it came from, or how long it would last. But who knows anything about good fortune, tight-lipped and capricious that it is.

"So now what?" she asked.

"Coffee," I said, forcing myself to my feet to head for the kitchen, leaving Amanda sprawled and semiconscious on the dew-soaked lawn. Eddie appeared out of nowhere and trotted along next to me.

"How did you let this happen?" I asked.

He looked unready to accept responsibility.

I was halfway through building a pair of double espressos when my cell phone rang.

"Ross wants to see you," said Joe Sullivan, referring to his boss, Ross Semple, the Southampton Town police chief.

"How come?"

"Oh, I don't know. A friend of yours is murdered. Ross is in charge of solving murders. Coincidence?"

I had an uneven relationship with Ross Semple, forged over years of complex and conflicted interactions. This was inevitable, for a variety of reasons. Jackie and I had interfered quite a bit in official police business, a chronic source of ill will, leavened by appreciation when things for his department worked out well in the end, aggravated when they didn't. Though like all complicated relationships, it went deeper than that, in ways neither of us quite understood.

"When?"

"Today would be good," said Sullivan. "Does an hour from now suit your schedule?"

I thought about the dovetail joints for a stack of drawers I was planning to cut that day. Frank Entwhistle, my stead source of work, was a very patient man, a quality I strove reinforce by relentlessly meeting his generous deadline built plenty of give in the timing of the current job, so off would have little or no effect. I just hated to lose t It was the principle.

"I'll be there in an hour. One hour for the inte I'm on my way back to the shop," I said.

"Wow, that's really good of you. A whole hour," said Sullivan.

"We don't need an hour."

"If it goes past that, are you going to leave?"

"No."

"I'll see you when you get here," he said, then hung up on me.

I checked the clock on my phone. Not even seven thirty in the morning and I was already preparing for combat.

MY EX-WIFE, Abby, and I probably shouldn't have married in the first place, a lament you hear all the time from divorced people. However, I can't express the same sentiment about sleeping with her, which resulted in a lot of memorable occasions, and most importantly, our daughter, Allison, our only child.

Allison had caused me great joy and nearly limitless grief. But I never once regretted her existence. I'd do it all over again, even if it meant all the grief and none of the joy. She wasn't an easy kid to raise, and as it turned out, not so easy an adult either. Though she and her mother stayed close after I left, Abby secretly called her The Apple, as in an apple that hadn't fallen very far from the tree. The tree being me.

This is probably why it took me so long to establish a relationship with Allison that involved more than relentless gales of hostility and recrimination. All generated by her and directed at me. My part was to answer the tempest with lavish praise and abiding affection, though making little effort to
n my own heedless self-destruction, which aroused much
er fury to begin with.

mehow we managed to stumble into an uneasy com-
. I took better care of myself and she redirected her
g toward boyfriends, employers, and the represen-
ur great civil institutions, whom she lumped under
rubric "worms."

It didn't hurt that she liked Amanda and Amanda liked her in return, enough to occasionally drive into New York where Allison worked as a freelance graphic designer so the two of them could shop, talk, and indulge in the kind of Broadway entertainment you could only get me to as a corpse.

I was about to leave to go see Chief Semple when Allison called me on my cell phone.

"I think Nathan might be sociopathic," she said, when I pushed the answer button.

"That's a pretty serious charge."

"Why else would he get another sales job?"

"Because he's a good salesman?"

"He gets a new job without discussing it with me? Without even considering the type of job we've talked about?"

"He might have considered it and decided it was a bad idea," I said.

"We're supposed to talk about these things. People who aren't sociopaths know this."

I knew taking Nathan's side was the wrong strategy if I wanted to advance his cause. Not that I cared much about his cause, having no say in the matter. I liked this kid better than the previous two dozen, though I avoided meeting him in person. As with new recruits joining a battle-weary platoon, you didn't want to make friends with people who'd likely be gone within the week.

"Why not let him work the job for a while and see what happens. Maybe he'll come to his senses."

"You hated your corporate job," she said.

"I loved my corporate job. I just hated the corporation. And its employees. Not all of them."

"He'll make enough money to afford an apartment we can both live in."

"Don't do it."

"Why not?"

"Never room with people you sleep with."

"Do you have any idea how ridiculous that sounds?"

"Are you still living on sour cream and potato chips?" I asked.

"You're changing the subject and sounding like my mother."

Allison somehow combined my intemperate approach to wellness with Abby's native gifts. In other words, she could trash her health, bypass the gym, and still look like a million bucks. Though she was still young and unaware that nature really does play a relentless game of catch-up.

"Your mother is an intelligent woman."

"She hates Nathan."

"There's a mark in his favor. Maybe you should move in together after all."

"I'm not going to. I probably never will. I wish I could blame it on you, but it's actually what I want."

"If he's worth anything, it'll be okay with him."

"I shouldn't talk to you about this sort of thing."

"No, you shouldn't. We can chat about hydrocarbon processing or the relative merits of structural composites versus dimensional lumber. Safer ground."

"He should have talked to me before accepting that new job," she said, her voice a low growl.

"He should have. Next time I see him I'll break his arms."

"Thanks, Daddy," she said, before hanging up.

I BROUGHT Eddie with me to the HQ. This was flagrantly manipulative. It took a heart of stone not to bend to Eddie's canine charms. And lucky for the plan, he was pretty indiscriminate about whom he charmed, assholes included who were in good supply at the HQ.

To be fair, the majority of police I've known are not only decent, hardworking, and principled people, they're mostly better than the rest of us. But positions of power have a way of attracting those who assume institutional prerogatives, resulting in a lot of struggle and strife for people like me who contend otherwise.

Since I was there for a command performance, I knew I'd easily breach the HQ's first line of defense, a female pit bull named Janet Orlovsky. Eddie did his part by jumping up on the bulletproof glass that sealed her booth and giving her the full force of his dazzling personality.

"Look at you, you handsome guy," said Janet, touching the glass that stood between Eddie's big black nose and her eager fingertips. "Don't tell me you brought along that curly haired, pain-in-the-ass Guinea."

"Mostly pain-in-the-ass Canuck," I said, which I often had to do. "Not that we favor ethnic pejoratives."

"Try being a Russian Jew," she said. "Then talk to me."

"My grandfather was a Polish Jew," I said. "On my mother's side. Eddie was a mutt left in the woods to die. Do you want to hire an ethnologist to determine which of us suffered greater persecution? Or do you want to call Ross and tell him I'm here?"

She kept her disdainful eyes on me as she dialed Ross's internal number. I held her gaze.

Without breaking eye contact, she buzzed us through the door. Eddie trotted along, staying mostly by my side with a minimum of urgent commands. The worst distractions were corners and baseboards, where the scatterings from hungry cops eating on the run had found their way.

Ross met me halfway through the squad room. I hadn't seen him in a few months and was surprised that he'd put on some weight. It always seemed his nervous intensity made up for a prideful lack of athleticism, though as noted, nature catches up with everyone eventually.

"Sam Acquillo," he said, "a sight for sore eyes."

"That's what eye drops are for."

"What brings you to our humble abode?"

"Sullivan said I had to come," I said.

He put a hand on his cheek.

"He did, did he? Follow me," he said, turning and walking back toward his office. I followed.

His office had been a dump when I first saw it, and over the years had gone downhill from there. The piles of paper on his desk were only distinguished from the piles on the floor by a difference in elevation. He sat in the desk chair and waved me into the only other chair you could actually sit in. Only Jackie Swaitkowski was a bigger slob, which defined their sole patch of cluttered common ground.

Eddie lay on a low pile of periodicals, local newspapers, and law enforcement trade journals after letting out a sigh that sounded more like acquiescence than satisfaction.

Ross offered me a cigarette, which I turned down. I looked around at the surrounding combustibles and took note of available exits.

"So you really gave it up," said Ross. "The smoking thing."

"I've confined reducing life expectancy to straight vodka and watching professional basketball."

"My dad smoked till the day he died, at eighty-five. Got hit by a car."

"The luck of the fathers doesn't always descend upon the sons," I said.

"You ought to hope that's true, if you don't mind me saying."

He meant that my father had been murdered in a restroom at the back of a crummy old neighborhood bar in the Bronx. Beaten to death, though the damage to his knuckles showed he didn't go easily.

"I don't mind, though I don't like talking about it."

"Who would. Speaking of untimely death, what's your take on Alfie Aldergreen?" he asked.

"No idea. Nowhere near enough data."

"I forgot. You're Mr. Empiricist."

"You didn't forget. You know I never speculate on things I know nothing about. Neither do you. Sometimes we have testable hypotheses. Tracks to follow. But not with this one. Not yet. Clean slate."

"Tabula rasa."

"So why all the questions?"

"I'm the chief of police. They pay me to ask questions."

I breathed in his cigarette smoke and fought the powerful urge to ask for one of my own. I'd quit the year before, and this moment confirmed what I already knew. Quit all you want; you're never free of it.

"What about you?" I asked. "What can you tell me? Not that the chief of police has to tell me anything," I added, sparing him from saying it himself.

"We got nothing," he said, pushing back in his battered desk chair and sucking in a huge drag of smoke. "I can't stop you and Jackie from sticking your noses into this thing. We know that from past experience. You're gonna do what you're gonna do. So let's try something different this time. You guys can go to places it's hard for us to go. But we're the police, and can do things you can't do. If we cooperate, if you communicate as you go, and tie us in as a resource rather than an adversary, it could mean a swift and just resolution to this tragedy."

That really was a first. Ross Semple, undisputed master of Southampton law enforcement, asking me and Jackie, unrepentant meddlers in police affairs, to let them in on our investigation, before we even had one.

The role reversal was so startling and abrupt, it almost wrenched my neck. Though I tried not to let it show.

He flung himself back in his chair and took another huge draw on his cigarette, causing the burning tobacco to outrun the paper, and consequently dropping a large dollop of glowing ash on his polyester pants. He brushed if off as well as he could, but I could imagine his dry cleaner confronting a constellation of irreparable pinprick holes.

"Sure, Ross. Whatever we find out, you find out. I'd like it if Joe Sullivan stayed on the case. Your other guy is a little competitive. But that's your call."

"Joe's on it," he said. "And me, too. My brother was wounded in Vietnam. Lived in a chair, like Alfie. Though not that long. Too many complications."

"I'm sorry," I said.

"I'm sick of conflict. I don't want to fight with anyone anymore, especially you. Maybe it's age. Just stay inside the legal lanes—Jackie knows what they are—talk to us on a regular basis and don't get in our way when things heat up."

Ross grew up like me in Southampton, but spent the first half of his career as a homicide detective in the most savage neighborhood in New York City during some of the bloodiest, crack-infested times. It was hard to overlook the weirdness, but the wise never underestimated the man.

"I hear you," I said.

His face slipped into serious.

"The same goes for that freckle-faced cyclone. Latitude doesn't mean carte blanche. Remind her of that, if you would."

"Jackie's her own girl, Ross. You know that. Anyway she's my boss. She tells me what to do."

"Interesting role reversal. You know you need a license to be a PI in this state."

"I'm not a PI. I'm a personal assistant."

"Right. You know Esther Ferguson accused us of harassing Alfie," he said.

"I didn't."

"He lived in the Village. Not even our jurisdiction. But he insisted that Town cops were threatening him."

"How so?" I asked.

"Looking at him, as it turned out. Even Esther backed off after that."

"The Town and Village have different uniforms, patrol cars."

"He described us," said Ross. "Pretty accurately."

"Alfie surprised me plenty of times."

"Terrible thing to be afraid of your own mind," said Ross. "It scares the hell out of the general public, but their fear is nothing compared to what people like Alfie go through. Did you know the incidence of violent crime perpetrated by paranoid schizophrenics is roughly the same as the population at large?"

"No, but it doesn't surprise me."

"I didn't think you were such a sensitive guy," said Ross.

"Sensitivity's got nothing to do with it. Simple fairness. Even lunatics have a right to life."

"You almost just improved my opinion of you, Sam."

"Always the underachiever."

"I've got another Alfie problem," he said.

"What's that?"

"Alfie himself. Can't find any next of kin. Carlo's okay keeping him on ice for now, but he'll be needing the drawer space.

"Jimmy Watruss might know," said Ross.

"I'll talk to him."

Despite all that talk about cooperation, Ross knew a lot more than he was willing to share, but it was all I'd get. So we tossed around the Latin allusions, semi-non sequiturs, and trivia one-upsmanship that served as conversation between us, and then I got the hell out of there.

ESTHER FERGUSON'S office was on the way back to the cottage, and it was still early, so despite some trepidation, I stopped in to see her.

The Social Services Department for Eastern Suffolk County was in a converted Victorian house in a mixed residential-commercial zone at the western end of Hill Street in Southampton. Not in the Village exactly, though not all the way out. The porch was deep, the ceilings high, and the smell was all damp, moldy rugs and stale cigarette smoke. The interior surfaces were freshly painted, though no one thought to strip off the underlayment. This turned the elegant old crown moldings and baseboards into congealed, linear blobs. I stood in the

foyer and tried to remember behind which of the unmarked
four doors Esther captained her social welfare ship.

I picked the one in least repair.

"Come on in," I heard in response to the knock. I walked
in and she said, "Sam Ah-cquillo. I been expectin' you."

"I figured."

I sat in one of her visitors' chairs. The office was sparsely
decorated, but bright and inviting, nearly elegant, as if the
shopworn foyer was a ruse to throw off intruders. The walls
were paneled in the original wide-board chestnut tongue and
groove, which nicely set off Esther's academic credentials
and accomplishments, including a master's in sociology from
Princeton.

Esther herself was equally well kept, slim, poised, and
handsome. Her perfume filled the room like a bunch of fresh-
cut flowers. Her face would have been pretty if it hadn't spent
so much time expressing wariness and assumed affront. Like
your mother always warned, if you keep crossing your eyes
like that, they're gonna stay that way.

"What went down with Alfie—wrong, wrong, wrong," she
said.

"Any ideas?" I asked.

" 'Bout what?"

"Who killed him."

"That's a leap. Somebody killin' him. Didn't just fall in the
water?" she asked.

"After he duct taped himself to the chair? Neat trick. I'd
like to see you do it."

"No you wouldn't. I'd prove you wrong."

"Probably would, but you know what I'm saying," I said.

"I do. It's just too depressing."

"So no ideas."

"You keep sayin' that," she said.

"What else should I say? I want to know who killed him.
Maybe you have an insight or two. You were his case man-
ager. Nobody knew him better."

"I already told the police what I know," she said, like that should be the end of the conversation.

"I don't care what you told the cops. I want to know what you really think," I said.

She sat forward in her red leather chair and gripped the arms, as if preparing to leap at me.

"You think I wouldn't be totally forthcoming with the police? You think I'm crazy, or just self-destructive?" she asked.

"What was Alfie's general mood in the weeks before he died? Anything unusual?"

"His mood was the same mood as always. Paranoid schizophrenic. The man was exceedingly clinical. Livin' right on the line. A little shove would've sent him right over."

"That's what he got. A little shove into the harbor."

She shifted papers around her desk without looking at them, since her eyes were fixed on mine.

"You know, Alfie wasn't the only character in town people would call crazy," she said. "That people would be scared to death of."

I couldn't tell if that was a threat or an insult, or both. I just knew I wouldn't take the bait.

"Jackie Swaitkowski thought he was more agitated than normal," I said. "More fearful."

"Some people are separated from society because of mental illness, or unfortunate circumstances," she said, not wanting to let it go. "And some are just antisocial."

"Not me. I got lots of friends."

"Yeah. Like Alfie Aldergreen. And look where that got him."

"If you'd locked him away like you wanted to, he'd be just as dead," I said, grabbing that bait with both hands.

And there it was. Esther had started the legal process of declaring Alfie incompetent and would have either moved him into an institution, or some group home Up Island where the state agency she worked for maintained the fiction that they integrated their jobless, drug-lobotomized clients into the community. I got in her way, and with the help of Jackie and Jimmy Watruss, had kept her at bay.

She'd lost an older brother to the streets, severely manic-depressive, after they closed the mental hospital where he'd lived for most of his life. This decided Esther's choice of careers, and also cemented her skepticism toward deinstitu-tionalization, a view that ran counter to the current thinking of the mental health profession. That said, a contrarian posi-tion suited her nature.

"Some people deserve to be locked up, no matter what the courts say. And I'm not talkin' Alfie Aldergreen."

She was referring to a persistent rumor that I'd gotten away with murder a few times. A belief unfortunately shared by important members of the law enforcement community, including Ross. She thought mention of that would be disturb-ing to me, but I'd heard it enough by then that it was old hat.

"Okay," I said, "I didn't think you'd be much help."

I got up and left her office. She was saying something as I walked away, but I couldn't make it out, either because she spoke too softly or I just didn't want to hear.

CHAPTER THREE

I went back to my shop and finished the drawer boxes for Frank's built-ins. The work was a good distraction from the troubling images of Alfie Aldergreen that kept bubbling up in my mind. I tried not to think about how frightened he must have been. Had he gone to his death thinking the dark forces of eternal evil had finally caught up with him? Or did he know the truth?

Amanda phoned earlier to tell me she was sleeping in that evening, not having fully recovered from the night before. Though I only had a passing familiarity with hangovers, a dubious blessing, I offered my sympathy and best wishes for sunnier times tomorrow.

"Well put," she said. "My head has been experiencing inclement weather all day."

After knocking around a few golf balls for Eddie, I cleaned off in the outdoor shower and climbed into fresh clothes. I left Eddie to guard the two houses, though the only threats he usually focused on were seabirds and colorful, inflated toys blown in from the Little Peconic Bay.

I drove into the Village in my '67 Pontiac Grand Prix, a car I'd inherited along with the cottage from my dead parents. My father bought the car only a few months before he was

killed. It was a surprising purchase for a guy without a drop
of sporting blood in his body. Until then, he'd driven nothing
more stirring than shabby, overpowered pickups, which his
mechanic's skills kept running well past their life expectan-
cies. After I discovered the preposterous vehicle in a shed at
the back of the property, it took some engineering skill to
get it pounded into legal shape. In hindsight the project might
have saved my life, as it substituted industry for the resolute
self-destruction that steered my life at the time.

The car had no reason to exist in the early twenty-first
century, but it was my car and would have to do. And given
its scale and latent ballistic force, other vehicles, both domes-
tic and imported—and even sturdy pickups—instinctively gave
it wide berth. Well advised, since none would survive a one-
on-one altercation.

My goal was the big bar and restaurant on Main Street
in Southampton. Jackie had told me she and her boyfriend,
Harry Goodlander, would be there. I liked the place well
enough. The food was overpriced, but the front of the restaurant opened up onto the street, letting in sea breezes and
the aimless chatter of passersby. And I liked the bartender,
an unreconstructed Brit who called himself Geordie. I was the
only one in town who knew why.

I parked in a remote spot, hoping to save the Grand Prix
injury from the swinging doors of neighboring cars. Rescuing
the old Pontiac from appropriate death (more than once) had
instilled in me unwarranted, but deeply paternal, feelings.

Jackie and Harry were already there. Geordie was engaged
with a swarm of wait staff at the service end of the bar, but
the hostess, another regular friend of mine, saw me working
through the crowd and made sure my usual Absolut on the
rocks was waiting for me when I got to my seat.

"Bon appétit," I said to Jackie before taking my first sip.

"That's for food. You're having a drink."

"Always splitting hairs."

"Learn to say 'Cheers.' Geordie will appreciate it."

Harry reached across Jackie with a hand the size of a catcher's mitt. I shook it as well as I could. The guy was around seven feet tall—lean, wide across the shoulders and stronger than a front-end loader. He lacked athletic grace, but that was a fine point to anyone stupid enough to challenge him.

"Hi, Harry," I said. "How's the logistics dodge?"

Harry shipped things around the world for a living.

"In constant motion. How's custom cabinetry?"

"Static, but pays the bills."

"Sorry about Alfie," he said. "He was a good friend of yours."

"Not a friend exactly, more of a nuisance. But I appreciate the thought."

"He was a friend," said Jackie. "Sam's uncomfortable with finer emotions," she added to Harry.

"Fuck all that," I said.

Geordie finally found his way to where we were sitting. He looked glad to see us, which I attributed to our sparkling repartee, though it was probably more about the tips.

"What can we do for you then?" he asked.

"We're good for now," said Harry, cheerfully.

"Did you know Alfie Aldergreen?" I asked, spoiling the mood.

Geordie grew serious.

"Knew him well. Bloody awful."

"Any ideas?" I asked.

Geordie was about forty, with a square head filled with thick black and grey hair and a blocky, fluid frame that served him well in a fight. I'd seen him in action, and though I respected his courage, I could see holes in his technique. I felt a little bad thinking things like that, but it was the habit of a long, occasionally violent fighter's life.

"Heard not a fookin' thing, man," he said. "No reason for it."

"You'll tell me if anything comes up," I said, leaning in a bit to give the exchange a conspiratorial feel.

"Aye. I want the bastards well as you," he said, just loud enough for me to hear.

"Should I be feeling left out?" asked Jackie, talking across both me and Harry.

"Not at all, Hinny," said Geordie. "We're just gettin' the odds straight on the Yankees."

"I'd've thought Newcastle United was more your thing," she said.

"And what would you know 'bout The Toon?" Geordie smirked.

"I was asking about Alfie," I said. "Geordie doesn't know any more than we do, but will keep his eyes and ears open."

"Alreet, then," said Geordie.

Jackie sat back in her seat, nearly satisfied with the answer.

"I'll ask the kitchen lads," said Geordie. "Sometimes they'd feed Alfie out the back. More a social thing than charity, mind. I told him he was welcome at the bar anytime, but there was an embarrassment factor. For him, not me."

I believed him. Geordie was committed to social enlightenment. And not afraid to provide teaching moments to the unenlightened.

"Sure," I said. "Is Tommy around?"

I was talking about a scrawny, good-natured guy from Pakistan who bussed tables at the place. He'd been at it long enough to earn a lot of friends, including me. Geordie picked up a phone behind the bar and called back to the kitchen. A few minutes later Tommy came out.

"Hey, Sam. What shakin'?"

"Not nearly enough. How 'bout you?" I said.

We all shook his hand and exchanged meaningless pleasantries.

"That thing that happen to Alfie," he said. "What the fuck?"

"What're people saying?" Jackie asked.

Tommy shook his head.

"Nothing but nonsense. Nobody know nothing."

"What kind of nonsense?" I asked.

"That there's a redneck cult out to kill cripples and Spanish people and this was a warning to them."

"That's ridiculous," said Jackie.

"Like I said, just nonsense. But don't blame *los caballeros*. Paranoia is the immigrant's life."

"No blame, Tommy," said Jackie. "I get it." She handed him her card. "If you hear anything else, even the ridiculous, e-mail me, okay?"

He took the card and recorded her contact information into an iPhone, then handed it back to her. He looked at me like I was next.

"No luck, Tommy," I said. "Don't even own a computer."

"Luddite," said Jackie.

When I ran R&D for that big industrial company, I wrote analytical if/then protocols that ran through a massively parallel processing array within a bank of mainframe computers covering about three thousand square feet. The room generated enough heat to melt Antarctica and is still one of the most powerful computational centers on the planet. Jackie knew this, so it wasn't worth mounting a rebuttal. And the truth was, she was basically right. I'd had a bellyful of technology, and if the digital revolution was happy to go on without me, I was happy to let it.

And you might think building custom kitchen cabinets and architectural detail was less complex, but only if you hadn't tried to build any.

After our chat with Tommy, the group went back to the core pursuit—drinking enough to anesthetize ourselves against our respective painful realities. Luckily all three of us possessed a heroic capacity, so only God and Geordie knew how much we drank and how little it showed to the outside world.

I HAD no trouble finding my old car, which I thought was parked well away from potential harm, so it surprised me to see the rear window smashed in.

The safety glass had sprayed into the backseat, where it formed a ground cover and small drifts, like a snowstorm. I never kept anything of value in the car, so there was no reason to worry about that. The ignition switch looked okay, so likely no attempt to start the engine. Though why would you? The antique value of a 1967 Grand Prix was basically zilch, and why pick such a hulking oddity in Southampton, the home of ultrararé collectible cars?

The answer was apparent. The point wasn't theft, it was damage. And not wanton, but with a purpose. I'd seen it before. It was a message, and I got what it said: Back off.

Bad strategy on their part.

FINDING A replacement rear window took some doing, but the people who rebuilt the car after a bad crash a few years ago had one shipped FedEx, and I was back in business a day after that. Meanwhile I got to borrow Amanda's Audi A4 Avant, which wasn't all that tough a sacrifice. I used it to go see Jimmy Watruss, Alfie's former landlord.

Jimmy lived in the apartment above a storefront on Main Street in Southampton. The store had a different tenant every summer. That year it was overpriced clothes for young women and older women who hadn't caught the article in Vogue on age-appropriateness.

The year before it was an art gallery. Before that, giant stuffed animals all the kids wanted to climb on, but weren't allowed to. This might have been to teach the lesson of thwarted desire to the children of the very rich. Which is why it immediately went out of business.

Jimmy owned the building, and several more in the Village, including Mad Martha's, the seafood restaurant and fish distributor, all inherited from his parents. It made for a nice living without him having to do a lot of work. This left plenty of time for Jimmy's other interests—working with veterans groups on drug and alcohol rehab and hanging around the neighborhood bars, usually his own. Always good to stay close to your subject matter.

So he was easy enough to find.

Mad Martha's, a few blocks from downtown Southampton Village, was half seafood wholesaler and half locals-only joint. Not that they wouldn't let the summer people come in for food and drink—none wanted to. Dark as a cave, with stained wood paneling on the walls and post-and-beam construction, the building had been converted from an eighteenth-century blacksmith's shop about one hundred years before. The walls were covered with paintings of fishing dories hard to the wind and whalers harpooning creatures that looked more like ferocious sea monsters than innocent whales. Artifacts of obsolete fishing technology also graced the walls and hung from the open beams overhead. The aroma of fish cleaning and packaging occasionally wafted in from the back, adding to the authentic ambience.

The patronage was largely Anglo construction workers who represented the last vestige of local, working-class guys born on the East End to families who'd been there since the first English ship stumbled onto shore. Their attitudes shifted between pride of survivorship and resentment as strong and deep as a concrete pylon.

My background wasn't that different, though they never quite got over the Italian name. Early on when I moved back to town, I had to establish my bona fides by kicking the ass of the first meatball who thought it would be fun to kick mine. Luckily that status didn't have to be renewed every year, a former boxing career having a definite shelf life.

Another inhibiting factor for the summer people was a sign above the bar: "None of that electronic shit allowed." An iPhone was stuck in the middle of the sign with a screwdriver. (Though this never discouraged Jackie from coming in once in a while, and I wouldn't want to be the guy who instructed her on the house rules.)

Jimmy was standing outside the elbow of the L-shaped bar, drinking a beer with a few of his regular mates. He was a lot younger than I, and like Joe Sullivan, meaty but far from fat. His complexion was the color and consistency of oatmeal, a liability somewhat relieved by a moustache and goatee. His lion's mane of dirty blond hair had witnessed few encounters with a comb, though you rarely saw him without a cowboy hat. Worked well with the cowboy boots.

He'd been chewed up by something over in Iraq, costing an eye, an ear, and two fingers on his left hand. Anything else, I wouldn't know. I never asked and he never told.

"Yo, Sam," he said as I approached. "I wondered when I'd see you."

"Hi, Jimmy," I said, and nodded to the other guys. They all nodded back.

"Pretty fucked up," said Jimmy.

"Yeah. What do you know?"

"What I read in the papers. And what I told Joe Sullivan. The guy didn't have any enemies outside of the ones in his head, and nothing was really much different lately. Not that I really knew. We were cool, but I didn't, like, hang with him all that much. Not like you."

I shook my head.

"I don't know anything either," I said. "Though somebody took a baseball bat to my rear window the other night. After I was asking around about Alfie."

I scanned the other guys, who took on that "Hey, it wasn't me" look.

"That old Grand Prix?" said Jimmy. "That's just wrong."

"I'm not happy about it, but I owe 'em a favor," I said.

"How so?"

"It tells me the people who killed him are here. So I probably don't have to go looking elsewhere. Not yet anyway."

"With all due respect, Sam," said one of Jimmy's friends, "who the hell around here would do something like that?"

"You think you know everybody?" another asked. "You don't know all them wetbacks."

He was referring to the Latino day laborers who congregated around the 7-Eleven every morning hoping to get a cash gig on a landscaping crew, or bull work on one of the monster construction sites around the East End. Since the real estate bust, there were a lot fewer of them to incite ethnic and economic hostility, but it was still there.

"Sam don't like that kinda talk," one of the other guys said.

"Well fucking excuse me," said the offending party, a young guy called Jaybo Flynn who stuck to Watruss like an extra appendage. Everyone assumed Jaybo was Jimmy's cousin or nephew, but I knew the kid's mother from high school. A classic pretty girl gone to seed, her only relation to Jimmy was living next door and needing some backup after her husband disappeared. Jimmy gave Jaybo a job in his restaurant and it turned out Jaybo was a pretty good cook, and well suited to the restaurant life. So by then he was managing the place and all Jimmy had to do was show up at the bar and convert the profits into free drinks.

"I don't like it, either," said Jimmy, glowering at Jaybo and putting a stop to further bigotry, at least for the time being.

I gently moved Jimmy out of the crowd so I could ask a touchier question.

"Apparently they can't find Alfie's next of kin. The medical examiner has his body up there in Riverhead in the cooler, but he needs to figure out what to do with it."

"Alfie's an orphan," he said, after a strangely long pause, as if reluctant to share the information. "I don't know what that means now that he's dead. But I'm pretty sure the VA will see to an honorable burial. Alfie was a soldier in good standing when he left the service. I'll take care of it."

"I'd appreciate it. And let me know if you hear anything at all about the murder," I said. "Tell Sullivan, but tell me, too."

"Sure, Sam," said Jimmy. "We want to get the bastards as much as you."

"That's what I keep hearing," I said.

It's not that they didn't. It was just human nature to quickly forget about a tragedy soon after it happens. The impulse was to turn away and allow the needs of the present to provide cover for natural apathy and indifference.

I had the opposite problem.

Chapter Four

I spent the next two days spreading the word around any of the joints, job sites, and social gatherings that could spread the word further. I had a simple message: know anything about Alfie's murder, tell me and tell the cops.

In two days, certain segments of Southampton society would be fully canvassed: the regular locals, the Latinos, documented and otherwise, and the people from Up Island who drove in and out every day to work.

Other segments would be oblivious. The professionals—doctors, lawyers, stockbrokers, retailers from the city —jewelers, antique dealers, art dealers. And the rich they served. I had a different strategy for getting to them.

"Did you ever have sex with that reporter from the *Times* who did a story on you?" I asked Jackie, when she answered her phone.

"No. Not that it's any of your business."

"So he might still be interested."

"You're suggesting if I *had* slept with him, he'd have lost interest in me?"

"We need him to write about Alfie Aldergreen," I said.

"It's possible a reporter could be interested in a story I brought him for reasons *other* than a chance at sexual favors," she said.

"Hey, how you do it is up to you. I just think it would serve the cause if something showed up in the *Times*."

"You can be such a jackass."

"But not all the time."

"Unbelievable," she said, and hung up on me.

I USED up the rest of the day in my basement shop putting the final touches on Frank's built-in unit and drawing up a detailed plan for the next round—a hemispherical china cabinet.

"Why do they want that?" I'd asked Frank. "Cost a fortune and adds a lot of wasted space."

"They have a fortune and ten thousand square feet to store the other dishes."

"I guess if it was rectangular, anyone could do it," I said.

"You're the custom woodworker, Sam. Can't get any more custom than a hemispherical china cabinet."

"Don't suppose you know how to do all those curves."

"If I did, I wouldn't need you," he said.

"Good point. Logical, even."

"I'm a regular fucking Aristotle, man. You know that."

Luckily, I had a secret weapon. My girlfriend, Amanda, a builder herself with a knack for sourcing exotic building materials. She claimed it was all on the Internet, but I knew it was her clever, clever ways.

As a result, I had a stack of catalogs on my drawing table from manufacturers who made products designed specifically for making things like curved cabinets. The choices were astonishingly extensive, as if the whole world needed curvy cabinetry. So what at first looked like an impossible mission was turning into a piece of cake. My biggest challenge would be to keep the myth of struggle and strife fresh in Frank's mind.

I WAS about to cash it in for the evening when the phone in my pocket vibrated. My Luddite ways aside, I'd given in to cell phones. While I wasn't keen on people calling me whenever the hell they liked, I liked being able to call them.

"We have a situation," said Jackie.

"Give me a headline."

"We're being summoned. I need you to agree before you hear who's doing the summoning."

"I'm not going to do that," I said.

"Yes, you are. I can't go through all the wrangling. It's too late at night."

"Okay, I agree."

"Edith Madison."

"No fucking way."

"You agreed."

Edith Madison was the Suffolk County district attorney. She once tried to put me away for murder. And even after the real guy confessed, I had firsthand knowledge that she still thought I was guilty. If not of that crime, undoubtedly some other.

"I take it back," I said to Jackie.

"You can't. The only reason the DA's office leaves you alone is they're too busy with easier cases. That doesn't mean they won't come after you like the psychotic goblins they are if you give them a reason to."

"What does she want?"

"I don't know. Consider it a good thing she called me first, your so-called lawyer. She wants us both in her office tomorrow. You're going to do this, Sam, so let's skip all the song and dance. Just pretend you're a reasonable person and say okay."

She was right. There was no point in resisting a foregone conclusion.

"Okay. What time?" I asked.

"I get nervous when you give in too easily."

"What should I wear?" I asked. "They'd tell you if this was an arrest, right?"

"It's not an arrest. That's Ross's job."

"In that case, I'm thinking blue blazer. Fresh khakis. My MIT tie."

"That's fine. Just leave your attitude at home," said Jackie. "I'll follow your lead."

"I said leave *your* attitude at home. My attitude's a different story."

The next morning she picked me up in her Volvo station wagon. I had two buckets of coffee, as she knew I would. She once supplied cigarettes for the road trips, but we'd both given them up, regrettable but necessary. You could still notice the faint smell of tobacco in her car, which made it all the harder to repress the nasty habit.

I compensated by telling her about my bashed-in window and conversations with Jimmy Watruss and other local luminaries.

"The window thing bothers me," she said.

"Nah, it's good," I said, repeating what I told Watruss. "Much better they know I'm on their ass. Helps shake them loose."

"Why do you say 'they'?"

"There were no wheelchair tracks leading up to the breakwater on Hawk's Pond. Alfie was carried. That means at least two people."

"So you like being bait?" she asked.

"Time is of the essence," I said. "You know that. Every day that goes by it gets harder to piece these things together. People leave town, evidence disappears, memories fade, cops get waylaid by other crimes. Since we don't know who these people are, we can't go to them. They have to come to us."

"Glad you said 'us.' I wouldn't want to feel left out."

"Just keep that Glock loaded and within reach."

THE DA's office was in Hauppauge, a town toward the western end of Suffolk County. I'd been there before, under more explicitly lousy circumstances, so I couldn't say it was

a pleasant homecoming. The security guys at the front desk
had me empty my pockets. They also made the mistake of
asking Jackie to dump out her duffel bag of a purse.

"Jesus Christ, lady," one of them said, "did you leave
anything at home?"

"The name's Attorney Swaitkowski, bub. Close associate
of DA Madison."

"You don't think she needs that stapler and solar-powered
battery charger?" I asked.

Since neither of us had anything more lethal than my
Swiss Army knife, which they retained, we got through. We
were met on the third floor by an administrative civil servant
wearing the requisite dour expression and frumpy clothes.
A standard that failed to extend to the upper echelons, as
demonstrated by Oksana Quan, the assistant district attorney
and the DA's right arm, who picked up our procession along
the way.

"Very nice to see you again," she said, shaking our hands.
"Edith will join us in a few minutes."

I doubted she was glad to see us, though in a way, I was
glad to see her. While there was no better put-together female
than Amanda Anselma, Oksana came in a close second—
with about a twelve-year advantage over Amanda in the youth
department. Her choice of formfitting skirt, dark pumps and
ostensibly modest white blouse made the most of her natural
gifts. And though I'm not as big on blondes as some people,
her version was so light and ephemeral, more platinum than
gold. And indescribably beautiful.

At our last encounter we stood side by side while the
judge dismissed the murder case against me, at the prosecutor's recommendation. I couldn't help but recall a faint note
of disappointment in Oksana's voice as she asked the court
to let me go, but maybe that was just my imagination.

"Can I get you coffee, water?" she asked, after ushering
us into a threadbare, but still stately, oak-paneled conference
room.

"Water, please," said Jackie.

"What do you have in the way of vodka?" I asked.

Jackie swatted me on the arm. Oksana showed something I hadn't seen before. The glimmer of a smile.

"That's okay," she said to Jackie, before leaving us alone. "I remember."

I sat down, put my hands in my lap and closed my eyes so I wouldn't have to see Jackie glowering at me.

We sat in silence until Jackie said, "Harry wants to get married. What do you think?"

I opened my eyes. Jackie was still glowering, though now for a different reason.

"Don't do it," I said.

"I knew you'd say that."

"So why'd you ask me?"

"I'm stupid. Or crazy. Or both."

"Has he been married before?" I asked.

"No."

"There you go. Doesn't know any better."

I closed my eyes again and tried to get more comfortable in my seat.

"My husband died," she said. "Not the same as your divorce."

"Would you still be married if he hadn't?"

"I'm not sure."

"There's your answer."

"Harry's different. I'm actually in love with him. He's good, and kind, and patient as Job. And he likes me as is. You don't know how rare that is."

I opened my eyes again and looked at her.

"I like you as is," I said.

"I know. Which is why you're my only friend."

"You have other friends. Dayna Red is your friend. So is Father Dent."

"Don't complicate things," she said. "The point is, I don't want to have children."

"This is something much better taken up with your other friends, like Dayna Red and Father Dent."

"Harry doesn't care if we have kids or not. So no pressure there. We make about the same amount of money, so that's off the table. We spend all our free time together. And did I mention he's a very big person?"

"If you're saying what I think you're saying, you can stop saying it."

"I'm saying I feel safe around him. That's a big deal in my line of work. He's already saved my life at least twice. What else does a guy have to do?" she said, in a plaintive way I didn't like. So I gave her the same advice I gave my daughter, since she made the mistake of asking.

"He can show some real courage and let you stay single like you want to," I said.

She stopped scowling, but took up tapping the surface of the conference table with her pen.

"Why do you always take the side of my least-sentimental nature?"

"I'm uncomfortable with finer emotions."

Oksana came back with a bottle of water for each of us. Moments later Edith Madison walked in. I stood up because my mother taught me to stand when women approached. Any woman, though Edith probably thought it was an honor reserved for her. I shook her dry, spidery hand.

Edith was still in her sixties, though barely. Her white hair was stacked up on her head in a tangled mess and her clothes, though likely expensive, were on extended duty. Her skin was the fair kind that wrinkled easily, though not enough to hide a bone structure chiseled out of New Hampshire granite.

"Counselor, Mr. Acquillo," she said, shaking our hands.

"Mrs. Madison, nice to see you again," said Jackie.

"I'm sure," said Edith. "How is Burton?"

She was referring to Burton Lewis, the founder of Jackie's pro bono law practice. Not only a philanthropist, Burton was a certified billionaire and notable among the prominent in

the city and on Long Island. The kind of guy people like
Edith Madison paid attention to. He was also a close friend
of mine, which was notable for me, since like Jackie, I didn't
have a lot of close friends.

"He's great as always," said Jackie. "I'll extend your
regards."

"Do so. It's been a long time."

I often wondered if Edith and Burton belonged to a covert
society of old-money WASPs who secretly ran the country.
A sort of Ivy League illuminati. Alfie had asserted that view,
and maybe he was right, though his other theory, that the
elves of Rivendell were in on the operation, undermined his
credibility.

"So what's up?" I asked, just to get things moving.

Edith and Oksana looked like it pained them to cast their
eyes my way.

"We're in possession of certain information," said Edith,
"the origins of which must remain confidential."

She waited for me to say sure, I can keep a secret.

"Certainly," said Jackie for both of us.

"You understand, the consequences of betraying this trust
would be severe," said Edith, pointing her bony finger at me.

"We understand," said Jackie.

We'd already said we'd keep our mouths shut, I thought.
You think a threat will make that promise easier to keep?

"This is extremely difficult," said Edith. "And I've chosen
this course of action with great reluctance. I've been convinced by a treasured advisor that it's the best of many dis-
agreeable options."

Yeah, yeah, I thought. Get on with it.

"If you want to tell us something, Mrs. Madison, I think
you should go ahead and do it. Or not," I said. "Till I know
what you're talking about, it's all a bunch of blather."

"You need to take this seriously," she said, sticking her
finger at me again, as if that would improve my mood.

"He will, Mrs. Madison," said Jackie. "I'll make sure of it."

That didn't seem to reassure her, though after a big cleansing breath, she pressed on.

"How well do you know Ross Semple?" she asked.

As much as anyone, I thought. I'd known him to say hello and banter back and forth in bad Latin since we were at Southampton High School together. A habit we took up again when he moved back from the city to run Southampton Town police. Though I didn't really know him, not in a real way. I shared that with Edith.

"We have it on excellent authority that a criminal enterprise has developed within the Town of Southampton Police Force," she said. "Mr. Aldergreen was not the only confidential informant to be murdered in recent weeks. In fact there were three. Our information suggests police collusion, or at least passivity."

Okay, I thought. That's something.

"Why eliminate your own CIs?" Jackie asked.

"Snitches are information hubs," said Oksana. "Not just one-way conduits into the cops. They knew too much."

"We're in a difficult position," said Edith. "Ross spent five years at Internal Affairs in the Bronx. His former partner now runs the state unit, the only organization qualified to handle an undercover investigation, but he refuses to help us, citing conflict of interest. If he worked for me, I'd fire him. But he doesn't."

She sat back in her chair and waited for us to absorb the implications.

"You want us to investigate the cops?" said Jackie, losing some of her professional reserve.

Edith still looked pained.

"Not exactly. Very competent assets have been deployed. But it would be very useful to have you both as confidential informants yourselves."

Jackie opened her mouth to speak, but nothing came out.

"How do you know we won't spill it all to Ross?" I asked. "He's a friend of ours, sort of."

Oksana dropped a fat manila folder in front of Jackie.

"This is the file we have on Mr. Acquillo. Read through it if you would, Jackie," said Edith, "then explain his chances in open court."

Jackie handed back the envelope.

"Not necessary. We get it," she said.

Edith nodded. Oksana just sat there like an exquisite figurine, both present and detached.

"You won't believe this," said Edith, "but I have some respect for your investigative skills. As an elected official of the State of New York, I'm obligated to uphold official legal process, but privately, I can say you two have had some impressive success. I know I'm taking a big risk even having these conversations, but the matter of police corruption is so serious, and problematic, that I'm willing to suspend my better judgment."

"That's okay with me," I told her, before Jackie had a chance to either cement the deal or leap like an Amazon warrior up on her high horse. "I like Ross fine, despite it all, and Sullivan really is a friend, but we'll play by your rules. For now, anyway."

"That's reassuring," said Oksana.

I shrugged.

"We'll take you at your word. Until there's a reason we shouldn't," I said.

Edith pointed at me again with no attempt to blunt the gesture. I felt like telling her, keep it up and I'll bite it off.

"That's the sort of impertinence I find so annoying," she said.

"I'll take annoyance. I've had worse from scarier people," I said.

Edith retreated back into her chair, the look of unresolved conflict in her eyes.

"Impossible," said Oksana.

"Agreed," said Jackie.

"Who are the other dead CIs?" I asked.

"Not sure we should share that," said Edith.

"Then the deal's off."

"Why?" Edith asked, looking startled.

"We'll find out anyway on our own, but it'll eat up time. We've got to know at least as much as you do. It's stupid not to tell us."

Oksana tapped the fat manila folder, probably unconsciously.

"If you want to stick any of that shit on me, go ahead and try," I said. "If I do this, I do it for my own reasons. And I do it my way."

"Our way," said Jackie.

"Right," I said, though I didn't exactly know what she meant.

Edith sighed and looked over at Oksana.

"Can you get the file?" she asked. Oksana got up and left the room, expressionless and unhurried. "We don't know what the police could be covering up. We assume it's one of the usual suspects—drugs, prostitution, shakedowns, even larceny. Given traditional patterns, it's unlikely that the participants extend beyond a small, tightly knit group. But we don't know that. Ross is such a competent chief, it's hard to imagine such a thing going on under his nose without his knowledge. Makes no sense."

"Less sense than Ross Semple corrupting his office?" Jackie asked.

Edith took off her glasses and rubbed her eyes.

"You think you know people," she said, leaving the sentence hanging in the air.

Oksana showed up with another manila folder, which she said contained a copy of everything they had. Jackie stuffed it into her giant purse.

"Please keep that confidential," said Oksana to Jackie, drawing a look I'd seen before. I knew what it meant, but I doubt the same was true for Oksana. "There's also a link with a password into our CI database. Good background information."

"I hope we aren't making a terrible mistake," said Edith, with a lot of sincerity.

"You shouldn't say stuff like that," I said, standing up. "You made a decision, stick with it. No second guessing."

"You can stop lecturing me," she said.

"Maybe you need it," I said, and walked out of there with Jackie and her emotions, all mixed up as usual, flowing along in my wake.

CHAPTER FIVE

The only thing I did the next day was the job I was actually paid to do—building architectural details in the basement woodshop of my cottage. I'd blundered into this work by doing finish carpentry for my friend Frank Entwhistle, who realized I could handle his fine woodworking chores at a far lower cost than he paid factory shops, with better quality, at only twice the time to completion that others promised but never delivered. This last discrepancy was allayed by an easy compliance on my part. I built whatever he asked me to build, which I reckoned was the job of a craftsman—not lecturing people who paid for the stuff on the idiocy of their requests. As much as I wanted to.

The way I saw it, this being the Hamptons, idiotic requests were more or less standard operating procedure.

The problem was one of an expanding universe. People living in three-million-dollar, eight-hundred-square-foot apartments could suddenly have a four-thousand-square-foot house for the same money. With no idea how to fill up all that space.

Ignorance rarely being a deterrent, these city dwellers were highly inventive in their dopey requests for interior appointments, and their architects more than happy to collect big fees for placing a single phone call to someone willing to accept the challenge, in my case Frank Entwhistle, who placed a call to me, who always said yes, and we all won.

A seamless and efficient transfer of wealth from the financial sector to the architects of their materialistic dreams, to the builders who translated architectural dreams into houses that wouldn't fall down, and lastly to me, the master of the finishing touch.

ALLISON CALLED me when I was about to rip a five-quarter piece of antique mahogany retrieved from a pile of wreckage behind an abandoned nightclub and hotel. The place was shut down two decades before when a club goer shot a bouncer. The victim's fellow bouncers responded by beating the gunman into a near vegetative state before bothering to call an ambulance, resulting in the original guy bleeding out on the dance floor.

The resulting blizzard of lawsuits and political hyperventilation overwhelmed the owners of the club, a pair of gay millionaires from Czechoslovakia, prompting them to simply close the doors and move back to Europe, where they still were as far as anyone knew.

Various vandals and enterprising salvagers had plundered the interior of what had once been a Victorian mansion, not realizing that the most valuable wood was locked up inside doors, windows, and architectural details covered in layers of paint, ripped out, and left outside to rot.

I had a separate section of my shop devoted to rough cleaning the stuff, the centerpiece of which was a cast iron planer about the same vintage as the quarried wood. With chipped blades and a DB rating comparable to a jet engine, it was a miracle I heard the phone ring.

"Doing anything?" Allison asked.

"Shaving off lead paint. You?"

"Nathan's quitting sales and going to work for a start-up."

"What are they starting?"

"I'm not sure. Half his pay is in equity."

"Getting in on the ground floor," I said.

"The other half won't cover his rent, so he wants to move in with me."

"Isn't this the kind of job you wanted him to take?"

"It is. I didn't realize the pay part," she said.

"Meet the Law of Unintended Consequences."

"I hate that," she said.

"So what're you going to do?"

"I was hoping you'd give me an idea."

"Try it for six months. And get a dog."

"To protect me from Nathan?"

"To have a friend, after you kick Nathan out of the apartment."

I let her run through another half-dozen speculative scenarios, filling in all possible permutations of each, until her options and my forbearance were both depleted. But it made her feel better, which I guess was the purpose of the call in the first place.

"I can't tell if you like Nathan or not," she said, as a parting thought.

"Me neither. Let's see how he does with the dog."

LATER THAT night, it was Jackie's turn. She called me when Eddie and I were rotting on the sun porch, him gnawing on a dinosaur bone, and me admiring the way the moon sketched flickering white lines across the blackness of the Little Peconic Bay. In other words, the two of us were thoroughly engaged in our favorite pastimes.

So it was a little annoying to see Jackie's name pop up on the cell phone's little screen.

"What."

"What's wrong with hello? Or, wow, Jackie! It's so great to hear from you!"

"I guess if it was."

"You love hearing from me," she said.

"Not at eleven o'clock at night, when most responsible people are either drunk or trying to get there."

"I read through all the files from Dame Edith and the White Witch. Do you want to hear what I found out?"

"You don't fancy Oksana? She seems kind of cuddly to me."

"If you like cuddling scorpions. Do you want to know what I learned or not?"

"I do."

I could hear wine pouring over the sound of her perennial sighs.

"Okay, Joey Wentworth. Son of Manhattan rich people, high school dropout after eleventh grade (idiot), skinny, pimples, white skin, heroin habit (even bigger idiot), dishwasher at Jacques and Valencia's for two years."

According to Jackie, he was slowly getting turned by the Southampton cops, specifically by the other Town detective, Lionel Veckstrom, whom Jackie and I generally referred to as "Prick Cop."

Few appreciate that the East End of Suffolk County, the farther reaches of which encompass the Hamptons, is essentially an island. A big swath of pine barren separates the East End from the rest of Long Island, and the Shinnecock Canal assures that the only way in or out is over a pair of bridges, unless you want to flee by way of the ferries to the North Fork, which run at the speed of number ten motor oil.

This was a big advantage for law enforcement, one Joey Wentworth recognized. And as a dedicated entrepreneur, figured out a work-around.

Speedboats.

"Joey had a twin engine picnic boat he could run to Bridgeport in just a few hours," said Jackie. "Stock up on the bad stuff and be back at Hawk Pond before nightfall."

"Nice gig."

"Until someone emptied a twelve-gauge into the cab of his SUV. Needed DNA to confirm his identity."

I knew Joey. Friendly, but twitchy guy. Docked his powerboat about five slips down from mine. Now I knew why I could hear the rumble of the big diesels five boats away and what was in the giant duffel bags tossed into his Range Rover, and why I hadn't seen him around for a while.

Next snitch up was Lilly Fremouth. Black father, white mother. Waitressed at a diner up on Old County Road. Had an infant daughter and a pimp, who also happened to be the daughter's father. Instrumental in busting a brothel and drug-retailing operation in Flanders, an impoverished backwater just south of Riverhead.

She was found strangled in her living room by her mother when she showed up to babysit for the grandkid.

"Ross has suspended all interaction with confidential informants while these killings are investigated," said Jackie. "Trouble is, snitches grease the gears of investigations. So effectively, the detective squad is half shut down."

"Might explain him letting us meddle in the Alfie thing," I said.

"Might."

"Is there a common thread?"

"Not that I can see. No evidence they knew each other. Joey was Veckstrom's, Lilly and Alfie were run by Joe Sullivan. Any thoughts on how we deal with that?" she asked.

That was the Big Thing. What to do about Joe Sullivan. A good, true, and loyal friend, when we weren't battling over alleged obstruction of justice or interference in police investigations. We'd all saved each other's lives and been through a load of crap together over a lot of years, so it didn't seem possible to hide this from him; the district attorney and her pretty pale assistant be damned.

"We tell him," I said.

"Of course we do," she said. "I just want to know how."

"Tomorrow night at the Pequot."

"Do I have to actually eat dinner, or just drink?"

We knew we'd find Joe Sullivan at the Pequot, Hodges's ratty little bar and grill serving the remaining fishermen of Sag Harbor and other diehard locals. His daughter, Dorothy, a Goth depressive, mostly ran the joint at this point, though Hodges was usually there to eat and lend unwanted advice.

The food was actually more than edible, contrary to Jackie's opinion, and the atmosphere truly distinctive, if your taste runs to red vinyl, weathered-grey wood, and the smell of fishermen fresh off the job.

"Drink all you want," I told her. "I'll drive you home."

"Then pick me up at six. Don't bother ringing the bell. I'll know you're there."

Jackie lived above a Japanese restaurant in Water Mill, a hamlet just east of Southampton Village. It wasn't a big place, just enough for an apartment and separate office. She'd know I'd arrived because the entire exterior of the building was under video surveillance, along with strategically placed alarms controlled by motion sensors.

I wasn't the only one on the team with a history of mortal threat.

Despite all that, when I got there, Jackie was sitting on the stoop eating out of a take-out container. As she stood, she had to pull down the hem of her dress to get it within legal distance above her knees. She wore high-heeled sandals and her big ball of hair was pulled back from her face.

"Jesus, Jackie," I said, "we're going to the Pequot, not Studio 54."

"I turn forty next year," she said. "Got to use up the wardrobe while I still can. What's Studio 54?"

"You're gonna give Hodges a heart attack."

"Then maybe he'll stop staring at my boobs."

Sag Harbor was an old whaling town bordering Southampton to the north. It had a lot of old houses densely packed together and a marina that accommodated giant yachts as well as the usual mix of merely unaffordable sailboats and cabin cruisers. Hidden away down a narrow channel on the other side of the harbor was the town's fishing fleet, once focused on commercial catches like cod and flounder, now as likely chartered out by sport fishermen who liked catching their bluefish and bass in more rustic surroundings.

The Pequot was off the marina's parking lot, so the fish was as fresh as the charter crews were ripe.

Sullivan was at his usual table for two, so we had to drag over another chair to all sit together.

"I don't remember the invitation," he said, as we plopped ourselves down. "What did you do with the rest of your dress?" he added, looking at Jackie over the top of his burger.

"She bought it off the midlife crisis rack," I said.

"Be thankful you're only at mid."

"We need to talk to you about something," said Jackie. "It's important."

Sullivan looked over at me.

"Do you like it when she says stuff like that?" he asked.

"No," I said.

"Sam knows it's important. He'd just wait till the end of the night to talk about it. I'm not that patient."

Sullivan held up his burger.

"What if we just wait till I eat this?"

"How come we're not drinking?" I yelled toward the bar, where Dorothy looked up from a conversation with another tattoo-festooned ghoul. She gazed through curved, three-inch-long black eyelashes, then walked slowly over to our table.

"Vodka, Pinot, and Bud," she said. "What's shakin'?"

"A vodka, a pinot, and a Bud," I said, "if they can find their way to our table."

"What're the specials tonight?" Jackie asked.

"Everything's special," said Dorothy. "Especially the wait staff. Certifiably awesome."

"You added something," said Jackie, studying Dorothy's face.

"Interesting," said Dorothy, "though consistent with clinical studies of the weak interplay between memory and casual observation."

"She took something away," I said, interpreting.

"Nose stud," said Dorothy. "Sick of it."

"In other words, eyewitnesses aren't worth shit," said Sullivan.

"How's the interplay between memory and drink orders?" I asked.

Dorothy patted me on the shoulder and sauntered back toward the bar.

"Seriously, Joe," Jackie said to Sullivan. "We need to talk."

He put his burger down with some regret, and stood up. We followed him out to the Pequot's rickety deck.

"What," he said, when we got there.

"We're going to tell you something you can't tell anyone we told you," said Jackie.

"I can't promise that."

"I know," said Jackie. "But when we tell you, you'll know why you have to."

Sullivan looked at me with more than a little exasperation.

"What the hell, Sam."

"There's something rotten inside Southampton Town Police," I told him. "The whole force is under investigation."

His frown was a complicated affair. Concern mixed with recognition.

"The snitches," he said.

"I didn't know Alfie was a CI," said Jackie. "What court would accept evidence from a full-out paranoid schizophrenic?"

Sullivan got more irritated.

"Who told you about Alfie?"

"Edith Madison," I said.

He pinched his lips together as if to throttle an ill-advised remark.

"How could anything he said be admissible?" Jackie asked, not ready to give up her point.

"They wouldn't know it was Alfie. That's why they're called confidential informants. Anyway, Alfie was more directional with his information than specific. Sam knows what I mean."

"He heard and saw a lot," I said. "Wouldn't necessarily know what it all meant."

"Where's Ross in all this?" Sullivan asked.

"Out of the loop," I said. "There's an official probe under way. No idea how they're going about it. But Edith Madison asked us to go CI ourselves."

"Get the fuck *out* of here," said Sullivan.

"Meanwhile Ross invited us to go ahead and dig around Alfie's murder despite the ongoing investigation," I said.

"What the hell's going on, Joe?" Jackie asked.

He didn't want to answer, but knew he had to say something after we'd shown him such unconditional trust and regard.

"I don't know. Don't even know how to think about it. Ross runs such a tight ship, no way he doesn't know. But if he knew, heads would already be rolling all over Southampton."

"Why did you jump to the snitches?" I asked.

"Three in a matter of weeks? Basically the whole snitch staff. Either an incredible run of bad luck, or somebody inside is dropping dimes. That makes sense up to the point it doesn't. Officially the only people who know who's snitching are me, Veckstrom, and Ross."

"Officially?" Jackie asked.

Sullivan let a little embarrassment intrude on his general air of defiance.

"First off you don't know who says what on the outside. Inside, none of us tried too hard to keep it confidential. Talk can be loose around the squad room. Occasionally a snitch will come in for a longer session, and never get booked, which was supposed to be the cover. Sloppy, now that I think about it, though you never think you have to hide stuff from your own cops."

"You know them all that well?" Jackie asked.

He thought about it.

"Sure, except for the new guys. One rookie from town and one transfer from Up Island. Both been there about a year. Normal replacements for two retirees. Just cops from what I can see."

"So nothing else?" Jackie asked.

Sullivan's face froze in place.

"Already said too much. If you don't mind, I'll be getting back to my burger before it turns into a block of ice."

Then he walked back into the restaurant, and we followed.

We flopped back at the table and ordered some food for ourselves and a few rounds of drinks, but it was a pretty subdued affair, not being able to talk about the thing most on our minds and too distracted to talk about anything else.

EDDIE WAS waiting on the lawn with a rubber ball between his feet. He looked down at the ball, then up at me, his face saying, "You know what to do here."

I'd never seen the ball, which looked fairly new. I hoped it was scavenged and not an outright theft from a small child on the beach, not unprecedented.

We went out to the Adirondack chairs where Eddie could perform his Rin Tin Tin leap off the breakwater. I was pleased to see Amanda sitting in one of the other chairs, slumped down with her head back, pitcher of cosmopolitans and a bowl of red grapes on the side table. I tossed the ball hard down the pebble beach and sat next to her.

"Don't let him fool you," she said, without opening her eyes. "I've been throwing that ball for hours."

"You can just say no."

"I did. That's when he went to wait for you. Sucker."

"Where'd he get it?"

"Don't know, but I heard wailing and assumed the worst."

"How was your day?" I asked.

She scrunched up her face and stuck out her tongue.

"I'd rather hear about yours."

So I told her everything I could remember. It took awhile since I had to answer perfectly reasonable questions I hadn't yet broached myself.

"Okay, so you had a worse day," she said. "Now I feel like a fool."

"It's not a contest. We're bad-day neutral here on Oak Point."

I couldn't see her very well in the pale moonlight, but I could sense her pulling back her thick hair to better see me.

"I find it hard to believe. It's about the last thing I'd think our cops would do," she said.

"You don't know all our cops."

"True."

"And though it looks like Ross and Edith have handed us the keys to the realm, I don't believe anything they say."

"I recall you once saying, 'Nothing is ever what it seems,'" she said.

"'Nothing' might be overstating the case."

"You can't possibly think Joe Sullivan is involved."

"He better not be. We just spilled the whole pot of beans."

"You told him?" she asked.

"We did. But if he's dirty, we've been transported to an alternate universe, one not worth living in."

"Speak for yourself. I might like it."

"It seems like Edith and Ross want people on the outside, but we need people on the inside. Which has to be Joe Sullivan."

"You like Danny Izard. Still a beat cop."

"Exactly. Too far from the action. It has to be Sullivan. Anyway it's too late to change course. The deed is done."

Amanda put her head back against her Adirondack chair and closed her eyes. She stayed like that for so long, I thought she'd fallen asleep. I occupied myself drinking and watching for subtle changes in the Little Peconic's ecosphere. So I was startled when Amanda, without moving, said quite clearly, "So what the hell is going on?"

I wanted to give her an entirely honest answer, so I thought a bit before answering the question.

"Unusual things are happening for sure, likely related, though maybe not. Everyone is suddenly behaving contrary to established norms. Unless I never really grasped those norms to begin with. There is almost no data, and no clear way to develop any, and the major players are either territorial, conspiratorial, manipulative, unreliable, or certifiably insane. Or all the above."

"In other words, you haven't a clue," she said.

"I haven't. All the more reason to refill the tumbler."

"I'll be here when you get back."

Chapter Six

The next day I was deep into coping joints for the cherry molding I'd custom-shaped for the built-in china cabinet when Jackie trotted down into my shop through the basement hatch. She wore flip-flops and a yellow cotton dress over a wet two-piece bathing suit.

Her frizz-ball hair was partially air-dried and the bright summer sun seemed to have added a few hundred new freckles.

"Welcome, I think," I said.

"You're always glad to see me."

She picked up a piece of the curved molding and examined the coped angle. "You know making this stuff doesn't seem possible," she said. "To the layperson."

"Seems that way to me, too," I said. "What's on your mind?"

"I really meant the compliment."

"Okay. Thanks. But you're not here to assess my carpentry skills."

She continued to study the wood pieces. "If someone gives you the keys to a house, where all but one of the doors inside are supposed to be locked," she said, without looking up at me, "but you're, like, really good at jimmying locks, so you do, because, what the hell, you're already in the house and all, so why waste an opportunity? What's the moral hazard?"

"I'm supposed to do the breaking and entering on this team," I said. "You're supposed to tell me not to and then I do it anyway."

"I'm speaking metaphorically. It's not actually a house."

"I guess that's good."

"It's a database."

"Maybe not so good. So you had access to a specific file and you hacked your way into other files you weren't supposed to see?"

"Not me personally. Randall Dodge."

Randall was a tall, skinny Shinnecock Indian (technically sort of an Indian/African American/Irish gumbo) and former cyber sleuth for the US Navy who ran a computer hardware repair and software training operation out of a storefront in Southampton Village. Jackie and I had taken occasional advantage of his technical skills in return for help with some legal entanglements.

"You had him hack the database," I said.

"I'd rather not use the word 'hack.' Sounds unseemly."

"No. Sounds illegal. Depending on whom you hacked."

"I guess I should know that better than you. From a legal perspective."

"So who's the victim?" I asked.

She stood there silently, indecision scrunching up her pretty round face. "You're going to tell me eventually. Stop wasting time and just get it out."

"The New York State Police?" she said, with enough upspeak to lift a truck.

"Not really."

"Really."

I put down the coping saw and sat on a tall stool. I looked at her face for traces of humor, in the hope it was just a bad joke.

"It's not a joke," she said, interpreting my look. "Tucked inside all the paper Oksana gave me was a link to the master CI file on the State Police server. I'm guessing there's a lot more information there than what Oksana gave us. It was password protected, of course, but I thought Randall might find it fun to see if he could crack the code."

"Fun? How much fun do you think he'll have in Hungerford State Penitentiary?"

"Randall doesn't get caught," she said, though with less conviction than she might have wanted to express.

"Not yet."

She reached in a pocket of the yellow dress and took out a flash drive. She held it up to the bright light of the shop. "It's amazing how much stuff you can stick on one of these things." Then she looked at me. "I don't suppose you'd want a look."

I didn't own a computer. I'd barely touched a keyboard since using the dumb terminal in my office to run technical analyses through a roomful of IBM mainframes. Getting cashiered from my corporate job had more or less killed my interest in digital technology, now preferring information delivered by the printed word or words spoken over the rim of a glass.

"No. I'm not even touching it."

She wiggled the drive in the air.

"I don't believe you," she said.

"Why take that kind of risk? What were you thinking?" I asked.

"That Edith wants to keep us in a tight little maze. That always makes me want to jump the walls and take a look around."

"Go ahead and look," I said, picking up the little coping saw and piece of molding, trying to remember where I'd left off. "I'll be working on my deniability."

She put the flash drive on my workbench and backed away.

"I might've accidentally dropped that on the floor. How would you know where it came from?" she said, then added, "It's a download. A copy. They can't know you're rummaging around in the attic. Just stay off the web while you rummage."

"Why's that?"

"I don't know. Ask Randall."

I looked at the drive, pausing over my work piece.

"What're we looking for?" I asked.

"You'll know it when you see it."

"You really don't know."

"I don't. I could do this all by myself, but four eyeballs are better than two."

She left the flash drive on the workbench on her way out. I ignored it for the rest of the day, concentrating as best I could on the cherry china cabinet.

After freshening up in the outside shower, I walked across our common lawn to Amanda's house—a creamy stucco- and blue-trimmed deal that looked like it'd been airlifted in from Provence. Amanda was out on her patio reading a thick, glossy publication issued by one of the bigger real estate agencies.

"Scouting the competition," she said, as I loaded up at the wet bar.

"How do you stack up?"

"Well in the running, buddy, if you filter out lovers of bad taste and ostentation."

"That covers a lot of territory."

"How was the woodshop?"

"Productive, despite an appearance by Jackie Swaitkowski."

"More on Alfie Aldergreen?"

"Sort of. Do you know how to work one of these things?" I asked, holding up the flash drive.

"I do. What's on it?"

"Dossiers on confidential informants, past and present. Illegally obtained."

"Eek."

"I'd rather not make you an accomplice after the fact, but I don't have a computer."

"I thought being an accomplice was the centerpiece of our relationship?"

"Let's boot it up."

We retired to her business office, an airy space with glass-topped furniture and white walls, darkened only by a shelf full of catalogs for building materials and household appliances.

"Jackie said to stay off the Internet when you're down-loading or accessing this information," I told her as she plugged the flash drive into a CPU on the floor.

"How come?"

"Some sort of security alchemy."

"That's comforting."

After starting the machine and clicking around folders and files, she stood up and offered me the mouse.

"Why don't you drive the car," she said.

It took a moment to remember how to use the mouse and navigate the file structures, but I got there. Like riding a bicycle.

"This isn't so hard," I said. "What's everybody talking about?"

"They aren't."

The first layer of the file structure was by date. Within that, it was broken out by police jurisdiction, a complicated thing in New York State where geopolitical bureaucracies are configured like a Russian nesting doll—Southampton Village inside Southampton Town, inside Suffolk County, inside New York State. I went into Southampton Town, started on current investigations, and burrowed down from there.

Two hours later, long after she'd wandered away, Amanda came into the office to announce dinner. I must have looked reluctant to move.

"You have to eat, darling. Your fingers need their strength."

After a tasty, but nearly silent meal—my mind being too cluttered with police procedure and jargon to manage a coherent conversation—I went back to the computer.

I was no stranger to the addictive properties of computer-aided research, but even I was surprised by how seductive it could be to rifle through utterly forbidden information. Another two hours passed before Amanda visited again, this time holding a big glass of vodka.

"I'm trying to knock you out so you'll abandon your new love and come to bed with me."

I looked up at her.

"I need another couple hours."

"Wake me up," she said, drifting back out of the room.

I could see why CIs could be such a crucial resource. Joey Wentworth, like Lilly Fremouth, was a fountain of insider information on the shipping, handling, and distribution of drugs. At the same time, they were both skilled in what to share and what to withhold. It was simple economics. If a snitch shared too much it reduced the value of the product, and often increased the possibility of getting caught by the snitched-upon. A bad career move.

With Alfie it was hard to tell. Sullivan was terse and to the point in his reports. Tempering with heavy qualifications any of Alfie's commentary. Unlike Joey and Lilly, who had a focus—heroin and prostitution respectively—Alfie was more generalized. A good example concerned an elegant woman with an indefinable foreign accent who frequented the more expensive boutiques in Southampton Village. Alfie noticed that she looked heavier leaving a shop than she did going in, and always seemed to be carrying the same bags every day. Sullivan worked with a Village cop named Judy Rensler to set up a sting, and sure enough, the woman was a professional shoplifter born and raised in Babylon on Long Island.

Other cases involved an old lady who picked up the wrong pug from where it was tied to a street sign, a team of teen-aged pickpockets—a girl and a boy who used the proceeds to buy surfing gear—and a skinny but lovely Latvian hostess at one of the restaurants on Jobs Lane who supplemented her income by giving blowjobs to anyone weighing less than three hundred pounds and in possession of an exotic sports car.

Hardly the stuff that should lead to summary execution.

Veckstrom, on the other hand, wrote like a career journalist with pretensions toward literary fiction. He had a law degree and a wealthy wife whose family's house on the beach in Southampton had been the original draw to the East End. The guy hated my guts, so it took a little effort to appreciate the intellectual sophistication beneath the arrogant sneer and relentless accusation.

He described his dealings with Joey Wentworth in terms of a psychological dynamic that had more to do with Joey's relationship with his rich, effeminate father and overbearing, but infantile mother than the kid's thirst for quick, sleazy profiteering. It was police paperwork in the form of Ibsen and O'Neill, though I admit it had me reading to the end, with Joey splattered all over the inside of his SUV, leaving Veckstrom at a loss over motive or perpetrator.

Not for lack of suspects. Everyone in the underground distribution chain had used his marine delivery services at one time or another, though no one really liked him personally, and he didn't like any of them.

No wife, no girlfriend—or boyfriend—no group affiliations or notorious feuds, just a low grade sociopath with a souped-up picnic boat and a penchant for risky business.

Despite the concentrated effort, there was more to read in the snitch files, but it was late, my eyes were sore, and a woman who made me promise to wake her up was quietly sleeping only a few doors away.

BEFORE I'D brought the Grand Prix to the repair guys to fix the rear window, I'd noticed in the daylight a rosy smear around an area that hadn't quite busted through. My first thought was bloodstain, a thought that vanished from my consciousness almost as quickly as it arrived.

Until I saw the plastic sour cream container in my shop that held the salvaged piece of glass. I picked it out of the container with a pair of pliers and looked at it under a task light. The stain was still there, now dried a darker red, but unmistakable.

I slipped the shard into a zip loc bag and stuck it in my pocket.

I worked another few hours in the shop, then called Joe Sullivan.

"Say Joe, how close are you with the ME these days?" I asked him when he answered the phone.

"No closer than I have to be."

"I think the guy who smashed in my rear window left a bloodstain. Do you think he'd run a DNA test for you?"

"I don't answer ridiculous questions when I'm off duty."

"They let you off duty?" I asked.

"Ask me tomorrow so I can officially say no."

"No?"

"We can barely get DNA from a murder weapon these days. They're backed up, like, fifty years," he said.

"He'd do it for you."

"No. But he might do it for Jackie."

"Really?"

"I can submit it as evidence," he said, "then she can tickle his tummy or whatever it takes to put it through sometime before the end of the century."

I shook off the unwanted image before it could take hold.

"Okay. Can I bring it over?"

"I said I was off."

"I know where you live. I'll bring coffee."

"Milk, no sugar," he said, then hung up.

BACK IN the early twentieth century when regular middle-class neighborhoods were growing up around Southampton Village, it was common practice to put a little free-standing apartment at the back of the lot, often over a garage, to have a place to store surplus relatives, sometimes a maid or gardener, or even rent-paying boarders. Municipal planning had outlawed the practice for new construction, for no good reason, though grandfathered "mother-in-law" apartments and guesthouses endured, instantly hiking the value of any property thus endowed.

Joe Sullivan lived in one behind the home of a friend's parents, local people thrilled to have such an eminent police presence in their neighborhood. Most of the other locals had sold out long before, converting the Hamptons's breathtaking real estate inflation into bigger houses in South Carolina and unexpectedly sumptuous retirements.

Though crime in the area was nearly unheard of, the old couple was unnerved by all the summer homes left abandoned nine months out of the year.

The cottage Sullivan rented was a miniature version of the main house, enclosed in mature shrubbery and made no less quaint by the unmarked Ford Crown Victoria parked a few feet from the front door.

I rang the doorbell, waited a few minutes, then rang it again. Sullivan swung open the door, greeting me with a snarl.

"Repeated ringing of a doorbell doesn't make a person answer any quicker," he said.

"Now you tell me."

He was wearing a sweat suit that loudly declared affiliation with the New York Giants. In his hand was a large coffee mug. On his feet were US Army desert-tan combat boots. I wondered where he'd stowed the lightweight .38 that never left his body.

He backed away from the door so I could enter a comfortable living area, unadorned, but clean and well lit, with a pair of plain fabric couches and a flat-screen TV.

"I brought reinforcements," I said, holding up a large cup of coffee bought at the corner place in the Village.

We sat across from each other on the couches. He stuck out his mug and I filled it up. The sour, sugary smell of metabolizing alcohol scented the air.

"How're you doing these days, Joe," I asked.

He looked unhappy with the question.

"Never better. What about you? What's with the grey hair?"

"It's what happens when it doesn't fall out."

"Great. Something else to look forward to."

Sullivan's wife had left him the year before. She cited, fairly, his career's lousy hours, dangerous working conditions, and short money. I'd never met her, but heard enough gritching in the background whenever I called him to guess the woman's nature. I didn't know how he felt about the whole thing, since we never talked about it.

"Or you could die early and avoid the whole thing," I said.

"Thanks for the coffee," he said, after taking a tentative sip.

"Pretty nice place," I said, looking around.

"You have to live somewhere."

I took the plastic bag with the glass shard and tossed it over to him.

"It's from the busted rear window of my Grand Prix. You can see the red stain pretty clearly. Makes me think the idiot used his fist to punch out the glass."

"Not easy to do," he said.

"But possible if you know how."

"Or you're too dumb to know better."

"Sure. If you're dumb, but strong," I said.

He put the bag in his sweatpants pocket.

"No promises."

"Any progress on Alfie?" I asked.

His scowl, nearly gone, regained purchase on his face.

"It's not going to be easy."

"I don't like that."

He pulled himself up so he could rest his elbows on his knees, moving closer to his argument.

"No witnesses, no prints, no forensics. No suspects."

"He was a snitch."

"Nobody knew that," he said.

"The cops knew. He said they were after him."

He banged his mug down on the coffee table.

"He was my CI. Nobody else knew."

"Ross knew. And Alfie could have spilled the beans to anyone. He was crazy, after all, as everyone likes pointing out."

"We're not talking Deep Throat here. He knew some shit, but nothing that should've got him killed. You think I'm happy about this? Tracking down killers is actually my job. And that freak was my responsibility. So take your fucking MIT, self-anointed moral paternalism and find somewhere else to peddle it."

"Edith Madison anointed me. And don't call her paternalistic. Would have to be *maternalistic*, but you'd know that if you went to MIT."

He shook his head and downed the rest of his coffee. He said I could make another pot if I wanted more. I took our mugs into the kitchen where I found an ancient Mr. Coffee on the counter and a half-dozen empty beer cans in the trash. The only thing in the fridge was a quart of milk. There were frozen bagels in the freezer, but the cupboards were empty. Three-quarters of a case of beer was under the sink.

"What're you looking for?" he called from the living room.

"Filters. Found 'em."

When I brought out the coffee I asked him if he wanted to go grab some lunch. He said no.

"Got a busy day planned," he said. "Checkin' the fences on the back forty, rebalancing my portfolio, and damn, when am I going to finish that collection of tone poems? My fans'll be at my throat."

"Suit yourself."

"That's all I do now, Sam," he said, falling back into his couch as if shoved there by an invisible hand. "And all I'm ever going to do for the rest of my life. What there is of it."

I left him there and went back outside where the summer
heat had draped a sodden blanket over the East End, though
somehow it felt more like a breath of fresh air.

CHAPTER SEVEN

I waited in Amanda's bedroom for her to come out of the shower. I sat in the overstuffed chair she used to read in at night before making the four-foot journey to her king-sized bed. I wore an off-white linen suit and a yellow silk tie my ex-wife bought me back when I had a wife and few defenses against the imposition of silk ties.

Amanda wore a white terry cloth towel on her head when she came through the bathroom door.

"What's the occasion?" she asked.

"Fund-raiser."

"Whose funds do they expect to raise?"

"Yours, presumably. All of mine are in frozen assets," I said, rattling the ice around the bottom of my vodka tumbler.

She threw the towel in my lap and retrieved an embroidered robe out of the clothes closet.

"I'll have to dry my hair, moisturize, decide on a lipstick, and all that. You're welcome to stay, though you'll find it all rather boring."

I wouldn't. Watching Amanda get dressed was almost as involving as watching the reverse. Though usually with less consequential outcomes. Still I did have other things to do. The tumbler was nearly empty, a flashy rose and magenta sunset was about to get under way over the Little Peconic, and my copy of *Candide, ou l'Optimisme* was still on a glass-topped table on Amanda's blue stone patio. So that's where I headed.

The sun was just under the horizon and the impression-ist's hallucination in the sky was in its full fury when Amanda joined me. So quiet was her soft footfall that I heard a rustling sound before I saw her slipping into her favorite recliner. My eyes left Voltaire as I watched her smooth the folds of her dress over the fronts of her thighs, brush invisible flecks from her shoulders, and adjust the drape of aqua fabric around her flat belly into a more satisfactory set.

"You are going to explain all this, I'm sure," she said, without looking up from her preening.

"Lionel Veckstrom's father-in-law was born with a brick factory."

"Not in one, presumably."

"The business was started by his great-grandfather, and run successfully by the heirs until the early twentieth century when they stopped making things out of brick."

"I'm building a brick chimney for one of my houses."

"Mostly stopped. Veckstrom's father-in-law had the fore-sight to dump the factory while it still had some value, enough to buy daughter Lacey a life without work, unless you count redoing her house on Gin Lane."

"And you know this . . . ?" she asked.

"He told me. Veckstrom's father-in-law, sitting on a bar stool at Mad Martha's."

"Pretty cheeky. I didn't know a guy like that could drink in a bar like that."

"Contrary to myth, Martha accepts US currency with no socioeconomic bias."

"Not what I hear."

"And as to Renard's cheeks, they glowed a nice bright pink."

"Wilson Renard? I knew him. He was one of my clients at the bank. Must have owned a very big brick factory."

"More like a brick factory town. He hated the business, though I'm sorry to say he wasn't much happier collecting investment revenue. Some people you can't please, though according to him, his late wife and Lacey took to the responsibilities of wealth with selfless enthusiasm."

"Noble."

"An important feature of which, as you know, involves lots of fund-raising parties where the participants are forced to eat unpronounceable finger food off silver trays while wearing their best guess at what the season considers au courant."

"That disqualifies us."

"Come on, you love finger food."

"And you hate fund-raisers. So why go to one thrown by Lionel Veckstrom's wife? What's the attraction?"

"Lionel Veckstrom."

To COMPLETE our disguise, we drove Amanda's zippy little Audi. On the way over to the ocean, I convinced her that crashing an invitation-only society event in the Hamptons was the easiest thing in the world.

"All it takes is money," I said.

"It seems my money's being freely recruited into the project."

"Nah, this one's on me."

Most people think the famous Gin Lane in Southampton got its name from the free flow of bathtub gin during prohibition, but it was actually the Puritan English settlers who called the cattle-grazing areas "gins." Hard to say which era's residents would be more horrified by the other's definition of the word.

The Renard property might have supported a small herd if they gave up the 3,500-square-foot guesthouse, twin tennis courts, and topiary garden. I parked the Audi along the road and we walked up to a pair of bouncers disguised as valets in white shirts, thin black ties, and black pants.

"I forgot our tickets," I said, rummaging around my inside jacket pocket. "I really hope we don't have to go all the way back to East Hampton."

The head bouncer, as identified by dominant height and girth, seemed unmoved.

"Sorry, sir. Tickets required."

"We're on the list, you have a list, don't you?" I asked, looking around him at a little table that showed no sign of a list.

"Is Lacey nearby?" Amanda asked, looking through the open iron gate.

"Need tickets," the guy said.

"Wait a minute," I said, pulling out a folded piece of paper. "Maybe this will work."

The guy took the paper, opened it up, then put it in his pocket.

"That works," he said, stepping out of the way.

Amanda put her arm through mine as we passed through the gate.

"So you had the tickets," she said.

"Just a hundred-dollar bill. A type of ticket."

"We bribed our way into Lacey Renard's fund-raiser?"

"Cheaper than a ticket."

A prevailing southwesterly breeze was blowing mist in off the ocean, cooling the air and setting a fuzzy halo around the half moon above. Some of the guests were warming themselves by a line of commercial grills operated by men and women in white chefs' outfits, though most were within gliding distance of the bars stationed at thirty-foot intervals around the periphery of the main tent.

The men's costumes were predominantly white or mixed colors you'd normally see in tubs of sorbet. Hair was mostly white or grey, where it grew, though younger, leaner, and less confident swells were well represented. The women could be safely divided into two camps—those with and without

artificial faces. The phony ones usually maximized the effect
with an excess of processed hair and enough gold and precious stones to sink an ocean liner.

I recognized a few of them, altered and otherwise, many
of them customers of Frank Entwhistle. One was a couple
named Joshua and Roseanne Edelstein. Joshua recognized
me despite the yellow tie and ran over as if he'd just redis-
covered a rich uncle.

"Hey, Sam. Sam Acquillo," he said, grabbing my hand in
both of his. "You remember Sam, right Rosie?"

Rosie was a pale, consumptive-looking thing in a pure
white dress and straw hat, and despite the late hour, sunglasses four times bigger than her featureless face could sustain. She dangled her hand in my general direction.

"I think I do," she said.

"That's okay if you don't. I can't remember my own name."
I held her limp hand and put an arm around Amanda's waist.
"This is Amanda Anselma."

"Sam built all the coolest stuff in the house," Joshua told
her. "The fun stuff."

"I'm not surprised," said Amanda. "Who's more fun than
Sam?"

"It's all still there," said Joshua. "Nothing's fallen on our
heads."

"There's a relief," I said.

"Did you do the Veckstroms'?" Rosie asked, still trying to
get me fixed in the right place.

"I certainly hope not," said Amanda.

"Lionel and I have had some professional involvement," I
said. "Professional for him, anyway."

"I don't know Lionel," said Rosie, as if relieved by the fact.

"Some place they got here," said Joshua, looking around.

"It's all Lacey," said Rosie.

"You don't know that," said Joshua, with gentle reproach.

She tilted her head away from him and I think rolled her
eyes, but they were hidden behind the sunglasses.

"I miss all that, Sam," said Joshua. "The building process. Who would have thought?"

"I would have," said Amanda.

"She's a builder," I said.

"The problem with finishing a house is, you're like, finished. You know?" said Joshua.

"Then you have to live in it," I said.

His eyes flicked over to Rosie and back.

"You do."

Rosie pinched a piece of his lime green and white seersucker jacket and pulled him away.

"Come, Joshua," she said. "The champagne is calling."

We let them retreat without resistance. Joshua saluted me with his cocktail, which made me wonder why he was drinking and I wasn't.

"Hearing a call of your own?" Amanda asked, reading my mind.

It wasn't until we'd hit one of the bars frequently enough to develop a relationship with the bartender that we ran into Lionel Veckstrom. Almost literally, as he spun toward me with a drink in each hand, barely avoiding a collision.

"Well, Sam Acquillo," he said, running his eyes over my suit. His was a three-piece in an antique cut, well complemented by tan and brown saddle shoes and a bow tie. Pushing his fifties, Veckstrom had a handsome, though fleshy, face with a weak chin and Paul McCartney eyes. His vest did a decent job of outlining a narrow waist and contoured upper body.

"Hi, Lionel."

"Didn't see you on the invite list."

"You probably haven't met Amanda Anselma," I said.

Amanda stuck out her hand.

"Sure," he said. "Mrs. Battiston from the bank."

He was referring to her former job as a personal banker, working for former husband Roy Battiston before he'd transitioned to a minimum-security cell in Upstate New York.

"I knew your father-in-law," she said. "From the bank. I was sorry to see him go."

"He had a good life," he said, as if still arguing the appropriateness of the old man's death. "If you don't mind," he added, holding up the two drinks.

We didn't. He left and we drifted into the general crowd, cleaving to each other and searching discreetly for a safe social harbor. Instead we ran into Oksana Quan from the prosecutor's office. She displayed her usual tightly wrapped beauty, somewhat loosened by a spectral white dress that fluttered haphazardly in the freshening sea breeze. I noticed the white nail polish when she extended her hand to Amanda.

"I remember you from the Milhouser case," said Oksana. "You sat in the back."

She meant the case her boss had hoped would get me a life sentence in a prison far more secure than Roy Battiston's. I thought I should look around for other legal people at the party so we could start a discussion group on my encounters with criminal prosecution.

"I remember you, too," said Amanda, the exact meaning of which was indecipherable to me but obviously understood by the two of them.

"Did you bring Edith along?" I asked Oksana.

"I don't bring Mrs. Madison anywhere. She brings me."

"I didn't know this was a political event," I said. "I thought they were raising money to neuter cats or something."

"Cats and dogs," said Oksana.

"Maybe we could throw in politicians," I said.

"I'll pass that along to Edith," said Oksana.

"Still doesn't explain what she's doing here," I said.

Oksana looked over our heads and scanned the crowd.

"Oh, the wealthiest fund-raising freaks on the East End. Oh, you think they might want to contribute to the election of the Suffolk County district attorney some day? Oh, gee, I don't know."

"I think you've got your answer," said Amanda.

"Maybe Edith would like me better if I pitched in a couple hundred bucks," I said.

"Consider it already returned," said Oksana.

I wanted to ask her if she had any information that would help our snooping around, but I couldn't let her know I'd spilled a highly confidential investigation to my girlfriend.

"How'd you get in to the prosecution business, anyway?" I asked her, with my usual gift for small talk.

She looked at me like I'd just asked her bra size, but managed to force out, "I interned in the city after graduating from law school. One thing led to another."

She took a sip from her drink, something that looked suspiciously like Diet Coke, and looked around again, this time to spot someone who could help her escape.

"Where'd you go to college?" I asked, on a roll.

"An art school," she said. "You wouldn't know it."

"Try me," I said. "My daughter went to art school."

Her attention suddenly swung back to my face, her eyes slightly wider despite a new furrow in her brow.

"Allison Acquillo?" she said. "Oh, God, I should have realized. How many Acquillos would the world allow?"

"You went to RISD?" I asked, actually somewhat pleased. It almost made Oksana seem like a standard human being to have shared a campus with my all-too-unstandard daughter.

"I did," she said. "And yes, it's not a conventional pathway to law school. But I decided I had to make a living."

"Allison makes a rather nice living," said Amanda, lightly, though I detected the slightest change in tone, an intimation of where things might go if we continued traveling this conversational path.

"I'm not surprised. We all wished we had her talent," said Oksana, using the moment to slip away as if her dress had finally been scooped up by the wind.

Amanda held her wine in the air, deciding between taking a sip, or tossing it at Oksana, as she walked across the grass. I clinked it to encourage the former.

"Let's keep moving," I said. "I could use the exercise."

I took her hand and we did a meandering turn through the milling humanity, around clumps of intimate conversations, fortifying at the round, munchie-laden tables and our new favorite bar. Thus occupied, we avoided further contact with other people until I saw Lionel again, speaking with a woman I thought was probably his wife, Lacey.

Again, Amanda did her bit by breaking the ice.

"Hello, Lacey," she said. "Lovely event. So good of you to support such an important cause."

Lacey looked pleased, though slightly confused, trying to place Amanda within her cohort of philanthropists and the merely aspiring.

"Thank you," she said. "I suppose these things come naturally to me. Lionel is so supportive."

I wanted to ask Lionel if proper neutering started in the home, but for once thought better of it.

Amanda complimented Lacey on the gush of summer flowers lining a nearby bed and asked if she wouldn't mind identifying the species. When the women were out of earshot, I asked Lionel, "Any luck on the Alfie Aldergreen thing?"

He stiffened, though his eyes looked amused.

"You get to bug Sullivan about that one," he said.

"But you have thoughts on the matter."

"None that I'd share with you."

"You want to hear mine?" I asked.

"Not really."

"Alfie was crazy, but observant. Didn't have much else to do but watch what was going on. I think he saw something he shouldn't have."

"Yeah, Southampton Village is a real criminal hotbed. Just the other day I saw a Chihuahua pee on a flower box."

I couldn't reveal I knew Alfie was an informant, which hampered the discussion.

"Did you get an ID on that pooch? I hear Edith Madison is here. She loves to prosecute."

"I'll never know how she fucked up Milhouser," said Veckstrom.

He meant the murder case against me.

"The killer confessed. That generally rises to a higher level of importance than 'I hate that sonofabitch Acquillo.'"

"I don't hate you, Sam. Any more than I hate the bugs we have to spray in the garden every spring."

"I thought I was the only Buddhist in town."

"Speaking of legal issues, you can tell Swaitkowski to keep her nose out of my investigations," he said. "I'm not a sucker for a short skirt like Sullivan and the captain."

"You told me Alfie was Sullivan's."

"Joey Wentworth's parents are wondering why she wants to talk to them. I am, too. If she shows up at their door, they're instructed to call the police."

"You're the police."

"I'd be happy to bust her for obstruction. It's long overdue."

I would have agreed with him, but there was no sense piling on.

"I thought you had a law degree," I said. "No honor among thieves?"

"I'd rather join al-Qaeda than work as a defense attorney."

"So why not be a prosecutor yourself? You could put innocent people in jail. Help undermine zoning regulations so rich fucks could ruin the beaches. There's plenty of that kind of work out here."

I'd call his expression blank if I'd ever seen him make any other kind of expression. To me, he was always blank.

"I think that falls in the category of none of your fucking business," he said, fairly enough.

"Noted," I said, saluting with my vodka.

"I'm going to see what Lacey is up to. I'm sure there are other people here for you to annoy," he said, leaving me on my own, exposed to the predations of the social set. Luckily Amanda got there first.

"How's Lionel?" she asked.

"He said he doesn't hate me."

"Could've fooled me."

"I'll just hate him twice as much to make up for it."

"Did you learn anything?" she asked.

"He suspects Jackie Swaitkowski of interfering with an official police investigation."

"That's shocking."

We made one more stroll around the event, talked to a few people we actually enjoyed talking to, drained off more of the hosts' free booze, and eventually grew intolerably weary of the whole thing.

"I'm ready," said Amanda.

"Oh, yeah."

When we reached the valet stand I was surprised to see Lacey there, sending people off. I told her as much.

"My father's doing. He always said farewells were just as important as hellos. It's amazing how that parent stuff sticks in your head."

My father always said a pain in the ass was better than a poke in the eye with a sharp stick, but I didn't share that with her.

"Thanks again, Lacey," said Amanda. "Your home is exquisite and the event just so."

That moved Lacey to surprise her with an enthusiastic hug. Amanda did her best to return the gesture, guarded of her personal space though she was.

"Did you get a chance to talk to Lionel?" Lacey asked, still holding Amanda with both hands.

"A bit."

"You know he's a good man," said Lacey.

"Why else would he be with you?" said Amanda, clearly confused. She wasn't the only one.

"So we have your support," said Lacey, then realizing Amanda hadn't immediately reacted, said, "The election. For district attorney. We're announcing tomorrow. You know

Lionel's the right man at the right time with the right vision
for Suffolk County."

"I'd say there's even more to him than that, Lacey," said
Amanda.

We didn't speak much on the way back to Oak Point.
I concentrated on driving and Amanda pretended to sleep.
Eddie was on duty when we got there and did a fine job herd-
ing us across the lawn to the Adirondack chairs, after we'd
paused at the cottage for pillows, blankets, Big Dog biscuits,
and two cups of coffee to guard against another night's sleep
on the grass.

The air was clear and warm, and calm, in contrast to
the blustery conditions over on the ocean. Once settled in, I
reached over and took Amanda's hand.

"Do you think he can win?" she asked.

"He's got the money."

"Don't tell me it's possible for a woman to buy her husband a political office. Even on the county level."

I didn't say anything, which was better than disappointing
her with the truth.

CHAPTER EIGHT

The next day I briefed Jackie on our time at the Veckstrom fund-raiser, in particular the conversation with Lionel and his feelings about her talking to Joey Wentworth's parents.

"I can talk to any goddamned person I want," she said.

"You can. And he can twist any goddamned thing you do into obstruction of justice. A disbarrable offense."

"I've heard that before."

"Let's switch. Let me take Veckstrom's CIs. There's not much he can do to me. You take Sullivan."

"What's going on with him?" she asked. "He's acting weird."

"I don't know. But it's not good."

"Is that an expression of concern for another human being? Are you sure you're Sam Acquillo?"

"How do I find Wentworth's parents?"

She told me, but then said, "I wasn't going there next. I got a lead on one of Joey's customers. Or more like a link in the supply chain. Mustafa Karadeniz. Harry knows him from the logistics trade. Turk. Owns Manny's Despatch out of Riverhead."

"Manny's?" I asked.

"Before I joined Burton's practice I helped him with an easement at his warehouse. It wasn't until I met Harry that I learned why the place was always half-empty. Keeps just enough stuff to maintain the front."

"What did he want to ease?"

"The driveway behind his warehouse was owned by a Jamaican bar and grill. We lost the case, but Mustafa was unmoved. A few weeks later the health department found the bar's kitchen infested with rats. Two weeks after that Mustafa bought the bar, tore it down, and shipped it to the dump, rats and all."

"Seems like a good place to start," I said.

"Be careful."

"Always."

"Right."

ON THE way to Riverhead, I stopped in the Village to charge my mug with French Vanilla from the coffee shop on the corner. The owner had devised a devilishly complex service layout, which mattered little off-season. In the summer the place was crammed with people from Manhattan, most of whom seemed invigorated by the challenge of competing for their coffee and croissants.

As a regular, I had a leg up. When the Guatemalan lady behind the counter saw me, she poured my usual and handed it over. This raised a lot of suspicion in the woman standing next to me, who rightly assumed I was trading on inside information.

"I've been standing here a long time," she said.

"Not as long as me," I said.

"You know the owner, you're taken care of. It's ever thus."

"Never met the guy."

"It's not what you know. It's who you know," she said, not listening.

"Envy destroys happiness," I told her, before muscling my way back through the crowd, and after grabbing a *Times*, settling onto a park bench to complete the ritual.

I was almost finished with the paper when I saw a headline in the City Section, "Many Questions in Death of Disabled Vet." The byline was Roger Angstrom, the reporter who'd written a long piece on Jackie after she'd saved one of her knuckle-headed clients in a dramatic enough way to attract the media.

The article laid out the facts pretty much as we knew them, leaving out the dead snitches. Predictably, the quotes from vacationers focused on such a cruel act taking place at the height of an idyllic Hamptons summer.

And at these rents, was the unspoken thought.

There was no mention of Jackie Swaitkowski, so he'd honored his source, though he'd managed to wrangle a quote from Ross Semple.

"The perpetrators of this heinous crime should be on notice. To us, a troubled man like Alfie Aldergreen is no different from the richest guy in the biggest house on the ocean. We won't give up until justice is served."

Despite the pat sentiment, I knew he meant every word.

RIVERHEAD IS a tough little town stuck in the crotch of the twin forks of Long Island. It was most notable these days for the strip development arcing over its northern territories. Mustafa's place was close to the original urban center, a vestige of small town America unmarred by the opulence of its Hamptons neighbors to the east.

The building was made of stone, unthinkable today with instant metal buildings and vanishing craftsmanship. I pulled into an empty parking lot, trying to sense the reggae music and oceans of Red Stripe that once flowed through the neighborhood.

I hadn't called ahead. Cops don't call ahead. Invading armies don't call ahead. It's never a good idea to call ahead if you don't want people to know you're coming.

The only downside is the quarry might not be there when you show up. This time I got lucky.

I rang the buzzer and Mustafa swung aside the giant sliding door. I assumed it was Mustafa, looking as he did like a dignified Turk confronted by an unannounced visitor.

He wore a pale white silk suit nicely offset by a green silk T-shirt. His hair was dyed a shade of black ill-suited to his broad, doughy face.

"What do you want?" he asked, reasonably enough.

"If you're Mustafa Karadeniz, I want to chat."

"I don't chat," he said, and started to slide the door back into place. I caught it with my foot.

"I just want a conversation. It could save you a lot of trouble down the road."

"What kind of trouble?"

He had the sort of gentle accent many foreign speakers acquired after long years in the United States. It was a type I could never distinguish between Spanish or Persian, German or Albanian, though I always liked the way it sounded.

"Legal trouble," I said. "It's headed your way. You help me, I help you."

He let the tension off the door, but didn't open it all the way.

"Who are you?"

"A guy was killed in Southampton the other day. He might have known people in a business you might know something about. Which means the cops'll come knocking on your door, sooner than later. The dead guy was a friend of mine. That's my only interest. I'm not looking at you. I just want a little information."

"What can you do for me?" he asked.

"Let's just say it's better if we're friends."

He looked at me more closely, in an unexpected way.

"I know who you are," he said.

That surprised me, which must have shown, because it made him smile.

"Sam Acquillo," he said. "I got a friend of my own who wants me to kill you. Nice of you to make it so easy."

Then he reached into his sport coat.

I'D LIVED long enough and done enough to have forgotten a lot more than I remembered. So I excuse myself for not immediately recalling who out there might want me dead.

At least not off the top of my head. If I'd had time to ponder things, I might have come up with a few candidates. But the analytical part of my brain was temporarily off-line while the survival instincts were busy dealing with the matter at hand.

I used my right fist to sock him in the throat. This is a really painful and frightening way to be socked, and if the socker isn't careful, he can easily crush the larynx and kill the guy.

Mustafa dropped to his knees, grabbed at his throat, and tried to get air flowing back through his lungs. I walked behind him, grabbed a headful of hair, stuck my knee in his back, and shoved him face down into the macadam parking lot. I sat on his back and frisked him, reaching every hiding place but the front waistline of his pants, an approach I didn't think Mustafa was stupid enough to employ.

I was about to let him go when he pushed up off the hard surface, and with surprising agility, rose to his feet. I wrapped my arms around his neck and hung on. Somehow he managed to get a piece of my forearm in his mouth. As he clamped down, I ripped my arm clear, leaving a piece of me behind. He reached back and grasped at my head, which upset our tenuous balance and caused him to fall backward like a felled tree. No problem for him, with me as a cushion.

The air in my lungs whooshed out, and it was a painful thing to suck in the next breath.

Mustafa pushed off the ground with his feet, arching his back and driving me farther into the pavement. Before he could do it again, I managed to partially twist out from under, which did little to stop him from rolling back on top of me. We repeated the same maneuver a few times, which an impartial observer might have thought a choreographed attempt by two angry men to tumble in tandem across the parking lot.

Wrestling is a contest most professional boxers eagerly avoid. Whatever skills and advantages we may have in throwing a punch, or dodging the other guy's, is entirely neutralized in a tight clench. Instead of bobbing and weaving, we're stuck wiggling and clutching, causing considerable damage to efficiency and dignity alike.

Not that Mustafa was any medal winner in heavyweight wrestling. His basic technique was to grab, claw, and toss ineffectual jabs, though his extra weight was a clear benefit, even if he squandered much of it with grossly inefficient flailing about.

"*Gelsene sikik! Götüne koyarım senin!*" he yelled, in evident frustration. It didn't take fluent Turkish to get the gist.

Suddenly he stopped writhing, took a deep breath, and lurched to his feet. He managed to break what I thought was an unbreakable lock around his neck with a massive heave of his thick shoulders. This in turn had the Newtonian effect of throwing us in opposite directions. Mustafa landed face down, and I landed on my back. In the race to our feet, Mustafa got there just ahead of me, so before I could regain my balance, he'd already launched himself like a linebacker straight into my midsection.

Down we went again, this time face to face, Mustafa's arms wrapped around my body and his shoulder stuck in my gut. I think the plan was to squeeze my torso until my head popped off like a cork. Workable if it weren't for my fists, which were now blessedly free.

It wasn't the best punch to the head, all arm and shoulder, with no body weight behind it, but enough to alert Mustafa to his strategic mistake. He let go of my waist and tried to scramble back on his feet, which only gave me freer reign to land two more sharp shots to his left temple.

The second one sucked half the fight out of him, allowing me to finally shake free and establish a legitimate fighting posture. From there I could pick any number of ways to finish him off, but there was no point.

He fell to his hands and knees and shook his head like a wet sheepdog.

"Fucking hell," he croaked out.

He sat back down on his butt and coughed, using his fingertips to delicately feel around his throat.

"I think I see what my buddy's problem is with you," he said, his voice a strained rasp.

"You said he told you to kill me."

"I didn't say I was going to do it," he said.

"You didn't say you weren't."

He reached in his inside pocket again, and this time I let him. He pulled out an iPhone.

"It was vibrating," he said.

He put the phone back and glared at me.

"Wouldn't mind knowing which buddy we're talking about," I said.

He shook his head and mumbled something that sounded like *hassiktir.* He went to get back on his feet, but thought better of it, and sat down instead.

"It's okay with me if we start fresh," I said.

"Fuckin' big of you."

Mustafa made another go at standing up. I held my stance and watched him. When he got there, he brushed off his suit with partial success, little rips and ugly smudges spoiling the sartorial splendor.

"Did you have anything else in mind besides beating me to death?" he asked.

"I said I just want information."

"Like what?"

"You knew Joey Wentworth?" I asked him.

He looked at me in weary disgust.

"Is that all you want to know? You could've just asked."

"Did you do business with him?" I asked.

He didn't like that one, for reasons we both understood.

"I already got interviewed about that," he said. "By some prick cop. I can't tell you anything without violating confidentiality."

"Sure, but you could anyway. Do a good deed. Purifies the soul."

"Nothing wrong with my soul, praise God. You want to come in the warehouse?" He jerked his thumb toward the door. "Get a cup of coffee?"

"Thanks, but I'm happy out here. I like the sunlight."

"You think it isn't safe?" he asked.

"You don't think Joey's killing could rub off on you?" I said.

He ran his fingers through his hair as if realizing his coif might have been disturbed in the scuffle.

"It's got nothing to do with me," he said. "I'm strictly moving and storage. This is what I told the cops, why the hell should I tell you anything different?"

"I'm worse than a cop. Once I start liking you, I never go away."

"What do you care about that second-rate messenger boy?" he asked. "You know how many Joey Wentworths are lining up to take his place? So I'm told," he added, getting a better grip.

"All I need is a name," I said. "Anyone who might've had a problem with Joey, for whatever reason."

"If I tell you something, will you stay the hell away from me?"

"If I get what I want, I will definitely stay the hell away."

He paused for a moment, then said, "The last time I saw him was here at the warehouse. He was jumpier than usual, which took some doing. I told him that sort of behavior would draw the wrong kind of attention. That made him laugh, and he said, 'Wronger than you know.' I told him none of that crazy talk around me. I don't like it. He keeps laughing and tells me, 'Just watch out for Greeks.' Thanks for the advice, I tell him, before shoving him out the door."

"Any idea what he meant?"

Mustafa had the look of a man done talking.

"You asked me a question, I answered it. I told you more than I told the cops. Be grateful I'm in a generous mood and get the fuck off my property."

"Okay," I said, taking a few steps backward.

"And stay the fuck off."

"Unless your lead turns into bullshit. In which case, I'll be back."

He looked incredulous.

"You got some kind of death wish, Acquillo."

"I've been told," I said, backing up a few more steps before turning around and heading for the car. I looked back once along the way and Mustafa was still standing there, watching, suppressed rage and bemusement skirmishing across his face.

CHAPTER NINE

I t was a few nights after my tussle with Mustafa Karadeniz.
I was on the sun porch at the little table I kept out there,
leaning over an assortment of gears, axles, bearings, washers,
and springs that had once comprised the working guts of my
starboard jib sheet winch. Earlier that week, a sudden tack to
that side in heavy wind had snapped the line in such a way
that some inherent flaw in the relatively new winch resulted in
a screeching failure, followed by highly confused operations
on the part of the captain and boat alike.

I was lining up the physical parts with their diagrammed
facsimiles when my cell phone vibrated in my pocket. I
growled out a mild curse at Jackie, the most likely offender,
getting it out of the way before answering the phone.

When I looked at the screen, it wasn't Jackie's number.
It was a New York City area code, though I didn't recognize
the rest of the number. I answered anyway.

"What."

"Mr. Acquillo?"

"Who's this?"

"Nathan Hepner. Allison's in the hospital. It's bad."

Even with a central nervous system conditioned to sudden
shock, these weren't words I was fundamentally prepared to
hear. So at first I thought I had it wrong.

"What did you say?"

"Allison's been badly hurt. She's at Roosevelt Hospital, unconscious. It was the closest emergency room. I didn't know where else to go."

"Hurt how?" I asked, now up from the table and stalking through the cottage toward the back door, checking for my keys and wallet. Eddie, on his bed in the kitchen, leaped up and looked at me, his broad sweep of a tail drooping toward the floor.

"Attacked in her apartment. I found her."

"Get me the doctor."

"I can't. They're all in the operating room. I can get a nurse."

"Okay," I said, then regretted it as the phone went silent. I wasn't done asking the kid questions. I was driving the Grand Prix toward Montauk Highway when a woman came on the line.

"Mr. Acquillo?"

"How bad is it?"

"I don't have any information for you at this time. The trauma surgeons are in with her now. We'll call you when . . ."

I hung up on her and waited about two minutes, then I called the number back. Nathan answered.

"What's hurt?" I asked.

"I don't know. There was blood all over her face and down her front. In her hair. Goddamn it all."

"She was breathing," I said, trying to confirm.

"They told me she was. I couldn't tell."

"Do you know who did this?" I asked.

"I just picked her up and ran down to my car. It was faster than an ambulance."

It sounded like he was speaking to himself as much as to me. There was a slight trill in his voice, though he seemed in control. One of the boroughs lay sturdy claim to his accent.

"What about the cops?"

"I talked to the one who chased me to the emergency entrance. I ran a few lights. He gave me a stack of tickets, but not before calling it in. He took my ID and told me to wait for the detective, like I'm going somewhere."

"What about her mother? Is she there?"

"She's in the south of France for the summer. I left a message on her phone to call me ASAP. I didn't know what else to do."

I told him that was good enough. I knew Abby would be there as soon as she could charter a jet, but I wasn't looking forward to it.

"What else?" I asked.

"There's nothing else. You better get here."

I pushed the end button and tossed the phone on the seat next to me. I drove brainlessly for about a half hour before a delayed impulse caused me to pick up the phone and call Amanda. When she answered I told her what had happened and that I was on my way into the city.

"Oh my God. Oh my God," she said. "I'm on my way."

"Jackie will feed Eddie. Just open the basement hatch. I'm calling Sullivan."

Amanda knew me well enough not to waste time asking stupid things, like how I was doing, or how I felt, or what was I going to do. I didn't know the answers to any of those questions and I was in no shape to think about anything but how to get to Roosevelt Hospital on the West Side of Manhattan in the fastest time possible without being delayed by speeding tickets.

My conversation with Sullivan was equally brief. He knew all I needed was a favor cashed in with a cop in the city who could pass the juice along to whatever precinct on the West Side had the case. I wasn't looking for a private investigative unit, just someone on the other end of the line who wouldn't treat me like a civilian.

From there the ride was a blank. Not because I forgot what happened—there was nothing in my mind but screaming pleas to all the divine influences I didn't believe in to please spare my daughter's life and deliver me from the eternal horror that would become my life if that couldn't happen.

As I crested the hill in Queens that gives you the first glimpse of the Empire State Building, I called Nathan.

"Nothing yet," he said. "She's still in there and they won't talk to me."

I put the phone in my lap and took a breath. Then I got back on and said, "Don't piss 'em off."

"I know. I'm just the boyfriend."

"Did you talk to the detective?"

"Yeah. He asked me if I did it. I guess he would."

"Did you?"

"I guess you'd ask, too. No."

There was no rancor or defensiveness in his voice.

"Any ideas?"

"No. Things were going well, but we weren't at the confess-and-tell-all stage. There's a lot about your daughter's life I know nothing about."

You and me both, I thought, but didn't say.

"Call me if you learn anything," I said. "You have my number."

"Mr. Acquillo," he said.

"Better if you call me Sam. Everyone else does."

"Sam, she could die. One of the nurses told me."

"I figured that."

"Allison told me you're a dangerous man."

"She exaggerated."

"You're not going to let this stand."

"I'm not."

When most of the traffic is home in bed, you can get into Manhattan and across town pretty quickly. The hardest part was finding a legitimate place to park the car at the curb. I had to choose between a no-parking zone and the parking garage. Better judgment told me to take the garage, and an extra five minutes probably wouldn't change anything.

It didn't. When I got to the emergency waiting room Allison was still in the OR and Nathan Hepner was there with his head in his hands. He looked up as I approached, his face rigid with worry. He was a skinny guy with a giant ball of soft curly hair that seemed better suited to a young child.

He shook my hand. It was an icy grip, with a slight tremor. I looked closer at his face. It was too pale, even for a city kid. I took his hand back and checked his pulse. He wobbled on his feet.

"Are you dizzy?" I asked him.

"A little."

I sat him down and told him to put his head between his knees. I went to the desk nurse and told her I had a guy in shock. She looked at me like I'd just vomited in her lap.

"What makes you think that?" she asked.

"Get somebody out here."

"The staff is . . ."

"Any nurse will do."

"All the nurses are busy," she said.

"How do you know that? You haven't even asked."

"I don't have to ask. I'm here every night."

"Are you a nurse or just a receptionist?"

"I'm an RN, but that's not the point."

"An RN and you won't take thirty seconds to . . ."

She glared at me.

"I'm sorry, but . . ."

I leaned into the hole in the glass that divided us, and whispered, "No, you're not. You're not sorry. You don't care if this kid lives or dies. You're an angry worm besotted with the misery of your failed existence. You have power over me, so you use it to frustrate my attempt to ease the suffering of an innocent person. I have nothing but contempt for you and all your ancestors whose decrepit genes tragically contributed to the forming of such a base and meaningless piece of garbage posing as a human being."

Then I went back to Nathan, who luckily was looking a lot better. I felt his forehead, which had nearly warmed to room temperature.

"Cover your mouth and take longer, deeper breaths," I said. "You're hyperventilating."

"I always wondered what that was," he said through his hands. "I thought it was a fake disease."

A security guy walked into the waiting room and approached the desk nurse. He was tall, black, and exuded dignified calm. Former military, I thought. After a moment with the desk nurse he came over to where we sat, both his thumbs tucked inside a black leather belt laden with communications equipment and ordnance.

"Everything okay with you tonight, sir?" he asked.

"Yeah. We're good. My daughter, his girlfriend, is fighting for her life in the OR, so we've been better. How're you doing?"

"I'm well, thank you. Sorry about your trouble," he said.

"We're desperate for information about her condition, of course, sir," said Nathan, "but Nurse Ratched over there thinks it's fun to keep us in the dark. I don't know how hard it would be to just say 'she's gonna make it,' or 'she's not gonna make it.'"

"What's the girl's name?" he asked.

"Allison Acquillo," said Nathan, spelling out the last name.

He nodded slowly.

"I can poke around, but I'm expectin' you to be here quiet and calm when I get back with a report."

"Absolutely," said Nathan.

The security guy glanced at me, then left through the same door.

"What did you say to her?" Nathan asked. "The nurse."

"Nothing. And she's not a real nurse. They're all back there saving lives."

"Thanks for the breathing tip. I'm feeling a lot better."

He looked a lot better. Enough blood had come back to his face that his natural olive skin tone had reemerged.

"Nice job with the security guy," I said.

"I'm not a physical person. I have to be nice to get what I want."

"Nice is best for everyone," I said.

"Allison said you sometimes hit people."

"Only if compelled to. It's rarely the right thing to do."

"It's good to hear you say that. Because, like I said, I'm not a physical person. I'm actually afraid of people who are bigger or meaner than me."

"You need to fix that," I said. "It's no good being afraid of people."

"With all due respect, I think that's in the 'easy-for-you-to-say' category."

The security guy came back into the waiting room. He brought a young man along with him, dark like the security guard but not of African heritage. His wad of black hair looked nearly identical to Nathan's. His eyes were alight, nearly furtive, but his face was stern and unexpressive.

"They stabilized her and relieved some pressure on her brain," he said. "She's unconscious and they'll likely keep her that way for another twenty-four hours. Vital organs are working, though they think there's some bruising of the kidneys that might affect function, though not permanently. Several fractured ribs. She'll need plastic surgery on her face. You can see her if you want, but she won't know you're there."

"Absolutely," said Nathan.

"You go ahead," I said. "I'll wait for Amanda. She'll be here soon."

"You don't want to see her?" Nathan asked.

I shook my head.

"I don't. It won't make me feel any better or any worse. And there's nothing it'll do for her."

"You're gonna see her eventually," he said, more a question.

"As soon as she wakes up."

"You're not supposed to be afraid of anything," said Nathan. I liked that.

"I am, though," I said. "I'm afraid of me."

CHAPTER TEN

Amanda arrived about when I thought she would. She sat down next to me and let me explain the situation as well as I could. She concentrated carefully on my words, her face serious, but calm. When I was finished, she asked, "Who could have done this?"

"I don't know. Maybe the cops do. That's my next stop."

"I can stay with her."

"She's not waking up for a while. We need to get a room."

"I can do that, too."

"Thanks for that."

I went to the window and told the desk nurse to get the security guy back. She looked unhappy, but didn't hesitate. The guy showed up about ten minutes later. I asked him if Amanda could join Nathan while I went to do some things. He said sure, room for one more. Before they disappeared through the door, he surprised me by shaking my hand.

"Terrible thing, a child injured by the hand of another," he said. "I been there."

"Thanks."

"Can make intelligent men do stupid things."

"You've been there, too, I imagine," I said.

"I have indeed," he said.

"So you won't mind keeping a close eye on her while she's here."

"We will, but it's a big hospital. Special attention equals overtime."

"I'll pay it. Through you. Just tell me how much."

"That's interesting," he said. "How do you know I won't just pocket it?"

"Because you're an honorable man. You can't hide it."

He grinned at me and shook his head, then he shook my hand.

"Deal."

I had to get all the way to the street before I could use my cell phone to call the detective on the case from the card he'd given Nathan. He picked up right away.

"Detective Fenton."

"This is Sam Acquillo. My daughter's Allison, the one here at Roosevelt Hospital."

"Mr. Acquillo. I talked to Mr. Hepner."

"I know. What can you tell me?"

"The door was unlocked and the chain intact."

"So she probably knew the attacker."

"Well enough to let him in," he said.

"Anything going on in the neighborhood?"

"Nothing special. And no, the neighbors heard nothing."

"Must be well-insulated apartments," I said.

"Yeah. And they're all wearing earplugs."

"What are you going to do?" I asked.

"Investigate. Catch the guy. Help the ADA put him away for as long as the law allows."

"You sound confident," I said.

"It's the only way to live, brother."

He said he'd call me if he learned anything substantive. I thanked him, and he said the usual things about having kids of his own, like he actually meant it. All in all, I felt we'd drawn a good cop.

I felt more that way when I got to Allison's apartment.
The door was open, and inside was a pair of CSIs guarded
by a short jerk in an NYPD uniform. I didn't actually know he
was a jerk when I first saw him, but sometimes first impres-
sions are pretty accurate.

"Nobody goes in," he said, thrusting out his lower jaw to
reinforce his position.

"I'm her father," I said. "The girl that was beat up."

"Allegedly," he said. "And nobody includes you."

"There's an interior fallacy in that statement. 'Nobody' is
the word for 'not a person.' Would 'anybody' then be allowed?"

He might have thought about that if thinking was something he normally did.

"It's a crime scene, pal. Move it along."

"Can I talk to them?" I asked.

"What part of 'move it along' don't you understand?"

"All of it."

He put his face up closer to mine, though it meant he
had to tilt his head back and rise up on his toes.

"Not everyone's afraid of hurtin' civilians," he said, quietly.

I moved my personal space back away from his invading breath and took out a little notebook I kept in my back
pocket. I wrote my name, cell phone number, and Amanda's
e-mail address on one of the sheets, tore it out, and folded
it four times. Then I yelled "Hey!" at the closest CSI. She
turned and I flicked the paper like I used to do with baseball
cards as a kid. It hit her in the breastbone, but she was quick
enough to slap it against her chest.

The cop shoved me across the hall and pinned me against
the wall with his right forearm.

"Listen, fuck," he started to say, but I yelled over him to
the lady investigator.

"I'm the girl's father. Anything you can tell me I'd appreciate."

The woman looked a little confused, but held on to the
folded paper. The cop gave me another shove, then let go
so he could shut the apartment door.

"Ten seconds to get out of here before I start clubbing you to death," he said.

So I left. I assumed this was all a waste of time and an unnecessary provocation of the cops, people I wanted on my side, but if I didn't do something I thought I'd rip my own skin off my body.

And yet I knew the worst was yet to come. Shock had flooded my bloodstream with deadening biochemicals, protective natural narcotics designed by nature to blunt the agony that a little time might make easier to control. When the wiser parts of the mind could take over and force the animal parts back into the dark.

This is what I was thinking as I hunted up a late night bar, with its promise of my preferred soothing agent, something clear, cold, and harsh on the throat. A bridge to daylight, when I might be able to imagine a future of something other than madness and fury.

I was looking at the ceiling of the hotel room, having watched it emerge with the meager sunlight that slunk in from the city outside, when my cell phone rang. Amanda stirred on top of the bed, like me, still in her clothes. I brought the phone into the bathroom. It was Nathan.

"They're going to start bringing her out of the coma this afternoon. Doesn't mean she'll wake up, they just won't be forcing her to stay under."

"What else?"

"Don't expect her to remember anything. The doc told me trauma like that wipes out big chunks of memory, usually of the traumatic event itself."

"Anything else?" I asked.

"That's it. I'm lying down now on a gurney out here in the hall. I hope to sleep a few minutes before they make me go back to the waiting room."

I hung up the phone and called Detective Fenton. It almost surprised me when he answered.

"Anything?" I asked.

"Sort of, though it won't make you feel any better."

"What."

"They took her computer. Not her purse, or any other stuff in the apartment, as far as we can tell. There was a nice digital camera and other fancy gear that's like candy to your average home invader."

"So it was just about hurting her," I said. "And hiding something."

"Not just hurting. The hospital people said she would've died if the boyfriend hadn't gotten her to the ER when he did. Hard heads must run in the family."

Busted-up heads, anyway, I thought.

"And they targeted her specifically. It wasn't random."

"That's my opinion based on experience, but nothing I could prove in court. It was somebody she knew well enough to buzz into the building and let into the apartment. That could be anyone from a close personal friend to a delivery boy. People aren't as careful as they ought to be." Spoken as if he knew Allison like I did. "Nobody else in the building was bothered. We're running prints. That'll take awhile. And checking blood, but that'll take even longer. It's not going to be a quick collar, so I'd get used to the long haul."

"What about you?" I asked. "Can you stick with this?"

"Not really, but I will. I don't get a lot of personal discretion, but I take it anyway. I blame this on my Polish mother. Very stubborn woman."

I took a shower after that, and woke up Amanda before I left the room. She told me she'd fix herself up as well, then go back over to the hospital. She told me she'd pick up some clothes and toiletries for me, and secure the room for a few days.

"Abby's going to show up eventually," I said. "Could complicate things."

"Surely she'll want what's best for her daughter."

"In her mind, that might include banishing her daughter's father's girlfriend."

"You're kidding."

"At the end of time," I said, "as the apocalypse descends upon this earth, it'll still be all about Abby."

"I won't make a scene. I promise."

"You can make anything you want, as far as I'm concerned."

She brooded on that for a moment, then let it drop, though I knew not forever.

"Do you know what you're going to do?" she asked, changing the subject. "About this whole thing."

"No. One step at a time."

"I'd rather not lose you, if that's all right. I've gotten used to those nights out on the Adirondack chairs. It's quite pleasant."

"Yes it is."

"Allison won't want to lose you either," she said. "She'll need you to pull through this."

"What's all this talk? I'm just going to nose around a little. Nothing new about that."

"No, it's new and you know it." I moved a wave of hair out of her eyes. She used the back of her arm to finish the job. She looked at me and said, "Don't worry, I won't bring it up again."

It was midmorning, and already getting hot. But I needed the exercise, so I walked the ten blocks uptown to Allison's apartment. There was a yellow crime-scene tape barring the way. I put on surgical gloves and used my key to open the door, peeling, then reattaching the tape before closing the door behind me.

The apartment was a one-bedroom deal, which meant it had a bedroom, a bathroom, and another room that included living area, kitchen, and a counter where two people could

eat. Allison was a freelance graphic artist, so the living space
was really a work area, with a professional computer set up
under a big task light, and a couple of file cabinets crammed
in the corner. Every square inch of wall space was covered in
photos, paintings, and fabric designs. None of it seemed to
belong together, yet it all worked well in the end. I guess that's
what happens when graphic artists decorate their apartments.

On top of her big monitor she'd duct taped a brass plaque
that said "Suffer Fools."

It was hot with the air-conditioning off, and all the rooms
were pretty badly tossed, though I'd seen worse. Fingerprint
powder, in a variety of colors, was everywhere, and the drawers and cabinet doors were all partly open, their contents
spread on the counters and floors. The coarse, woven rug
was good at hiding stains, but there was a lot of blood. Also
on the hardwood floors and up one of the walls. I hadn't seen
much of the place over the years. Allison was a certified slob
and was usually embarrassed to let me in. Or she had a man
tucked away in there and was reluctant, for some reason, to
expose him to her gentle, unassuming father. So I wouldn't
likely know if there was anything abnormal, any sort of tale
the apartment's inanimate objects might tell.

I sat at the computer and turned it on. Nothing happened.
I looked under the desk and saw a tangle of severed cords,
then remembered that the CPU, the brain of the computer,
was gone. I looked around the apartment, knowing it was
a waste of effort. Whoever beat her up took the computer.
Maybe because of what was on it, or he was just taking pre-
cautions. Or simple theft, though that was unlikely. Too much
else was left behind.

I took out my cell phone and called Randall Dodge—
Shinnecock Indian, occasional sparring partner and go-to geek.

I asked him if he could break into my daughter's e-mail
account, which I assumed lived somewhere in the cloud.

"No guess on the password?" he asked.

"Nah. I'm more likely to lock it up from too many wrong tries."

I told him I'd get Amanda to forward one of Allison's messages as soon as she could get back on her computer.

"No guarantees, but I'll give it a go," he said. "You might tell me why."

I told him, and he expressed sympathy and concern through a few simple words. This was one of the reasons Indians make good friends. Not a lot wasted on unwanted sentiment.

Before leaving the building, on impulse, I knocked on the door of Allison's next-door neighbor to the left. No one answered, so I knocked on the door to her right. The door opened as far as the chain would allow and a sallow young face with a dusting of beard and shiny skin peered out. The hall was hotter than Allison's apartment, and the air flowing from this guy's place hotter still.

"What do you want?" he asked.

"You know the girl next door was assaulted?"

"Yeah. Thoroughly shitty."

"Did you hear or see anything?"

"I told you guys already, I didn't see or hear shit because I wasn't here. I was at a meeting and if you want proof, I can line up people from here to Paterson, New Jersey."

"Anything when you were here? People coming around threatening or acting abusive?"

"Look, detective. I love Allison. Totally unperverted by the mindless, predatory exploiters she had to work for to pay the rent. Quiet, respectful, nonjudgmental, and generous with her pharmaceuticals whenever asked." I let that last bit roll by unexamined, helped by a rise in the guy's amplitude. "So I'm a lot more *upset* about this than you'll *ever* be and I'd do anything to nail the mother*fuckers* who did this to the fucking *wall* and carve off their fucking genitals and feed them to their *puppies*, but I wasn't here when it went down." His voice dropped down to its original volume. "So, sorry."

"Okay then," I said to the door, after it was closed delicately in my face.

I was out on the street when I got a call from Joe Sullivan.

"Jesus Christ, Sam, what the hell."

"If you had anything to do with Detective Fenton getting assigned the case, thank you."

"Not a thing. Though they say he's one of the better ones, if you get past the booze and bad rapport with senior police officials, which makes him sound like every other cop I know."

"There's not much to go on. Looks like she knew the guy, though no witnesses and forensics running like a slow boat to China."

"By the way, Ross put in a word for you as well," said Sullivan. "Much better than mine, given his hitch in NYPD homicide."

"Thank him for me."

"I got a shitload of time off banked if you need company," he said.

Right after feeling a wave of gratitude, I remembered that thing I was working on when I got the call from Nathan.

"What about the Alfie investigation?"

"Jackie and Veckstrom will have to get along without us," he said.

"They might make progress, but getting along is not a possibility. Anyway I'd be grateful for the help."

"You get the room and don't forget the minibar."

I'm ashamed to say I rarely remembered the details of my conversations with Allison. I could follow the big picture, but when she named names from work or off time, or referred to performers, TV shows, or other useless junk from popular culture, I'd put my attention on hold. So it was a bit surprising

I remembered one of her regular clients, a design firm called Brand & Weeks, just because the name stuck in my head.

It was high up in a tower in Midtown, near, but not on, Madison Avenue. The crack security guy at the desk had me sign my name in a book, and even looked at my driver's license. I asked him if he thought the picture was a decent likeness. He didn't answer, just handed back the card and told me which floor to get off.

The elevator opened onto a basketball court, though not one you could actually use to play basketball, given the eight-foot ceilings and tiny parquet floor. A very small young woman in a form-fitting dress and nosebleed pumps sat at a table at center court. The only thing on the table was a desk phone. I walked up to her.

"I'd like to talk to the person who hires freelancers," I said.

"You need to go online and post your book," she said, loneliness nearly overcoming the tedium of repeating the line. "Somebody will call you. Or not."

"I'm not a freelancer. It's a police matter."

"Oh," she said, perking up. "That's different." She picked up the phone and punched in a number. "There's a cop here who wants to talk to you," she said into the phone. She looked up at me.

"Do you have identification?"

"I'll show it to the person who hires freelancers," I said.

"He says he has to show it to you," she said into the phone. "Probably police procedure."

She nodded and hung up the phone, telling me Althea would be right out. I thanked her. Althea showed up a few minutes later, and instantly filled up the reception area. Six feet tall, or a little more, big around the middle, but not fat, scruffy clothes, and sloppy white hair barely restrained by a red headband, blue jeans and knee-high laced boots, a loose chambray shirt, and a drafting pencil stuck in her mouth. She shook my hand, or rather cranked it like you would a recalcitrant pump handle.

"Cop, huh?" she said. "Love cops, when they aren't arresting me. Just a joke. Not a very good one."

I showed her my driver's license.

"Not a cop," I said. "I'm Allison Acquillo's father. Somebody beat her up yesterday bad enough to put her in a coma. I was hoping you could talk to me about her work life."

"Fucking shit. You are fucking kidding me."

"I'm not. Can you spare a minute?"

"Yeah," she said, in the two-syllable way people do now when they mean of course. "Follow me." She led me into a big room full of long tables at which mostly young people clothed as haphazardly as Althea worked side by side at computers.

"Interesting setup," I said, as we wormed our way down a narrow aisle.

"We did away with private offices, then cubicles, and now we all work at whatever work station is open when we get here. Two thirds of our people work remotely. I don't know where they are. I think a few of them are on the moon, but I can't prove it."

She led me into a room with a door, walls made of whiteboards covered in script and sketches, and a few overstuffed chairs.

"War room," she said. "For the big pitches and projects."

"Tough business."

"You have no idea." As soon as we were in the comfy chairs she said, "Allison is one of my favorite designers. Great left brain/right brain thinker. Not that common."

"She got the best of her parents," I said, leaving out that she also got some of the worst of me, but I didn't have to.

"Not first rate in the interpersonal department, no offense I hope."

"So she had some enemies," I said, "if that's not too strong a word."

"Will it surprise you to learn that creative people can have delicate feelings? No, enemies isn't too strong. It's a tough

business even when you get along with people. I call Allison
for the work that's so tricky and complex it makes your hair
hurt. But never as part of a team. Growing up, did she share
her toys and play nicely with the other children?"

"You probably know the answer to that."

"I put her on staff once for about a week. Disaster. I sent
her back home with a plaque that said 'suffer fools.' Probably
threw it out."

"She didn't. Can you tell me who had a bad beef with her?"

"Bad enough to beat her up? No. Designers specialize
in stabs to the back, though entirely metaphorical. I'm really
sorry about this. Terrible thing. Do you want some coffee?"

I admitted I did. She called somebody on the phone and a
few minutes later two mugs were brought in by a young guy
attempting to grow a beard, maybe to balance out his glasses,
which had frames made of thick, black plastic.

"Do you know who else hired her?" I asked.

"Other than Brandon?" I must have looked confused.
"Brandon Weeks, my former partner. The only writer who
could work with her. Just as smart and difficult, but a lot
crazier."

"Explains the name of the place."

"I bought him out in the nineties when he was trying
to single-handedly sustain the Manhattan cocaine industry.
Laudable, but not business friendly. Rehab saved his life but
didn't do much for his people skills. He makes Allison look
like Dale Carnegie. Though I think they've been on the outs
the last couple years. They used to sweep the awards shows.
Now it's just her. I don't hear much about him. I don't care.
Some people are so toxic you'd need about a million years
to even look at them without a beta blocker."

"I don't know any of this," I said, mostly to myself.

"Kids don't tell you shit. I have two sons who work in theater and nuclear biology, respectively, and live in apartments
that I can find on a map and that's about all I know. Oh, one

of them has a cat and the other dated a girl who liked him to wear dresses. Don't ask me how I found that out."

We talked a little more about all the changes going on in her business, how the Internet had turned everything on its head, which I could have guessed on my own even though I didn't own a computer. She promised to think about whom Allison might have worked with beyond the already mentioned Brandon Weeks, and anything else that might shed some light. I thanked her, gave her my cell phone number, and got up to leave. She stood up and loomed over me.

"I probably gave you the wrong impression about me and Allison," she said. "We actually get along great. I love her even if she keeps me at arm's length. I just figured she had a lousy childhood or something. Oh shit, I just said that to her father. I'm sorry."

I shook her offered hand.

"Don't worry about it," I said. "Interpersonal skills aren't all they're cracked up to be."

And just to prove the point, on the way out I told the kid with the wispy beard if he ever wanted to get laid to get contacts and shave off the stupid beard. Althea said, "Listen to the man," and crushed my knuckles with a handshake that sent me back to the street thinking that fools weren't the only people worth suffering.

CHAPTER ELEVEN

A bby managed to time her appearance at the hospital a few minutes before the doctors let us into Allison's room so we could watch her come out of the induced coma. Abby's husband was there as well, a man with a handsome chiseled face and slicked-back hair that started halfway up his skull, bestowing an even greater air of gravity and importance than his substantial résumé and investment holdings already conveyed.

Amanda was back at the hotel, wisely reducing the awkwardness of the moment to the merely surreal.

Abby looked great. Only a few years younger than I, it didn't remotely show. The same gifts that made her such a neck-snapping beauty when we met in our twenties up in Boston hadn't flagged, rendering an unachievably fine specimen of middle age without a lick of surgery or prosthesis.

Her family always assumed I married her for her money and social standing, when in fact it was for her body and its rapacious appetites, no less a foolishly unsustainable motivation.

"Samuel," she said to me in the waiting room, offering her cool, dry hand and a dig she liked to give my long-dead proletarian parents for officially naming me Sam. She, on the other hand, insisted everyone call her Abigail.

"Hello, Abby."

"You better brace yourself. We're in for a long haul."

"I knew living in this city was a terrible idea."

Handsome as she was, her face was taut with worry. Her husband, Evan Quirogo, in turn was clearly worried about her. He put a thick arm around her, pinning her arms, and spoke in his musical accent a few inches from her ear.

"We'll get through this, darling. I promise you."

She nodded, eyes downcast.

"I know, Evan. I'm just so frightened."

I might have done things a little differently with our daughter if I'd been around more as she grew up, but I knew as a matter of faith and observation that Abby was a good and caring mother. It wasn't easy for her to see her rampant and groundless fears become not so groundless after all.

"Do they know who did this?" Evan asked me.

"Not yet," I said, "but they're working on it."

"I should hope so," said Abby, betraying to my sensitive ear her abiding conviction that all official institutions were inherently incompetent.

The East Indian doc who'd first briefed me and Nathan came into the room with Nathan at his side. Abby was polite but cool when shaking Nathan's hand. She thanked him for getting Allison to the hospital. Evan chimed in with "Good show."

"Experience tells me her eyes will be open, but don't expect much awareness," said the doc. "That'll come along slowly."

"So she'll recover?" Abby asked.

"How far we don't know. Not yet."

He described the procedures needed to get her through the initial stages in medical terms I mostly understood. I knew Abby didn't, but she nodded along with confidence, then led our party behind the doc as we made the short trip into the ICU.

Having seen the cliché of people lying still in a hospital bed with their heads wrapped in bandages was inadequate preparation for the real thing. Especially when the person in question was the dearest being in the universe whose safety and well-being had been an all-consuming obsession for more than thirty years. Abby actually staggered on her sensibly shod feet. Evan and I each took an arm. Nathan took Allison's hand.

With the doc's help, Nathan described what all the tubes, wiring, and electronic monitors were for. I didn't follow it very well, though I was glad someone was speaking, saving me from talking through the wad of anguish stuck in my throat. Abby just wept while Evan murmured reassurances in her ear.

"We're pretty liberal about visiting hours," said the doc. "It's good to talk to her, even if she's nonresponsive. It'll help her regain consciousness."

"I'm here for the duration," said Nathan.

"Good of your employer," I said.

"I quit that job. Allison didn't want me to take it anyway."

"That kid'll do anything to get her way," I said.

Abby frowned at me, though mostly out of long habit.

"We need to open up the city place," said Abby, "but then I'm available. We can take shifts."

I left them to figure that out and scrammed out of there as quickly as good form would allow. I hated hospitals to a degree you might call phobic, though more importantly, they could look after Allison better than I at this point, and there was no place for them in what I had to do.

JOE SULLIVAN met me and Detective Fenton at a bar in Midtown. When they shook hands I learned Fenton's first name was Bill. They didn't know each other, but had a lot of common acquaintances in different police units in and around the city. Most prominently Ross Semple.

"You heard about the shoot-out in Bed-Stuy when Semple and his partner went to interview a homicide witness and stumbled into a drug deal," said Fenton.

"Ross doesn't talk about his time here," said Sullivan. "We just hear it from guys like you."

"The people in the apartment thought the cops were the buyers, which they went along with. Then the real buyers show up. Semple shot his own partner in the arm to prove his cred. The sellers then start shooting the real buyers, and after the smoke clears, Ross is the last man standing. Said he couldn't hear for a month."

"What happened to the partner?"

"Became a gym teacher over in Lindenhurst. Semple pretty much worked alone after that. You can understand why."

"Any new thinking on my daughter's situation?" I asked, hauling the grinning cops back to the present.

Fenton nodded.

"We're interviewing everybody she worked with, including the attack-of-the-fifty-foot-tall woman at Brand & Weeks that you apparently softened up for us."

"She didn't help much," I said.

"Employers usually don't. Most don't ask about their workers' personal lives and most workers don't tell."

I could attest to that. When I supervised a few thousand people I kept the rules to a minimum, but one was keep the home junk at home. Abby saw that as another misanthropic impulse blocking my rise up the career ladder.

"Did she tell you about Brandon Weeks?" I asked.

"Sure. The wacky partner. He's on our list."

"I was going there next."

"Be my guest," said Fenton. "Joe and I can canvass the neighborhood and pay calls on the local low life. She let the guy in, but that doesn't mean she knew him that well. People do stupid shit like that all the time. Sorry. No offense."

"People in this town keep thinking they're offending me," I said. "You need to get to the Hamptons where nobody cares what you say."

"Offensive comments are sanctioned by municipal code," said Sullivan.

They left after that and I sat at the bar and called Randall Dodge, the computer warrior working on the hard drive from Allison's computer.

"I like her stuff," he said when I told him who was calling. When he cracked Allison's e-mail account he opened some of the attachments.

"Me, too. Got it all from her mother."

"Not so sure about that. There's a lot of engineering under those designs."

"What's in the e-mail?" I asked.

"Usual boring stuff. She could use a little help with her bedside manner. Would get more business."

"Anything stand out, hostility-wise?" I asked.

"Lots of drama with some dude named Weeks. Your basic fuck-you-he-said, fuck-you-she-said. Whatever happened was off camera before the e-mails started. Sounds bad, but who knows. Allison's a pretty straight-ahead communicator, a little too straight ahead, but writing to Weeks, she gets positively poetic. And we're not talking Emily Dickinson."

"Sylvia Plath?"

"More like it."

"Anything else of note?" I asked.

"Can't say yet. Just started digging around. How much time do I have?"

"Take all you want."

"Say hi for me when she wakes up," he said.

"I will."

I put the phone down and ordered another drink, feeling that it was fair recompense for taking up bar space, even though there were only two other guys on the other stools. To make the time even more productive, I called Jackie Swaitkowski.

I let her tell me how sorry and angry she was over what happened to Allison. She asked me if there was anything she could do and I had an answer for that.

"Don't let up on Alfie Aldergreen," I said.

"I'm not. Carlo told me he conveyed the disposition of Alfie's remains to the VA, who'll give him a decent burial in one of their cemeteries. Jimmy Watruss is taking care of the details. I still want to have a memorial service, though, when I get you back in town."

"You don't have to wait for me," I said.

"I know. But I'm going to wait for you. Carlo also gave me the results of the blood sample off your rear window."

Sullivan was right. Jackie could move the ME to feats of speed unavailable to his official clients. I didn't ask her how she did it.

"And?"

"He's a cow."

At first I thought she meant Vendetti.

"More like a skinny rooster," I said.

"No, I mean the guy who busted in your windshield. The DNA was from a cow. Could have been a bull or a steer. Clearly bovine."

I had to think about that for a moment, so I was quiet on the phone. Jackie hates dead air.

"Say something," she said.

"Be careful out there. When livestock go rogue, who knows what's next."

"Sullivan's there with you?" she asked.

"Yeah. He's hanging out with the plainclothesman they put on Allison's case."

"Speaking of plain clothes, there's an article in the *Times* today on Veckstrom running for DA. They actually think he has a chance."

"The better candidate?"

"The richer. Edith Madison never had to do much in the way of fund-raising. Lived off connections, but a lot of those are dead, or moved to Florida. You can tell she hasn't the stomach for an all-out fight. Too unseemly."

"Who cares. A pox on both their houses."

"You know that fat manila envelope Oksana kept waving in front of your nose? Veckstrom gets the job, that's the first place he's going to look."

"I'm not worried about that. I got a good lawyer."

"She'd be better if you actually paid her."

"I know I took Joey Wentworth's parents, but I'm a little distracted. What do you say?"

"I said I'd help, but they're right there in the east eighties."

"Okay. I got it," I said. "After I visit Brandon Weeks."

"Who's that?"

"Someone Allison hated, apparently. I assume he hated her back."

"Don't do anything stupid," she said.

"This is what lawyers are good for. Wise and temperate counsel."

I went outside and looked at the piece of paper with Brandon's address that Althea gave me. It was in a part of Greenwich Village that I knew well from my young years as an urban desperado. I didn't know if the neighborhood would be the same as I remembered it.

It wasn't. It was a lot cleaner, flush with active commerce and free of the day-to-day impoverished specters that used to haunt those environs. Brandon had a walk-up in a building that had started life as a townhouse, long ago succumbing to subdivision. I pushed the button on the outside panel.

"You're kidding me," the intercom squawked at me.

"Not yet. Haven't had the chance."

"I don't take deliveries unannounced. Call and make an appointment."

"It's not a delivery," I said. "It's about Allison Acquillo."

"Oh that's priceless. She's not suing me is she?"

"Somebody tried to kill her. She's in a coma. Buzz me in."

"Oh my lord. Are you the cops?"

"No. The father. Talk to me now or talk to me later. But you're gonna have to talk to me."

A moment went by, then the buzzer buzzed and I walked in the building and up the three flights to his apartment where he was waiting for me. With a sharp nose, high forehead, long neck, and thick round glasses, my first thought was startled terrier.

"When did this happen?" he asked, his voice crisply modulated and much deeper than it sounded over the intercom.

I told him the basic facts as they currently stood. He listened without moving in or out of the doorway to his apartment. He wore a starched white shirt and bow tie, suspenders, and old-fashioned armbands that held the french cuffs away from his wrists. I asked him if he was going somewhere.

"No. I'm working. I guess you can come in."

The apartment was about the size of Allison's, though opposite in decorative exuberance. What furniture was there was all right-angled leather, chrome, and glass. A brushed aluminum laptop was open on the desk. A huge black and white woodcut of abstract agony covered one wall. He sat at the desk after offering me the only other chair in the room.

"I never met Hepner," he said. "I just heard she was dating."

"I don't know much about what Allison did for a living," I said. "Maybe you could tell me."

"Advertising. Or, as I call it, narcissists, neurotics, and infantilized fanatics in the service of free enterprise."

"Something a writer might say."

"A copywriter. The only way to make more money with fewer words is a ransom note. Someone else wrote that line. Though I could have, I'm sure."

"So Allison's in charge of the pictures," I said.

"How elegantly put. Yes. Though creative teams tend to concept together before crawling off to our respective holes to complete the work. Do you have any idea who could have done this thing to her?"

"I was hoping you could tell me."

He blinked at me from behind the round glasses.

"Not a clue. But then again, I haven't worked with her for more than a year. We had what's euphemistically called a falling out. I'd call it more of a tossing off the cliff."

"Who tossed whom?" I asked.

Like other people I've known who made their living with words, Weeks took a few extra beats between question and answer, putting a dash of craft into every response.

"You wouldn't think such a slender girl could toss a chap so far."

The image didn't fit that well with the one of her lying in that hospital bed, but I pushed both aside.

"Sounds like a tough business, all these words and pictures," I said.

He gave a nearly silent laugh.

"The words and pictures are the easy part. It's the politics that'll get you."

"I hear that from a lot of people."

"I wish I could help you more, Mr. Acquillo, but I'm on a ferocious deadline."

"Actually you haven't helped me at all."

His blinking sped up considerably, and a bit of flush formed on his prominent cheekbones.

"I don't think I'm required to tell you anything," he said, in a quiet voice that crept up a half register. "Even though I have, out of respect for your situation."

"It's your situation, too. You don't have to help me, but pretty soon two hardnosed cops will come calling and if you think evading their questions is a good idea, try it. What really went on between you and Allison?"

He lips grew tight as if trying to prevent any further words from escaping, to no avail.

"Not what you're suggesting."

"I'm not suggesting anything."

"Call me anything you want. I'm not a thief."

"Is that what she called you?" I asked.

"Among other things. Quite a few actually. Just because I started a job with her and ended it with another."

"So you stole her ideas."

He slapped the top of his thighs in the first natural gesture I'd seen him perform.

"You collaborate in a team, who knows where the ideas come from. Somebody sparks something, you build on it. You go together down different paths. It's the process. Anyway she got paid. That's how it works. You get the money, you forfeit all right to ownership. And you stay professional. She's your daughter and you're upset. I don't blame you, but I'm not going to be the one to educate you on the niceties of Allison Acquillo's sweet and subtle personality. Though I can see where she got it from."

I had to give him points for perception as well as chutzpah, even if he didn't realize how close he was to getting my fist crammed down his throat. But even a guy as sweetly subtle as me knew that was an unproductive strategy.

Instead I told him when I learned things he could have shared with me I'd be back, assuming he had even more to tell. Despite the brief show of guts, he didn't seem happy at the prospect. I got out of there more quickly than part of me wanted, the part that knew I was leaving important stuff on the table. But I wasn't sure I could trust the rest of me being in such close proximity to any creature toward whom my precious daughter held such enmity.

I stopped at the sidewalk to gather up some New York City air, cleaner than it used to be, so the big lungfuls had a calming effect, which was better than choking to death, which a completely different part of me likely would have welcomed.

CHAPTER TWELVE

My relationship with Allison followed the dreary arc shared by a lot of fathers I know. Until she was about twelve, the sun and the moon and all the stars rose and set through the beneficent ordering of her father. I didn't know how to conjure this sort of devotion, and neither did I try, it just happened.

Abby did nothing to encourage or discourage the mutual adoration that throbbed between us—the code words, stolen looks prompting uncontrollable mirth, the desperate clench around my neck, and tears that came upon us both unexpectedly over seemingly nothing.

But then puberty and the demands of my job and Abby's emotional sabotage all converged and blew apart that happy union. I can't tell you when it started, but it ended with me drunk in a hotel bar, having lost my job, my house, my wife, and all of my money, watching Allison walk away from me, and thus, losing her, too.

That's when Abby really went to town, believing that preserving that separation was the only way to save Allison from the fate that was me. Luckily Allison had by then developed her own antisocial tendencies, thus forming some common ground upon which a fresh start could take root.

It took a lot of work, but we got there eventually, more or less.

THE BUILDING the Wentworths lived in had two doormen, one inside and one out. Getting past the first was no guarantee with the second, not without forewarning by one of their residents, which I didn't have.

So in a departure from standard form, I tried calling them on the phone.

As soon as Mr. Wentworth got on the line I dropped my friend Burton Lewis's name hard enough to put a hole in the sidewalk. Wentworth didn't remember meeting me at Burton's house, probably because he hadn't, but I'd been to the place often enough to create a plausible story. He had a high-pitched, scratchy but cheerful voice, which didn't falter when I told him I was part of a murder investigation Burton's law firm was engaged in that might have a connection to his son's death. I asked him if he could let me come up to their apartment and he surprised me by saying yes.

Both doormen were courteous bordering on obsequious, reminding me how much easier it was to have an official purpose in this world.

I knew the Wentworths had a lot of money, based on the house they had on the ocean in Southampton, not far from Burton's. It didn't quite prepare me for stepping out of the elevator and into an enclosed foyer, since the Wentworth apartment encompassed the entire floor. I hadn't quite taken in the art on the walls when a pair of double doors opened and emitted a short round guy stuffed into a melon-colored shirt, with white pants and shoes. He carried an unlit cigar, though the stench of it followed him into the foyer. We shook hands.

"How is my favorite fruitcake?" he asked, referring to Burton, who was gay, and a man of such dignified poise and decency that I felt a surge of insult on his behalf. But I was there to do a job, so I swallowed it down.

"Burton's doing quite well," I said. "I'm sure he would tell you so himself."

He waved me through the doors, which led to a long, broad hallway pierced by an occasional arched opening. More art lined the walls, along with antique tables on which pottery and sculpture waited to be knocked over by visitors like me bedazzled by the extravagant display of square footage.

I followed him as he shuffled into a sitting area lit by floor-to-ceiling windows shrouded in gauzy curtains. A thin, white-haired woman was perched on the edge of a chair that belonged behind a velvet rope. She waited for me to go over to her and offer my hand. Hers felt skeletal, though the grip was forthright and strong.

"Nice to see you again, Mr. Acquillo," she said, also buying into my social fiction.

"Call me Sam, if you would," I said. "Everyone else does."

"Everyone calls me Mrs. Wentworth," she said, "though I prefer Sally. Jack and Sally," she added, gazing over at her husband who stood at a glass table with a decanter in his hand.

"I hope you drink, Sam. There's still plenty left in this bottle."

I assured him I did, which was a relief to Sally as well. Jack also lit the cigar after offering one to me, which I declined with a touch of tobacco-addicted regret.

"I appreciate you letting me barge into your home here to talk about something I'm sure you'd rather not talk about," I said.

Jack's head was the type of bullet-shaped thing that benefitted from fashion's new acceptance of slick baldness. Neither of the Wentworths had wrinkles, without any obvious plastic surgery, though Jack's skin was pinkish where Sally's was as white as her hair, and nearly translucent.

"Not at all, Sam," said Jack, speaking with a slight lisp that reminded me of Truman Capote. "Especially since that asshole from the Southampton Police told me to stay away from you people."

"He told me to stay away from you," I said.

"As noted, an asshole."

"I'm sorry to bother you with this stuff," I said.

"We lost Joseph a long time ago," said Jack. "His death was a formality."

"We have four other children," said Sally, as if that explained their seeming indifference. "All doing quite nicely."

"Joseph didn't fall in with a bad crowd," said Jack. "He was the bad crowd."

"Though we loved him, Jack, you know that," said Sally, not that convincingly.

"Had you talked to him much before he was killed?" I asked.

Jack gestured at Sally with his cigar. She nodded.

"I'd speak with him on the phone. Every week. It was a habit begun when he was in boarding school."

"Never made it to college," said Jack. "Too busy with my lawyers keeping him out of jail."

"Was there anything different in those last days?" I asked. "Anything that said he was in deeper trouble than usual?"

Sally had been sitting with her knees turned to the side and her hands in her lap, as if posing for a portrait. Now she sat back and crossed her legs, cocktail glass in hand.

"Definitely," she said. "He was quite excitable by nature, but he seemed much more distressed. Though fatalistic, which he often seemed as well. Joseph always had trust issues."

"Paranoid is what he was," said Jack. "You'd be, too, if you were ass deep in the drug trade."

"He lived hand to mouth but never took a dime of help from us," said Sally, a bit off topic. "We tried so hard to help."

"Did he say anything about Greeks?" I asked.

Sally looked puzzled.

"I don't recall, though he said he met people from all over working import and export." Jack guffawed. Sally seemed undeterred. "He didn't just deal in drugs, I'm certain of that."

"What about cops? Any talk about them?" I asked.

"He told me they couldn't be trusted," said Sally. "Though he felt that way about everyone."

I wondered if their opinion of their son would improve if they knew he was a police informant. It half made me want to deliver the news. But I couldn't tell them, since it was still under wraps.

"You referred to Detective Veckstrom. Did Joey ever talk about him?"

Sally looked over at Jack, but when he didn't say anything, she said, "He really didn't like Mr. Veckstrom."

"He called him a Nazi fuck-wad," said Jack.

Sally looked away, toward one of the big windows that cast upon her such a flattering, diffused light.

"I have no idea what that means," she said.

I suddenly wished I were somewhere else, despite my wonder at making it into their apartment in the first place. Jack looked at me, his fat face looking even fatter from the effects of the double bourbon in his hand.

"So there you have it," he said.

I got the feeling they were the type of couple that needed a third party in the room as a mediator, or an audience to bear witness to private truths otherwise never spoken.

"Do you believe in genetic predestination, Mr. Acquillo?" Sally asked me.

"You mean, that kids can be born goofed up? Yeah. But are genes destiny? Not so sure about that. I used to blame everything I didn't like about my daughter on her mother, though in retrospect it was probably more my fault."

"You have just the one?"

"Yeah. Unlike you, I have no way to contrast and compare. Of course, neither does she."

"Complicated shit, huh?" said Jack. "Kids."

"Except the unconditional love," I said. "That part's pretty simple."

"What exactly do you do for Burton?" Sally asked.

"Mostly fill up space in his private box at the Garden. Sometimes a little finish carpentry. He prefers to do that stuff himself, but I can teach him a few things."

She looked more confused than disappointed.

"I thought you were an attorney."

"I just work for one. She runs Burton's operation. I'm in this because one of her clients was murdered. A disabled guy named Alfie Aldergreen. They dropped him and his wheelchair in Hawk Pond. Did Joseph ever talk about him?"

Jack perked up.

"The wackjob with the cammies and saxophone," he said. "Buzzed around the Village. Public hazard."

"Paranoid schizophrenic, technically," I said.

"Joseph knew him," said Sally. "We were having lunch on the sidewalk, and I'd just given my son this lovely outfit. He dressed so oddly. Your wheelchair person rode by and Joseph put the boxes right in his lap."

"Fat load of good that did," said Jack. "Wheelchair person only wore fatigues."

"His name was Alfie," I said, then asked Sally, "Do you remember what they talked about?"

She shook her head.

"No, but they did one of those funny ghetto handshakes. And there was quite a bit of laughter. They were friends."

"What the hell, Sam. The kid could have hung with movie stars and billionaires and instead he's palling around with some fucking nutbag cripple."

Half of me wanted to tap my fist on the top of that bald noggin, but the other half couldn't help but hear the pain and longing in his voice. I sympathized with his plight, caught as he was within the baffling force field of a father's love.

I MET up with Sullivan and Fenton at the bar where we'd started out. Fenton was about the same vintage as Sullivan, though in much worse physical shape. I often wondered why some cops are so committed to going to seed where others have bodies like Captain America well into old age. Maybe it's the same with any other group, though it seemed like cops clumped at the opposite ends of the sliding scale.

Fenton looked like he could really use a shower and someone to tell him how to comb his hair and straighten his collar. Both were red faced from the heat, made worse by the lightweight jackets they used to hide their guns. Of course, there was no better way to telegraph to the dumbest criminal in the world that here were a couple of cops.

It was off-duty time, so Sullivan ordered a beer. Fenton a double Scotch on the rocks with a side of water, with the kind of enthusiasm that made me think off-duty status wasn't as essential as it was with Sullivan.

"What'd you learn?" I asked them.

"The west nineties aren't the shithole they were when I was coming up," said Fenton. "It's making me nostalgic."

"Still plenty of dirtballs," said Sullivan.

"None of them knew anything," said Fenton, "though some tried to act like they did. Junkies don't make very good liars."

"So you're crossing local actors off your list," I said.

"Not yet, but I'm not feeling it," said Fenton. "Don't get a lot of home invasions around here. I'm thinking outsider."

As you often hear, New York is a city of neighborhoods. People like to live, shop, eat, and mug other people in familiar surroundings.

"Targeted," I said.

"That's what I'm thinking," said Sullivan. "Though it's early yet."

"I'm thinking the same thing," said Fenton. "She buzzed the guy in. Could have been a delivery. You can get a stick of gum brought to your door at three in the morning in this town. But my street contacts would know if there was a bad guy working that angle. Unless he's just startin' out. That could be."

"So friends and family," said Sullivan. "Sorry, Sam. You know what I mean."

"I do," I said. "And coworkers. I talked to two of them today. I'm not ready to like Weeks, but he's worth a closer look. I think I've prepared him for the tender mercies of the NYPD and their Long Island cousins."

"We'll be delivering that tomorrow," said Fenton, waving the bartender over to refill our glasses. Some time went by while that got sorted out, along with an order of bar food meticulously specified by our host cop.

"I stay away from the chicken wings," he said. "Spent too much time in Guangdong."

I didn't know what that meant, but I didn't ask.

When things settled down I told Sullivan that I'd paid a visit to Joey Wentworth's parents at their apartment on the East Side. I filled him in on the conversation as well as my memory would allow, leaving out the psychodrama.

"I know their place off Wickapogue Road," said Sullivan. "About the size of the Pentagon."

"They like a lot of elbow room," I said.

"So Joey knew Alfie."

"He did, but who didn't. Alfie was always around."

"Alfie was the DB in the wheelchair," Sullivan told Fenton. "Joey Wentworth was another CI that got ventilated with a twelve-gauge the week before. We're wonderin'."

"No wonder to me," said Fenton. "Somebody's dropping dimes."

"That's what it looks like," said Sullivan, "though I've been living with those people a lot of years, and it just doesn't add up."

"It's the ones you least expect," said Fenton.

"I hear you," said Sullivan.

"You do have two new guys on the force," I said.

Fenton looked at Sullivan like he probably looked when one of his street contacts tried to hold out on him.

"I've known Pete Cermanski since he was still wiping his nose on his sleeve," said Sullivan.

"You don't still do that?" asked Fenton.

"What about the other guy, Bennie Gardella?" I asked.

"Bennie fucking Gardella?" asked Fenton. "You're shitting me."

"You know him," said Sullivan.

"Sure. Did some serious undercover during the Giuliani glory days. Compared to him, Donnie Brasco could have been in witness protection. Very highly regarded guy, even if he did spend a few years at the Retreat and went on desk after that. Sort of a PTSD thing, is what I think."

"What's the Retreat?" I asked.

"Rehab central for cops and firemen. Does a brisk business, not a big surprise."

"I didn't know any of this," said Sullivan.

"Your chief does. Ross ran Bennie when he first went undercover in the South Bronx. Those two went through shit I hope my brain's too stupid to imagine. Talk about PTSD."

I remembered Edith Madison saying she had assets at Southampton Town Police. I assumed covert, meaning hidden from Ross, so that couldn't mean Gardella.

"Goddammit," said Sullivan.

"I probably just fucked up," said Fenton, smelling Semple's obvious breach of trust seeping into the air.

Sullivan made one of those hand gestures meant to make the last statement go away.

"No, *I* did," he said. "I'm glad you leveled with me. I'll respect what you said." In other words, not let on to Ross that he knew Gardella's story.

"I appreciate that," said Fenton.

After that, to the relief of both cops, we switched topics to local sports teams, the greedy ways of every living and dead politician, and whether the slightly outsized rear end of the bar's only waitress constituted a net plus or minus.

"Personal preferences are a strange and wonderful thing," said Fenton, to which we all nodded, basking in equanimity.

Eventually we decided the wise choice was to retreat to our respective beds while we could still hail cabs without tripping on the curb. Out on the sidewalk, we shook hands and exchanged thanks and upbeat words of encouragement for the upcoming efforts. In the middle of this, Sullivan asked if I could look into Bennie Gardella, since he was a cop and thus off-limits. And anyway, I'd do a better job with a fellow guinea. Fenton laughed.

"That's what everybody thinks," he said, "but Bennie's no guinea. Family's from some weird place in the toe of Italy. He's a Griko."

"What the hell's a Griko?" asked Sullivan.

"They're Greeks. That was Bennie's code name when he went undercover. The Greek."

CHAPTER THIRTEEN

As predicted when Allison woke up she remembered nothing about the attack. She could barely hear, so we were left to communicate with her by writing in a pocket notebook. Abby told Allison she'd obtained the notebook at a darling little shop somewhere in the south of France. I knew you could get the same thing at nearly any bodega in the city, but didn't think it worth mentioning.

You want people you love in these circumstances to just wake up and start blabbing away, but that's not how it works. Allison looked to me like she knew some horrible thing had happened to her, but was just too sick, sore, and drug-addled to do much about it but stare and try to make out what we were trying to tell her.

Abby's instinct was to express a kind of ersatz cheerfulness that was unnatural to her normal disposition and likely unconvincing, if not disturbing, to Allison. Abby's husband, Evan, kept his focus on Abby as if waiting to catch her as she fell, though that never seemed a possibility.

Nathan talked to Allison as if they'd just gotten home from a busy day at work and were having a good-natured moment of decompression. She held his face with her eyes, watching his mouth form the words she couldn't hear. As he scribbled away on the notebook, she reached over and took his hand.

Amanda was there as well, having broken the ice with Abby in the waiting room. Like most of these things, the fearful expectation was wasted. They shook hands, Amanda expressed concern for Allison and all others involved, Abby said that Allison spoke very highly of Amanda, and so on. There was plenty of cool reserve in the air, but good intentions and civility more than made up for lack of warmth.

"So what are we looking at here?" I asked the doctor, before he had a chance to scoot out of the room.

"Prognosis? Not sure. Pretty major traumatic head injuries, internal trauma, though there she is, eyes opened, seemingly cognizant of her surroundings. She'll live. The question now is restoration of function. I'd be optimistic."

"Because pessimism won't make things turn out any better?" I asked.

"Something like that."

I let the other people in the room do all the talking and pad writing, but Allison knew I was there, because every once in a while her eyes, poking through the bandages, would drift over to mine. I didn't know what they might have been trying to tell me, but I tried to tell her with mine that we'd talk when she was able. Meanwhile I'd be busy doing things I was better suited to than cooing reassurances I didn't necessarily believe.

AMANDA CHOSE to stay for a few more days at the hotel in the city, but I needed to get back to Southampton to take care of a few things, like my work for Frank Entwhistle and the care and feeding of my once-feral mutt.

I knew Jackie would do a good job looking after him, but Eddie liked things the way he liked them, and that included having me around to hit golf balls and feed him Big Dog biscuits.

In honor of both these obligations, I spent a couple days in my shop in the basement of the cottage, leaving the hatch open so Eddie could come and go as he pleased. Amanda kept me informed from New York by telephone, but as predicted, there was no significant news to report.

The same was true of Sullivan and Fenton. Another two days scouring the neighborhood turned up nothing either in suspects or productive information. We were entering the long slog phase; that was certain. But both men seemed up for it, eager even, so that was encouraging.

On the third day, I went over to Amanda's and got back on her computer so I could look at the ill-gotten file on confidential informants. I'd been focused entirely on our local snitches, but Jackie and Randall had swiped the entire state file, so I wanted to see what might be there on The Greek, Bennie Gardella.

There wasn't much. In fact, no mention at all of his undercover work, not surprising. Success in that arena, which included survival, was highly dependent on secrecy. It was likely the only people who knew what he actually did were Ross and the DA, Edith Madison's counterpart in the city.

I pulled out the flash drive and went on the Internet so I could look at the Southampton Town Police website. That's where I learned that Detective Gardella had transferred to Southampton Town Police as Sergeant Gardella to oversee suspect processing and record keeping.

I called Jackie and asked her if she could find out where Gardella lived.

"You know the Internet has all sorts of ways to find people," she said. "It's not that hard."

"I know. I just pick up the phone and call you, and bingo."

To keep her company while she looked, I told her about my conversation with Detective Fenton about Bennie Gardella, and Ross and Gardella's time undercover. Also what Mustafa told me Joey Wentworth told him. To watch out for Greeks.

"So you think there's a connection?" she asked.

"I don't know. Joey's mother hadn't heard anything about it."

Then I told her about the conversation with the Wentworths in their big Upper East Side apartment.

"I actually met them at Burton's," she said. "They're okay, if you don't mind Jack's bitchy insinuations and the iron pole up Sally's ass."

"Who would?"

"I never heard them talk about their son Joey. I guess they were pretty embarrassed by him."

I realized she'd done a better job understanding the Wentworths' underlying state of mind. Regret and disappointment, sure. But for people in their world, it was mostly embarrassment, a far stronger emotion.

"A. Benedict Gardella, in Hampton Bays. I'm guessing that's the guy," said Jackie.

"Sounds like it."

"I don't know if knocking on his door would be such a good idea," she said.

"I could send a calling card. See if he wants to have tea."

"If he's in Hampton Bays, maybe he goes to Sonny's."

Sonny's was a boxing gym up in the Pine Barrens north of Hampton Bays, not far from Southampton Town Police HQ. It was popular with cops, firemen, and ex-military living in the area, people who wanted a good workout without enduring the spandex and self-love of the gyms favored by people from the city. I'd been going to Sonny's ever since moving back to Southampton for all the same reasons. And as one of the few guys there who actually had a professional boxing career, however brief, I was often dragged into ad hoc training sessions delivered ringside during sparring matches.

I'd never seen Gardella there, but I usually went after work and he might have favored early morning.

"That's thinkin'," I said to Jackie.

"I do have a good thought once in a while."

"You're always thinking. Maybe that's your problem."

"Who said I have a problem?"

"I don't know. Think about it."

SONNY'S WAS owned and run by a retired Town cop named Ronny, one of the central mysteries of the place. Ronny had a small face in the middle of a big head with the type of fleshy neck that flowed seamlessly into his shoulders. He wore thick glasses on his florid face and had a giant potbelly. In short, the person who looked in most need of Ronny's establishment was Ronny himself.

I found him in his office, where he spent most of his time, doing what I don't know. How much office work would it take to run a boxing gym in the woods that never advertised and charged a flat fee of fifty bucks a month?

"Hey, Sam," he said. "What do you say?"

"Not much that's worth saying."

"I heard about your daughter. Truly sucks."

News travels fast in cop land. Worse gossips than hairdressers.

"Thanks, Ronny. We're working on it."

"I heard Sullivan's in the city as we speak, on personal time."

"Yeah. Hope that doesn't cause a crime wave in Southampton."

He thought that was funny. Ronny liked to laugh. But then he got serious again.

"Then there's the vet in the wheelchair," he said. "How fucked up is that?"

"His name was Alfie Aldergreen," I said. "If you hear anything that might be useful, you can tell me. I'm in daily touch with Sullivan."

"Haven't heard shit, but will do."

"Meanwhile do you ever see the new guy in Southampton, Bennie Gardella?"

"Almost every day. He's usually waiting for me to open up the place. What about him?"

"I just want to chat about a few things. He doesn't have to know that."

Ronny understood, trusting me not to do anything that would make him feel disloyal to a fellow cop. Even one from out of town.

"He's a quiet one, Gardella, just so you know. Keeps to himself. Power lifter on the free weights. Works the bag like he knows what he's doing."

"Sound like your typical desk jockey?" I said.

"That's what I've been wondering, though I haven't shared the thought with anyone."

I thanked him and he wished me luck with everything. I took the opportunity to change into my gym clothes and spend a little time on the bag myself. If you've ever done any of that, you know how mesmerizing and soothing the practice can be, once you get into the zone. It was one of the few ways I could get my mind to stop nattering at me over all the things I should be thinking about and all the things I shouldn't, which was most of it.

So THE next morning I was waiting at the front door of Sonny's with a giant cup of French Vanilla in my hand and cobwebs woven inside my brain. I don't really have a problem with mornings, it's more about what happens the night before. And before you start making assumptions, too much sleep is usually the bigger problem. Give me six hours and a pot of coffee and I'm right as rain.

Bennie Gardella, on the other hand, looked like it was the middle of the day when he climbed out of a new Chevy Malibu wearing jeans, black T-shirt, and a lightweight nylon jacket you often saw on cops and punks from one of the families. His face might have been handsome to women who liked gaunt, angular features. He had all his hair, combed back Bobby Darin style, though it was mostly grey. He didn't have to open his mouth for me to know what he sounded like, or what he thought about a variety of subjects. I knew the type completely, having hung around with them when I visited my father in the Bronx. He was me and I was him. At least on the outside.

He saw where I was standing and walked right up to me.

"Took you long enough," he said.

"To do what?"

"You were here yesterday, talkin' to Ronny. I figured you'd be here today."

"You know a lot," I said.

"I know you're Sam Acquillo. Ross told me you'd be nosin' around. I expected it sooner."

"I got distracted. Somebody beat up my daughter in the city. She's just coming out of it."

"You know who did it? Oh, wait a minute. If you did, you'd already be in Rikers on a manslaughter charge. At best."

He stood just outside of my reach with his hands in the pockets of his windbreaker, his feet set apart in a ready stance. I stepped back far enough to lean against the outside wall of the gym, my hands in my jeans, awkward and vulnerable. His shoulders relaxed a little, but his eyes, light blue in a dark face, kept their stare.

"I'm too old for that stuff," I said. "And not that stupid."

"Those things go together."

"Why were you leaning on Joey Wentworth?" I asked.

He worked his face into something like a smirk, or maybe a snarl, or maybe something in between.

"First off, I'm a police officer who doesn't respond to questions from civilians. Secondly, I don't know what the fuck you're talking about. And third, I am the last person on earth you want to fuck with. I read your file. I know your shit. It doesn't impress me. I knew we were going to have a conversation. Consider this the one and only time."

"So you're not really here to work on Southampton's record keeping. Too bad. Probably could've used some sprucing up."

He shoved by me and tried the door handle. It was locked. He looked around as if expecting Ronny to leap out from some hiding place.

"Ross brought you in because something's going down in his operation that he doesn't trust anyone on the inside to deal with. You're the go-to. The star player from the glory days."

Gardella just looked at me, enjoying his own silence, his own cocky defiance. I kept on anyway.

"That's good," I said. "Maybe you'll be some help. Just don't get in the way. It's hard enough without some flatfoot cop gumming up the works."

He gave his head a little shake, as if trying to clear his ears. As if he wasn't sure he just heard what he heard.

"Don't push it, Acquillo."

"Push what? Alfie Aldergreen was probably killed for being a snitch. Like Joey Wentworth. They knew each other. Buddies, even. Did you know that?"

"Not my jurisdiction. I'm in record keeping."

Ronny pulled up, in a Japanese roadster that rocked a little when he got out, keys in hand. He opened the door to the gym and I watched Gardella go in, but I didn't bother to go in myself. I had what I wanted. For now.

LIONEL VECKSTROM stood between the big white columns on the steps of Southampton Town Hall when he formally announced his candidacy for district attorney of Suffolk County. He made the case that only an experienced police detective really knew the dark inner workings of the DA's office, yet only an outsider, politically, would be able to effect the drastic reforms he believed were required. He also managed to cite his law degree and five years working for the DA

in Manhattan, something I hadn't known, as further credentials in support of his candidacy.

His wife, Lacey, stood at his side, reinforcing another
credential, his ability to outspend the other candidate. She
seemed ready and eager to jump millions into the fray.

In a statement released to the media, Edith Madison
responded by calling Veckstrom a distinguished police officer,
an honorable servant of the people of Suffolk County, and
a worthy opponent. Somewhere in the fine print she also
proffered the hope that more people vote for her than her
opponent so she could continue in the office she had effectively managed through a half-dozen terms.

You wouldn't exactly call it a barn-burner defense of her
candidacy.

I got to watch it all on TV at Burton's house, where I met
up with Jackie and her boyfriend, Harry Goodlander, for the
occasion. Neither Amanda nor I had a TV, so it was a novel
experience. What Burton had was more like a small movie
screen in what's known as a home theater, though his was
barely distinguishable from the real thing. He'd built the room
and installed all the equipment himself, so the motivation was
more about projects than pretense, since Burton was the least
pretentious super rich guy I knew.

A bit younger than me, with a weathered but handsome
Waspy face and the type of brown hair that inflicted the term
boyish, Burton Lewis was a big disappointment to women
everywhere and an aspiration to every gay man. Wary as
he was of gold diggers of all persuasions, he'd still had a few
satisfying relationships, though at that moment he was on
his own.

Amanda was still in the city, alternating visits to Allison
with Abby. She'd told me that Allison mumbled something,
so she decided to hang in there for another few days in the
hope she'd hear some coherent words. I expressed the hope
they'd be the name of the bastard who did this to her, and
Amanda said I'd be the first to know.

After the political TV was over, Burton and his guests all
went up to a big room with removable glass walls, tile floor,
and two paddle fans languorously turning in the ceiling. Burton's housekeeper, Isabella, had rolled out an industrial-sized
chrome cart stocked with enough food to sustain us for the
rest of the summer.

"Do you think he has a chance?" Jackie asked Burton,
when everyone but Harry was settled on the heavily cush-
ioned wrought iron furniture. Harry was still piling assorted
meats on a plate, forgivable given his colossal size.

"Better than others in the race," he said.

"Better than Edith?"

"Possibly. She's never had to actually campaign before.
Finds the whole thing tremendously distasteful. I can't blame
her, but it is an elected office. Campaigning comes with the
territory."

"Veckstrom seems to think she hasn't run a very tight
ship," said Harry, joining us in the seating circle.

"Who knows what he really thinks," said Jackie. "He'll
say what he needs to win. I'm no fan of Edith Madison,
who considers defense attorneys a notch or two below rabid
vermin, but I can't say she's been a lousy DA."

"How long do you think she can keep it a secret that all
three people just murdered in Southampton were confidential
informants?" I asked Jackie.

"I can't see how that would be much help for Veckstrom,
either," she said.

"Unless he solves the case, or cases," said Burton. "Given
the timing of the election, and the usual period for a big case
to go to trial, he might get to prosecute as well."

"If he figures out who killed Alfie, I'll vote for him," I said.

"So no progress there," said Burton.

"Not sure, Burt," I said. "Alfie himself thought the cops
were after him. Joey Wentworth was worried about Greeks,
and it turns out an undercover from Ross's days in the South

Bronx is embedded in the Town police force. They call him 'The Greek.' Sullivan was with me when I found out."

Burton didn't like the sound of that.

"Joe needs to be discreet," he said.

"I've got him busy with a cop in the city. Keep him out of trouble for the time being."

"He's not in a good way," said Jackie. "It's worrisome."

"Loss of a spouse, however shrewish, can be unsettling," said Burton. "Compounded by a loss of faith in his own police force, his only stabilizing influence."

"Except for Sam," said Harry. Everyone looked over at him. "Sam can be a good influence," he added, somewhat defensively.

Burton took that moment to ask if everyone had adequate refreshment.

"But you're happy with Detective Fenton," said Jackie, moving things along.

"I am," I said. "He's the kind of cop who likes to chew on a bone."

"Allison may simply identify the perpetrator when she comes to," said Burton.

"She might," I said. "Amanda will be there for that. I asked her to tell me, then Fenton, with the hope that he gets to the guy before I do."

"Don't even joke about that," said Jackie.

"Nobody's joking," I said.

Burton cleared his throat, ever the conciliator.

"Has anyone interviewed people connected to Lilly Fremouth, the third CI?" he asked.

"I'm having trouble there," said Jackie. "With Sullivan out and Veckstrom in the lead role, I've got to be a little careful. I know it's not like me, but I'm worried about Prick Cop with this campaign thing. If he wants to get political, I'm a sitting duck."

"Maybe I should pay a call," said Burton.

"That's good of you, Burt," I said, "but let me. I can't get any worse with Veckstrom."

"Very well," he said. "But don't forget, I'm always available for assignment."

"We won't," said Jackie, who would rather sever one of her limbs than put Burton in a dangerous situation. "I'll go with Sam. Between the two of us, we may manage not to fuck it up."

"There's that can-do attitude," said Burton.

With little settled, but comfortably sedated by food and drink, I went home to the cottage on the Little Peconic and the dog, who held no rancor toward me for leaving him when I went into the city. In fact when I came home, he seemed glad to have me back. I'd say the easy forgiveness of dogs is one of their finer qualities if Eddie didn't occasionally resent my decision to rot in an Adirondack chair and stare at the water instead of hitting golf balls on the beach for him to chase and triumphantly return.

That night he likely sensed that rotting in the Adirondacks was the only option, so he joined me, lying shoved up against my feet and acting like this was a source of great contentment.

CHAPTER FOURTEEN

I had to go into the Village the next day to buy some weird little fasteners you can only buy from the hardware store on Main Street. After several years in the construction trade in Southampton, I'd begun to think the place stocked at least one of everything that has ever been made.

First, though, I stopped at the coffee place on the corner to resupply my giant travel mug drained on the ten-minute trip from the cottage. The shop was packed with the usual summer crowd, but I practiced patience and forbearance and got out of there after only growling at one young jerk in an exercise outfit who was too occupied with his smartphone to avoid bumping into me.

At the hardware store, I caught up with the various Latinos, Poles, and craggy old Anglos who worked the place, suggesting that my five-dollar sale likely assured the owner's mortgage that month.

From there I walked across the street toward the bank and got hit by a big white van.

I was at the crosswalk, where an urgent sign in the middle of the road should have provided enough warning to the driver, and in fact, I saw him slow down as he approached. But then a woman behind me on the sidewalk started losing

149

control of the little dog she was holding. Her insistent commands and the dog's yelping pulled my attention away and
by the time I looked forward again the van was right on top
of me. I jumped back, literally, but too late to avoid getting
clipped by the big truck's left fender.

Even at low speed, the ballistic energy of a multiton vehicle is a lot more than the average human body is built to
withstand. Even if you spend as much time in the gym as I do.

I spun like a skating routine gone terribly wrong and landed
hard enough to hear the crack of my jaw as it hit the pavement. I'd been punched there a few times during my boxing
career, but it didn't prepare me for the shock to the brain
and special effects that lit up before my eyes. My elbows and
knees were also involved, though I was more interested at
that point in staying out from under the wheels of the truck.
I heard screams from the sidewalk and the screech of tires.
And somebody yelling "son of a bitch," though I think that
was me.

When I stopped rolling I was hard against the curb. I
looked up and saw a bunch of people staring down at me
saying things like, "Is he dead?" One of the faces got a lot
closer, and I recognized him as the driver. Jaybo Flynn, Jimmy
Watruss's young buddy driving Mad Martha's refrigerated
fish van.

"Holy shit, Sam, I'm so fucking sorry," he was screaming.
"Are you okay? Oh man, somebody call an ambulance. My
fucking foot slipped. Jesus Christ, are you dead?"

"I'm not dead, Jaybo," I said, pulling myself up. "I'm not
even all that hurt, unless this blood means something."

I looked at the red smear on my hand that came from
feeling around my chin.

"Jimmy's gonna fucking kill me," said Jaybo. "I'm not
even drunk."

"He's not going to kill you," I said, trying with some help
from Jaybo and the other gawkers to get up on my feet.
"Though I might."

"I don't know what happened. I thought I was hitting the brake and I hit the accelerator instead. It's not my truck."

Jaybo had another guy in the truck with him who looked even more shook up than Jaybo.

"That's totally what happened, man," the guy said.

"Forget about it," I said. "I should've been more careful."

The crowd tried to help me to one of the park benches that line Main Street, but I shook them off and got there on my own power. I was suddenly aware that my ribs where the van hit were burning, and I knew I'd be pretty sore in a few hours, but thought everything else was still in working order. No breaks or strains among the moveable parts.

"If you want to be useful, get that for me," I said to Jaybo, pointing to the paper bag filled with my fasteners where it lay in the street. "I might never find those things again."

A Village cop I didn't know sat down next to me on the bench. She was stocky and serious, her belt bristling with equipment, her face kind and concerned.

"We need to get you to the hospital," she said.

"No we don't. I'm okay."

"You don't know that."

"Yes I do. I've been beat up by bigger guys than that truck."

The little crowd around me dissipated with the arrival of the cop, much to my relief. Jaybo and his buddy were still there after retrieving my little paper bag. He looked even jumpier than usual, consumed with worry.

"Jaybo, it's all right," I said.

"Oh, fuck," he said, looking away from me. I followed his eyes to where Jimmy Watruss was striding down the street.

"Jimmy, I'm fine," I said, drawing his attention away from Jaybo. "I did a stupid thing. Wasn't Jaybo's fault."

The young cop said to Jimmy, "Maybe you could convince Mr. Macho to let me take him to the hospital." I looked at the name on her name tag.

"I'll go with you, Roza, if you tell Jimmy it's no big deal," I said.

"It's no big deal," she said.

Jaybo looked at Jimmy with a look that said, "See?"

"His name is Sam," Jimmy said to the cop. "Put him in cuffs and take his dumb ass to the hospital."

None of them knew, though, about my phobia of hospitals. All that soothing pale paint, blinking machines, people in blue outfits carrying syringes. Images of Allison in her bed all hooked up flooded my brain. Almost made me want to run out into the street and find another truck to finish the job.

Instead Officer Roza Dudko gently dragged me up off the bench and toward a waiting patrol car, which took me to Southampton Hospital, only a few blocks away. I was met by the ER king, an oversized Jamaican doctor named Markham Fairchild, who'd seen me there before.

"Not my fault," I said to him, as he used his pizza-platter-sized hand to check my pulse.

"Never your fault, Mr. Acquillo. What is it this time?"

"Fish van hit him on Main Street," said Officer Dudko.

"I'm fine," I said. "Both of you, go look after people who need looking after."

Markham stuck a tiny flashlight in my eyes and felt around my skull.

"One of the harder heads in Southampton," he said to Officer Dudko. "I've seen the X-rays."

She noted that, then agreed to leave us and go back to more useful work. Markham poked and prodded a bit more, and after a physician's assistant put a few stitches in my chin, decided I was a waste of his time. I heartily agreed.

"Of course now I'm at the hospital and my car's in the Village," I said.

"Don't worry, Mr. Acquillo. We have special transport for our repeat customers."

So a nurse just getting off shift had the dubious privilege of driving me back to my car. She didn't seem to mind. On the way we traded names of people we knew in town and agreed that the world would be a better place if Markham ruled everything.

"Can you have an ER-Docracy?" she asked.

I LEARNED a few things about injured ribs. They get a lot worse a few days after the injury and then stay that way for a very long time. You can avoid the pain by not walking, sitting, standing, lying down, laughing, coughing, sneezing, or breathing. I still managed to resist the painkillers they prescribed, certain the evil things would've instantly turned me into a heroin addict.

Part of the recovery plan was to avoid allowing people to hear me cry out in agony, so I stayed away from the public for about a week, though I spoke to Amanda every day on the phone.

"As we thought, she doesn't remember a thing," she reported on the occasion of Allison waking up. "We had to explain everything to her. Nathan did the heavy lifting. He's an interesting young man."

"How's Abby taking it?"

"She's been good. I think Allison was glad to see everybody."

"But me."

"She doesn't want you there, not in the condition she's in. How did you know that?"

"Because that's what I would want."

"Though you are coming soon, I trust," she said. "If the ribs allow."

"I'll make it in tomorrow," I said. "Better to surprise her."

"You can drive?"

"The Grand Prix basically drives itself."

"So no progress on who did it," she said.

"Sullivan's on his way back. He's stopping by to tell me what they have, though I know what he'll say."

"They got nothing."

"Probably less than that."

SULLIVAN DID stop by about an hour later. He looked as if his time in the city had done him some good. Brighter eyes and quicker movements. More irritation and less resignation, like the old Sullivan.

He fussed over Eddie like he always did, then agreed to carry some beers out to the Adirondack chairs so we wouldn't die of thirst while we talked. Given my ribs, it took awhile to get out there, so I had time to tell him what happened. He'd had a similar injury, so it pleased him to share the experience.

"It's a fucker, right?" he said.

"It is."

"I did mine falling down the basement stairs carrying a stack of pizzas. Wish it was a better story."

"How did the pizzas come out?" I asked.

"Worse than me, but we ate them anyway."

When we finally got to the breakwater, all I had to do was drop into the chair while stifling the usual little yelp. I was partly successful.

"You really fucked yourself up, didn't you," he said.

"Jaybo Flynn fucked me up. Though he didn't mean to."

"I think that kid would fuck up signing his name if it weren't for Jimmy Watruss."

Then he told me about Allison's case, and as expected, they had bubkes, despite a lot of talk with informants and associates of Allison's and people in the neighborhood.

"Thing is," he said, after downing half his beer, "this actually tells us something."

"You've eliminated first order variables."

"I would've said exactly that, if I knew what the hell it meant."

"The solutions to most puzzles are almost always the most obvious," I said. "So you go there first. When those fail, you know you're facing the nonobvious, which changes your approach."

"Where'd you learn that?"

"Fixing oil refineries," I said.

"They break?"

"Sometimes."

He concentrated on downing his beer and opening another. The night was warmer than you'd expect, even for that time of the summer. The breeze off the Little Peconic had momentarily flagged, reminding me that nothing works all the time.

"What's obvious to me is that Allison knew her attacker," he said. "That he wasn't from the neighborhood. That it has nothing to do with money, which usually means it's about sex or information. I'm crossing off sex after talking to the Hepner kid, who's about as stand up as you can get. Sorry," he added, remembering he was talking about my daughter.

"No need."

"So what's left is information. Somebody tried to waste Allison because she knew something she shouldn't have. She's only alive because he didn't know how hard it is to kill an Acquillo. That's my two cents, for what it's worth."

"It's worth a lot."

"Yeah?"

"I'm grateful," I said.

He shrugged, dismissing the sentiment, though an even less sensitive person than I would have seen it pleased him.

"Okay, good," he said. "I better get back to my place. See if the help has restocked the wine cellar."

I let him go without leaving the Adirondacks. Eddie stuck with me, even lying hard up against my legs again, which was a little out of the ordinary. Maybe he was telling me he liked

COP JOB

our arrangement as is, and not to screw it up by getting run over by any more trucks.

I told him okay, though I wasn't sure I could deliver on the promise.

THE NEXT day the pain in my ribs was slightly less startling, so I took a chance on driving me and Eddie in the Grand Prix to the hospital in the city where they had Allison. Riding in the car is one of Eddie's transcendent delights, proven by frequent trips to and from the rear seat and long periods with his head stuck out the window.

When I first got him, he was startled by a big dog that barked at him from the bed of a black pickup. Since then, he barks at every black pickup, assuming it conveys its own threatening dog. Or maybe he thinks the truck is the dog itself. I'm not sure, but on the way to the city, no black pickup escaped his wrath.

At the hospital, we made it past the battle-ax at the front desk and all the way to the nurses' station in Allison's ward before being told dogs weren't allowed in the hospital. Eddie responded by putting his front paws on the desk so the nurse could reach over and scratch the top of his head. I told her he was a trained therapy dog, which she didn't believe, but let me through anyway.

I told Eddie to go find Amanda and followed him as he sniffed his way down the hall and into Allison's room, where Amanda and Nathan were using her sheet-covered legs as a black jack table.

"Hello there, Eddie," said Amanda. "Want to play?"

"Never trust a mixed breed with a deck of cards," I told her.

"We have news," said Amanda.

"They're busting Allison out of here," said Nathan.

"Into a nursing home," said Allison. "Not exactly out out."

Her voice was hoarse and the words slurred, but you could understand her.

Amanda gathered up their cards and shuffled the deck before handing it back to Nathan.

"Technically she's being transferred to a convalescent facility where they can maintain care and start rehab," said Amanda. "It's a big step," she added lightly, squeezing Allison's knee.

"She means they need the bed for the next bleeding bag of bones," said Allison.

"We're a little fussy today," said Nathan.

"That's my girl," I said. "A sure sign she's on the mend."

"What's with the chin?" Nathan asked, pointing to the scuff I got from hitting the pavement on Main Street. "What's the other guy look like?"

"The other guy was a truck. Looks better than me."

I put my hand over my wounded ribs out of habit. Amanda saw me and asked how I felt. Sore, I told her, but mobile.

"Allison has some very interesting pain medicine," said Amanda. "I'm sure she'll share."

"I might take her up on it. Those things can be expensive."

"Her stepfather's paying for everything not covered by insurance, which is quite a bit, I'm appalled to note," said Nathan

"He doesn't have to do that," I said.

"Are we about to look a gift horse in the mouth?" asked Amanda.

Allison had her eyes closed, but she opened them again to give me a stare.

"We're not," she mumbled.

"Okay, but she's not going into any nursing home," I said.

"She can't stay here," said Amanda.

"No, but you've got plenty of room at your house," I said. "For you and Allison, and Nathan, if he's serious about looking after her."

"I'm serious," he said.

"The nurses and physical therapists can come to us," I said. "Allison can have the guest suite on the second floor. It's got its own bath and plenty of room for rehab equipment."

"Can you just do that?" Nathan asked.

"My father often thinks he can just do things," said Allison.

"It's certainly fine with me," said Amanda to Allison. "I'd love to have you at my house."

It took a lot more to convince the discharge people at the hospital. At one point, they brought in one of the docs who gravely lectured me on the importance of full-time, institutional care for a case as serious as Allison's. I listened politely before telling him to collect his kickback from the nursing home for warehousing some other poor schlub—he wasn't getting my daughter. For some reason, he found this offensive, and stormed out of the office before I could further enlighten him. Though I did get a chance to chat with a hospital administrator who subsequently appeared, another imperious asshole who thought I'd be cowed by threats of legal action. I told him my friend Burton Lewis was richer and more powerful than any of his friends, and anyway, there was nothing legally he could do as long as Allison chose to go with us of her own free will.

After that, the best he could do was tell me to stop bringing my dog to the hospital. Eddie handled the insult as graciously as usual.

When I could use my cell phone out on the sidewalk I called Abby and told her our plans. Except for a half-hearted offer to use their apartment instead, she agreed it was far better for Allison to be surrounded by people who loved her, in a real home and away from the antiseptic, dehumanizing medical world.

I heard Evan yelling in the background that he not only would pay the added freight, he knew how to set up all the necessary in-home care and rehabilitation. Before I got off the phone I told him through Abby to go ahead and make the arrangements. What the hell, he was paying.

There was another reason I wanted Allison on Oak Point, which I hadn't yet shared with anyone. I had some faith in the security people at Roosevelt Hospital, so far justified. I might not be as lucky at the next place. I needed Allison out on Oak Point so we could keep an eye on her. Whoever beat her up hadn't meant to stop there. Whatever motivated him still existed. And as long as Allison lived, so did the motivation.

So the odds were better than even that he'd try to finish the job.

Unless I got to him first.

CHAPTER FIFTEEN

E van had been true to his word. Within days we had a hospital bed, medical gear, monitors, and assorted scary-looking rehab equipment, plus a continuous flow of visiting nurses waiting for Allison after they discharged her from the hospital and drove her and Nathan out to Southampton in an ambulance.

I was there to watch over the delivery, but I didn't need to be. Everything was handled very smoothly and professionally. The only thing I did was carry Allison up to the second floor so they didn't have to negotiate the wheelchair. It wasn't a hard task, even with the bum ribs, she'd lost so much weight. Though her grip around my neck was stronger than you'd think possible, and I took advantage of the moment to breathe in the aroma of her hair, something I hadn't been able to do since she was an early teen.

After we got her and Nathan settled in, I told everyone that Paul Hodges was signed up to handle security.

Amanda was happy about it, Nathan not so much.

"You don't think I can protect her," he said. "You think I'm just a pussy nerd."

"Have you ever shot anyone?" I asked.

"No."

I took him down to my shop in the basement and gave him a .45 automatic I'd lifted off a guy who'd once tried to kill me. We both survived, but I thought the wiser choice was to keep his gun. I showed Nathan how to load the clip, free the safety, and aim with both hands.

"Go for the body," I told him. "Makes it harder to miss."

We designated Amanda's master bedroom next door for the security detail and put her in another guest suite on the first floor. As arranged, Hodges showed up around dinnertime so Amanda had a crowd to feed and water. She seemed to like it, though I wondered for how long. Amanda and I got along pretty well partly because we liked spending a lot of time on our own. Just another issue to push out into the indefinite future.

When all the commotion calmed down, I went back to my cottage and out to the Adirondacks with Eddie to find my own seclusion, happy though I was to have the crowd next door. Safe for now, I hoped.

JACKIE PICKED me up the next day in the rolling storage container she used as a car. She cleared a space for me in the passenger seat by heaving the stacks of paper, cosmetics, ice scrapers (useful in the middle of summer), bankers boxes, bulging tote bags, and changes of clothes that usually lived there into the back, which may or may not have had the seat unfolded.

"When was the last time you checked for wildlife?" I asked her.

"Get it out of your system now. I'm not listening to this all the way to Riverhead."

Jackie had tried to arrange a visit with Lilly Fremouth's mother, but the woman was so deranged with shock and grief after finding her murdered daughter that she was essentially mute and nonresponsive. But Lilly's father, divorced for many years, said okay. He lived in a section of Southampton in the north, hard up against Riverhead, called Flanders. It didn't look much like Belgium, though it was home to a famous building in the shape of a duck where they used to sell authentic Long Island duck eggs.

It wasn't a part of the Hamptons that showed up in any of the slippery, four-color magazines that littered the Village all summer. Up there nobody preened for society photographers or rode polo ponies. Instead they mostly worked hard jobs with landscaping crews and painting contractors, worried about their families, and tried to stay clear of the police.

Ben Fremouth was in many ways an exception. He'd retired ten years before from teaching history and social studies at Westhampton Beach High School. He had a well-tended house on the same street where he'd grown up. There weren't many places a black kid could grow up out here in those days, but after the Civil Rights movement, he could have moved out, but didn't.

Jackie told me all this on the ride up, but couldn't explain that last one.

A family passed by on foot on Ben's street as we were getting out of the car, but they hardly looked at us. They were Latinos, who had become a much bigger percentage of the population over the last decade. I said *hola* anyway before following Jackie up the stone path.

Fremouth was tall and gaunt with long enough hair to nearly qualify as an Afro. He stooped closer to our level when he opened the screen door and squinted at us through heavy glasses. Jackie told him who we were and he nodded, backing up to let us into his living room.

Books lined one wall and surrounded an easy chair. It was the type you could sit in for about a thousand years. The smell of the books, not unpleasant, filled the room, as did a mix of floral and leather aromas the source of which was not immediately apparent.

"I can offer you tea. Or Diet Coke," he said. "That's all I have here."

We said we were all set, and he said he'd have some tea himself, since that's what he drank throughout the day.

"Used to be coffee, but then my central nervous system started to rebel," he said. "Getting old seems to be a process of serial deprivation."

Once he was back in the room in his chair, and we were on a sofa, Jackie started to apologize for bothering him about something he likely didn't want to discuss, but he cut her off.

"If I wasn't willing to address the subject I wouldn't have agreed to talk," he said.

"Of course," said Jackie.

"It was inevitable, what happened to Lilly," he said. "Only a matter of time."

"Why was that?" I asked.

He looked at me as if I were blind to the self-evident.

"Once they become addicted to heroin, the odds of recovery are sadly long. It's the financial pressure. Imagine having to buy something on a daily basis that you can't afford, that's illegal, that has no quality control, that is retailed by people of no conscience, social or otherwise, whose only goal is to ensnare you in further illicit activity, where is that going to end?"

He spoke in a flat, matter-of-fact way that failed to entirely obscure the same anguish I'd heard in Jack Wentworth's voice. Anguish without socioeconomic borders.

And as with the Wentworths, part of me wanted to tell him at least Lilly had enough conscience of her own to help bust some of that low life, though I didn't know the girl personally. Maybe it was only for the money.

"Did Lilly seem different before she was killed?" Jackie asked. "Was she fearful, distracted?"

Fremouth put a finger alongside his nose, in what looked like a habit of deliberation.

"Yes. Not that we had much in the way of interaction. She only lived a few blocks from here, but I refused to aid in her lifestyle choices, to put it in the euphemism of social services. So I wasn't much worth talking to."

"But enough to know something was up," I said.

He nodded.

"She stopped by with my granddaughter, a certain way to have me let her in the house. I gave her tea. And braced myself for the money pitch, though it never came. She only seemed to want to talk. I was happy to accommodate that, and allow my granddaughter to sit on my lap and perform indignities with my reading glasses."

"What did she talk about?" I asked.

"It was a desultory conversation. No particular themes. I mostly listened, since I never asked her about herself, wanting neither the truth nor a passel of lies."

His gaze had been mostly directed at the floor a few feet in front of where we sat. Now it drifted up toward his over-flowing bookcase, as if the books held the answer to his life's tragedies.

"Did she talk about the cops?" Jackie asked. "Mention any by name?"

He shook his head, tentatively, as if unsure that was the proper answer.

"Not by name, but she did ask me if I thought the police who patrol Flanders were on the take, as if I'd know the answer to that. I've never spoken to any of them, with the exception of one fellow who I had as a student. I would see him occasionally. Actually more often lately in his cleverly unmarked police cruiser, as if anyone even more unschooled in law enforcement than me would be fooled by that."

"A plainclothesman," said Jackie.

"Is that what they're called? In the nineteenth century they wore identical bowler hats and morning coats. No more convincing a disguise."

"Can you tell us his name?" I asked. "If you don't mind."

"Joseph Sullivan," he said. "I also taught his two older brothers. Both went into the military. One killed in the Gulf War. I read the other was in the State Department, but that might be very old information. I liked Joe. Had the wits of his brothers, but lacked confidence. I think he found his footing on the police force."

I didn't want to break the news that Sullivan's footing had been a little precarious of late. So I asked another question.

"Did Lilly ever mention him?"

He didn't think so, but reminded us that communica tion with his daughter had been hit or miss in recent years. Then he veered into a description of Lilly's mother, and how he thought her own battles with prescription drugs, legally obtained, had contributed to Lilly's addiction. He said he didn't want to cast judgment, but the scent of recrimination hung in the air.

"Did she talk about any of the other detectives?" Jackie asked, ignoring the fact that we'd already asked that question. Fremouth took note.

"You seem to have some focus on the Southampton police," he said. "That's interesting."

Jackie tried to backpedal.

"Not really," she said. "Just talking here."

"You brought it up," he said.

"Do you have any idea of who might have killed your daughter?" I asked.

"Do you think I don't wonder that myself nearly every waking minute of every day?" he said. "This neighborhood has been my home for my entire life. I'm old, but I still know a lot of people who tell me things. If it could be known, I'd know it. Everyone assumed her boyfriend was the culprit, but he was out of town, and frankly, lacks the courage for such a monstrous act. In my opinion. For people who live here, the police are a fact of daily life. A necessary evil much of the time, though often more evil than necessary. Though nothing leads me, or anyone I know, to believe they have any complicity in this. Does that answer your question?"

"It does," said Jackie, too quickly for my taste.

It didn't look like we'd get much more of use from the elegant, exhausted man, though we gave him the chance to tell us anything we hadn't already asked about. So we thanked him, and were nearly out the door when I remembered what I'd meant to ask all along.

"Mr. Fremouth, did Lilly know a mentally ill white guy in a wheelchair named Alfie Aldergreen?" I asked.

"The one who was drowned in Hawk Pond?" he said. "I have no idea."

"What about another guy, Joey Wentworth?" said Jackie, catching the drift.

Fremouth was standing at the door about to usher us out. He looked bothered all of a sudden.

"He was killed as well," he said. "You think there's a connection to Lilly's death?" We stood there immobile, unable to answer. "Yes," he said. "Wentworth was a local operator. If I knew that, Lilly surely did as well. So there might be a connection. I'll think about it. At this point, there's really nothing left to do."

When we got in Jackie's car, I saw him still standing in his doorway like the monument to sad forbearance that he was, watching us, likely wondering whether agreeing to talk to us was a blessing or a curse.

I NEVER go out of my way to follow the news, but if you want to listen to reasonable music where I live you have to listen to public radio, and if you do that, you can't avoid bumping into a news story or two, even if you're fast with the on-off button.

That's why I heard the next day a report on Edith Madison that said she'd been treated for clinical depression and anxiety for several years following the death of her husband. Since this was only about six years ago, some people were concerned that she had hidden this malady while continuing in her official duties at a time when her office was heavily involved in serious and sensitive prosecutions.

The story was a big enough deal to make the national news, and apparently solid enough to meet the journalistic standards of National Public Radio, despite the anonymous sources. As her leading competitor in the upcoming election, Lionel Veckstrom was asked to comment, but demurred, sounding statesmanlike in his reluctance to discuss such a personal matter as the DA's psychiatric status, even bemoaning the stigmatization of people with emotional disorders.

A nice bit of damning with faint principle.

I called Jackie who just said "Holy Crap" when she answered the phone.

"What does this mean?" I asked.

"I don't know, but it can't be that great for Edith."

"What does it mean for our snitch project?"

"Don't know that, either. Of course I'm wondering if her asking us to nose around about the cops was in any way improper, or God forbid, illegal. Not that there's a connection with her health issues, but once there's blood in the water, the sharks aren't far behind."

"We need to talk to her," I said.

"Oh, goody. That sounds like fun."

"Worse than talking to the parents of murdered children?"

She huffed.

"No. Of course not."

"So call over there and get an appointment."

"What am I, your secretary?"

"Hell, no. You're the boss. They wouldn't even take my call."

She huffed again and hung up.

A few minutes later, she called back.

"I didn't reach Edith, but Oksana gave me a date for next week," she said.

"That was quick," I said.

"Do things you hate immediately or never do them at all. That's my philosophy."

"*Carpe odious.*"

"That almost sounds like a real thing," she said.

"*Ad libitum absurdum.*"

"Just stop it," she said, and hung up again.

I SPENT the following days buried in my workshop catching up on Frank Entwhistle's projects, taking occasional breaks to walk next door and visit with Allison. She was frustrated by what she thought was lack of progress in her recovery, but otherwise lighter and brighter for being in a house and out of the hospital.

During the day a regular flow of cars and vans went in and out of our common driveway carrying nurses, physical therapists, and an assortment of specialists focusing on who-knows-what. I had to hand it to Abby's husband, Evan. He delivered.

Amanda and Nathan filled in between nurse visits, to a fault, until Allison reminded them that prior to the beating she spent most of her time alone hunched over her computer. Consequently Amanda was able to spend more time on her own day job rebuilding houses and Nathan was invigorated by the challenge of finding common conversational ground with Paul Hodges.

I talked every few days with Detective Fenton, who rarely had anything of substance to report, though I felt he wasn't giving up on the investigation. I told him I understood that it was a slow process and appreciated his efforts, which I know he appreciated in return.

The only bit of worthwhile news was a phone call from the female CSI I saw that day in Allison's apartment. She told me what I already knew from Fenton, that there was no match for the assailant's fingerprints or DNA in the CODIS database. I asked her if the DNA told her anything else.

"It was a man," she said.

"White man? Black man? Green man?"

"Don't know. From a mitochondrial marker perspective, race is a meaningless concept."

"I thought DNA could tell you anything," I said.

"I can tell you where your guy's ancestors came from, which in America is usually a mix of everywhere, but not the color of his skin."

"I came from a disappointed white lady and a first class son of a bitch," I said.

"If there's a marker for SOBs, I'm sure your guy would have had it."

I promised her I'd keep our conversation confidential and thanked her for acting like a human being. She reminded me that most people did, which was useful for me to hear.

After what happened to Allison, my view of humanity needed all the burnishing it could get.

CHAPTER SIXTEEN

Getting to Edith Madison might have been a bit of a chore, but talking to Ross Semple, chief of the Southampton Town Police, meant simply driving over to the HQ and knocking on the door.

Metaphorically. The actual task was to knock heads with Janet Orlovsky. But nothing like that happened, because Orlovsky wasn't there. Instead a much younger woman with the face of an elf and a voice filled with good cheer.

Her name tag said Lucille Lausanne.

I barely had a chance to ask for Ross before she was on the phone telling him I was out in reception. Seconds after that, she buzzed me in.

"He said you know where to go," she said, her eyes bright with achievements present and future.

I did know, and got there unimpeded. Ross was waiting for me at his office door.

"I've been expecting you," he said, after I walked in the office and found a clear spot to sit down.

"What did you do with Orlovsky?" I asked.

"She's out on leave. At her request," he added, making an important distinction.

"She all right?"

170

"Her husband left her yesterday."

"That happens a lot around here," I said, thinking of Joe Sullivan.

"Don't get used to Sergeant Lausanne. She's my new adjutant."

"Though a nice change of pace. You gotta admit."

He moved effortlessly through the mountains of crap on the floor and around the desk and dropped into his swivel chair. He lit a cigarette and blew the smoke in my direction. I didn't take the bait.

"Tough thing about Allison," he said. "How's she doing?"

"Okay. Not great. We moved her into Amanda's."

"Better to heal?"

"Better to keep an eye on her."

"You think the perp will try again?" he asked.

"You don't?"

He shrugged.

"Depends on his objectives. That he almost killed her doesn't mean he meant to kill her."

"Not according to the ER docs, though you might be right," I said.

"But that's not why you're here," he said. "You're reporting progress on the snitch murders."

"Progress might be an overstatement."

He sat back in his broken-down chair so far I thought he might topple over.

"How 'bout that Edith," he said. "Full of surprises."

"You know better than me, but I guess it's going to get messy."

"Messy is one way of putting it. One of my key subordinates is trying to take her job."

"I don't know politics and I don't care," I said.

"You'll care if Veckstrom becomes DA. Your file will blossom like the midsummer sun."

"But it won't affect you," I said.

"You think it won't? You're right. You don't know politics."

"How come you didn't tell me two other snitches were killed the same time as Alfie?"

"And deprive you of the joy of discovery?"

He stubbed out his cigarette and immediately lit another.

"Alfie and Joey knew each other," I said. "Lilly probably knew Joey, maybe Alfie. More reason to think the killings are all connected."

"*Cum hoc ergo propter hoc.*"

Basically, correlation doesn't equal causation.

"*Lex parsimoniae,*" I countered, shorthand for "The simplest explanation is usually the right one."

"I concede the point."

"I don't expect you to tell me why you wanted me and Jackie to get into this thing in the first place, but if I were a person given to speculation, which I am, I might think you're lacking trust in your own police force."

"That'd be a terrible thing for the chief of police, wouldn't it?" he said, in a neutral way I could interpret however I wanted.

"It would explain the arrival of a cop who once trusted you with his life, and vice versa. Breeds a different kind of loyalty."

"If you're referring to Bennie Gardella, he's here to clean up our case files. It might surprise you, seeing as how I manage my own paperwork, that it's an area where the squad's performance has been less than exemplary."

I looked around his office at what you'd more fairly describe as an unregulated landfill.

"Everyone needs a good cleanup guy," I said.

"So do you have anything interesting to share, or is this really a pleasant social visit?"

"When I talked to Bennie, he was pretty threatening. You might tell him I'm on the same side."

"There're no sides, Sam. Unless you count the living and the dead."

"I don't know the woman, but Edith doesn't seem the type to use a shrink," I said.

"Nobody knows what goes on in anyone else's head. Especially a self-contained head like Edith's. She saw it happen, you know."

"Who?"

"Her husband. He was an accountant in the city. Until he went splat on the sidewalk outside their apartment on the Upper East Side."

"Really."

"Fell out the window," he said, looking over at a window in his office, probably four feet off the ground. "Who does that anymore?"

"Jesus."

"But the cat lived."

I went to MIT during a period when they thought it was important for their science and engineering students to be exposed to the wider intellectual tradition, in particular philosophy and religion. This is how I ended up in a class on Zen Buddhism, which changed my perspective on reality and provided excellent preparation for these conversations with Chief Ross Semple.

"Don't they always?" I asked.

"The cat liked to sit on a ledge outside their apartment window. It was perfectly happy out there, but Edith's husband couldn't bear the thought of the little kitty being within inches of certain death, so he'd lean out and grab her, and in so doing one night, leaned a little too far."

"They make screens."

"Not according to their super, apparently."

"I don't know politics, but I think her campaign will survive this," I said.

"Me, too. Women voters will lap it up. Cat lovers all."

There didn't seem much point in hanging around after that, so I left and took a long, circuitous route back to the cottage on Oak Point, hoping the soothing imprecision of the Grand Prix's ancient suspension would help calm my mind enough to have a few coherent thoughts about the dead snitches, the alien Long Island politics, architectural wood-work, and most importantly, Allison's attacker, still out there hidden in some hole, planning God knows what.

But all I achieved was more mental chaos, more existen-tial unease.

When Jackie and I finally got to Edith Madison's office, she'd flown the coop. According to Oksana Quan, it was a strategic withdrawal after issuing a statement on her emotional health. The idea was to force the media to focus on the statement by avoiding follow-up questions and the usual hectoring attempts to shove her off balance.

Jackie read it to me as we drove over there, and I had to agree, it was a nicely written defense of her personal pri-vacy, acknowledging the importance of transparency from public officials while combining a hearty condemnation of the bastards responsible for leaking the story, and a gentle dig at unnamed people for twisting simple grief counseling into an ugly political smear.

The press, in turn, leaned more or less the same way, so it looked like an ultimate win for the Madison camp.

Oksana met us as we were about to pass through security and asked if we could take it outside instead. The day was bright, cool and breezy, so that wasn't a hard sell. She led us over to a picnic table, giving me a chance to watch the pleasing way the wind ruffled her silky summer clothing. As we walked over the grass to the table, she slipped off her heels and tiptoed the rest of the way in bare feet.

"That sun feels great," she said, as we settled at the table. "I've been virtually living in that office since the leak. I already look enough like a ghost."

I wanted to say the afterlife suited her fine, but Jackie got in my way.

"Edith's statement was pretty impressive," she said. "Seems to be doing its job with the media."

"I wrote it," said Oksana. "With Edith, of course," she added quickly. "And her political people, whom she isn't ignoring for a change."

"Any idea who leaked it?" I asked.

"No, but when we find out, my plan is to personally eviscerate him."

"Politics can be ugly," said Jackie.

"We're actually here to update you and Edith on our snitch investigation," I said. "If you can call it that."

"I'm all ears."

I told her most of what I told Ross Semple, which wasn't much, in particular leaving out mention of Bennie Gardella. I knew that was the type of info the women were most keenly interested in, but something told me to keep that card tucked out of sight.

"So you really have nothing to report," said Oksana.

Jackie rose to our defense.

"It might look that way, because we think your central thesis is flawed," she said.

Since we hadn't discussed this in advance, Oksana and I were both keenly interested in what she meant.

"In order to believe that the police had anything to do with the deaths of Alfie, Lilly Fremouth, or Joey Wentworth," said Jackie, "you have to disregard everything you know about the people involved. To think that Ross Semple, Joe Sullivan, or even Lionel Veckstrom could possibly commit or condone murdering their own confidential informants is beyond the pale."

"There are other cops," said Oksana.

"True, which is why we're still looking in that direction," said Jackie, "but this emphasis on the cops could be diverting us from the real culprits."

Oksana sat silently with her hands in her lap, in a near parody of a woman deciding if she should give voice to her internal thoughts. I knew then what Jackie was up to.

"We're willing to run with any decent theory, but there's no basis here," I said. "If it's political, then we won't be of much help."

Oksana probably hated hearing that, but you wouldn't know it from her blank affect.

"Joey Wentworth didn't die immediately from his wounds," she said. "We were able to have what you might call a death bed interview."

"Who's 'we'?" said Jackie.

Oksana let her eyes drift over to Jackie as if reluctantly noticing she was sitting at the same table with us.

"I'd rather not say," she said.

"And?" I asked.

Oksana sighed in a way that made her sound almost girlish, surprisingly.

"Joey said he was sitting in his truck waiting for a meet. With a representative of the Southampton Town Police."

"Lionel Veckstrom," said Jackie. "He was assigned to Joey."

Oksana seemed a little unsettled at that, until it registered that she'd given us the CI file.

"Normally, yes. But not that night. Joey said his information couldn't be trusted with anyone but top, top management. Because it had to do with the cops themselves."

It was our turn to be a little unsettled.

"Ross Semple?" Jackie asked, incredulity dripping from her voice.

"Unfortunately, yes," said Oksana. "Ridiculous, right? So I asked him point blank, and yes I was there for the interview. Wentworth said he didn't see the shooter. Just saw a shape. But the greater point is that no one else should have known about the meet. And by the way, every crazy story you ever heard about Semple's time in homicide in the city is an understatement."

I didn't often see Jackie at a loss for words. I would have marveled more if I weren't so much at a loss myself.

Just to make the moment more unsettling, Jackie's cell phone started to ring. After looking at the caller, she jumped up with a gush of apologies and ran off with the thing stuck to her ear. Oksana huffed.

"I guess people have their priorities," she said.

"Jackie's are usually in the right place," I said.

Oksana gave the slightest hint of a shrug and sought a more comfortable position on the picnic bench. The result displayed about another six inches of naked leg, pale and smoothly muscular.

"What do you care, as long as you have that Anselma person," she said.

"Her name is Amanda, and I care plenty about Jackie. Though I don't know what you're getting at."

"Sounds complicated."

She shifted again, this time causing one of those ghostly legs to run hard up against mine. I held my ground.

"It's not complicated at all," I said, looking over at where Jackie was chattering into her cell phone, "If you believe in faith and loyalty. You know something about that, working for Edith Madison."

She moved closer to me to emphasize what she wanted to say.

"I would do anything for Edith," she said. "There's never been a more noble woman."

I believed her, distracted though I was by the smell of her platinum hair, now close enough to flutter across my face and get stuck in my three-day stubble of beard.

"Glad that's settled," I said.

"Nothing's settled," she said, leaning even closer in. "Anything can happen. Even the most surprising things. If you have the imagination. You do have an imagination, don't you, Sam?"

Luckily Jackie picked that moment to come back to the picnic table, stuffing the phone into her pocket and begging forgiveness. Oksana put a little air between us, though she held her gaze to mine as she went back to her story.

"We have our share of local drug problems in Suffolk County, but the greater concern is all the product coming into the East End and traveling through," she said. "The stakes are high on both sides of the legal divide, and with that comes a lot of loose money. We had information that some of that money was finding its way into the Southampton Town police force. That's why we brought in our assets in the first place. We thought we were making progress when suddenly three of the squad's confidential informants are killed. Not a coincidence, in our opinion, and damaging enough to our efforts that Edith felt compelled to take the highly irregular step of asking for your cooperation."

That last line was meant to tell us it was all Edith's decision. No surprise there.

"The dead snitches are a message not lost on anyone thinking of a career in snitching," said Jackie. "It makes it a lot harder for the cops to get intel off the street."

Oksana nodded.

"That's essentially the situation," she said. "The case has gone dark and everyone's clammed up. Significant in itself, but nothing that helps us move forward." She closed her eyes and leaned her head back to bathe her face in the deep summer sun. "Normally, it wouldn't matter so much. With time, cracks always open up. Somebody starts talking. But the election is complicating everything. Creating time pressure."

I caught myself almost feeling sympathy for their situation. Then I reminded myself that they'd never feel the same sympathy for me.

"Okay," I said. "Thanks for your help. We'll get out of your hair." Literally, I thought to myself.

Jackie looked a little surprised, and she might have had more questions, but I wanted to get away from Oksana so I could think more clearly on what to do next. Jackie took the cue and got up to leave like it was all her idea. Oksana looked happy enough to let us go.

"My expectations for you aren't overwhelming," she said, "but it would certainly help the cause to be finished with this distraction. It would also be advantageous for both of you to earn a little of Edith's appreciation."

It's interesting to me how some people can damn, threaten, and coerce in the same sentence without seeming to do any of the three.

"I ALMOST started feeling sorry for them," Jackie said when we were back in the car.

"What did you think about what Joey Wentworth told them?" I asked.

"Are you asking me a question you already have an answer to?"

"No. I really want to know what you think."

She looked down and pulled the hem of her skirt closer to her knees, more of a nervous gesture than any act of modesty.

"I think Ross Semple is easily the strangest man I've ever met. Opaque, flaky, ruthless, occasionally a colossal asshole. Did I mention a teeny bit creepy? But he's the ultimate cop's cop, intellectually fighting well below his weight. Just not possible."

"You're sure."

"No. I'm not sure about anything but the love and devotion of my boyfriend, Harry Goodlander, who's merely colossal."

"You still shouldn't marry him."

"Oksana's right. This whole thing feels like it's stuck shut."

"It is."

"So what are you going to do?" she asked.

"Find a crack."

"What if you can't?"

"Make one."

CHAPTER SEVENTEEN

I called Joe Sullivan to see if he wanted to have a questionable dinner at the Pequot, but he'd already committed himself to Mad Martha's unquestionably great local seafood. I told him I'd meet him there, unless he already had a date.

He said not a chance, though he might get lucky at Martha's.

"Like, if an actual female that doesn't look like Mike Ditka's grandmother happens to walk into the place."

I checked on Allison as I did whenever I left Oak Point for any extended period of time. She was okay, but still not what I hoped for at this point. Amanda was back at work, but Nathan was there, so I asked him how things were going.

"We've been acting a little bummed lately," he said. "The visiting nurse said depression was common at this stage with trauma victims. She said it'll pass."

"When wasn't Allison a little bummed?" I asked.

Nathan just stood there looking pretty gloomy himself. I walked into Allison's bedroom.

"Hey, Sunshine," I said.

"Don't believe him," she said, or more accurately, growled. "I'm fine."

"I believe you," I said.

She didn't seem to like that, so I switched subjects.

"How's the therapy going?"

"Painfully. Not that it matters."

"Course it matters," I said. "Get you back on your feet."

"My feet are fine. Therapy won't do anything for my face. I never liked it, and now it's gone."

"Anything's fixable," I said.

"I took off the bandages and looked. Nothing's going to fix that mess."

She picked at the sheet that covered her legs, as if plucking off invading bugs.

"Jackie got her face blown up by a bomb," I said. "She looks better now than before."

I didn't add that Jackie was also an angry lump of misery during the months of restoration, though maybe I should have.

"Jackie's naturally tough. I'm more like a tub of cream cheese."

"Not what I hear."

"You never listened very well," she said.

She had me on that one, so I didn't answer and a little dead air started to build up.

"Okay. I guess that's that," I said, giving up. I got up to leave.

She glared at me.

"That's that?" she asked.

"Let me know when you've run out of self-pity."

The glare deepened.

"Tough love?" she said.

"Love for sure."

JOE SULLIVAN had one of the tables near the bar at Mad Martha's, so we were able to drift in and out of the conversations between Jimmy Watruss and his retinue of regular barflies. They all thought of Sullivan as more or less one of them, though having the big cop within earshot took some of the spice out of the subject matter.

The salubrious effects of his stay in the city had worn off a little, though his appetite was good enough to tackle a small mountain of local seafood and a pitcher of beer.

"I heard from Fenton today," he said.

"They got anything?"

"He's still liking that copywriter, though more on principle than proof. Him and Allison apparently had quite a catfight. You wouldn't think those artistic types would have anything to fight over."

Sullivan was a very smart guy, but a lifetime on the East End among people like Mad Martha's clientele had left some gaps in sophistication. He was sensitive about it, so I tried to be careful.

"When there's money involved, that's all the reason you need," I said. "That and envy, jealousy, ambition, self-delusion, and raging insecurity."

"What about terminal stupidity?"

"That, too."

Jaybo came out of the kitchen in his chef's outfit. He saw us and walked over to our table.

"How're the ribs?" he asked me.

"I thought we were eating fish," said Sullivan.

"A lot better, Jaybo," I said. "It wasn't his fault," I added to Sullivan.

"What?"

"I hit him with the van," said Jaybo. "It wasn't my fault."

"I thought a dog was about to run out in the street. It distracted me."

"Oh."

Jimmy saw us talking, slid his bulk off the bar stool and pulled up a chair. Jaybo went back to the kitchen.

"Anything you can tell me about the Alfie case?" he asked Sullivan, though also looking over at me.

"Not really," said Sullivan, "but I have a question for you."

"Shoot."

"Did Alfie ever mention a woman named Lilly Fremouth? Black dad, white mother, lived up in Flanders?"

Jimmy thought about it, but shook his head.

"Don't think so, though like I told Sam, I didn't spend that much time with the guy. Looniness aside, he was a pretty quiet tenant. Like everybody else, I just saw him rollin' up and down the sidewalk, or behind the restaurant when he'd cop a free meal. The kitchen guys were on notice to give him whatever he asked for."

"Generous," said Sullivan.

Jimmy rubbed the stumps where his two fingers used to be.

"Not really. Alfie was a vet. Unit cost of a meal is a lot less than I charge customers. No skin off my teeth."

"He was grateful for what you did for him," I said. "For what it's worth."

"It's worth something," said Jimmy. "But plenty of people around the Village helped him as well."

That gave me a thought.

"Did you get much trouble from Esther Ferguson after she tried to save him from the streets?"

Jimmy snorted.

"Not really. Though I'd see her talking to him on the sidewalk, and she tried to get permission from me to check on his apartment. I told her to stick it, politely of course."

"How did he end up living there in the first place?" Sullivan asked.

Jimmy sat back in his chair, which made it harder to hear him, especially since he dropped his voice a notch or two.

"Alfie was in my national guard platoon in Iraq. I'd heard he'd mustered out on a 464, a psych thing, but I didn't know how bad it was till I saw him at the VA center. Fucked-up head and mangled spine, he wouldn't have lasted long cooped up like that. So I moved him into the gallery apartment. I do a lot of stuff for vets, but it's kind of my personal business, if you know what I mean."

"I do," said Sullivan, "but I appreciate the information."

"I just hope you catch the motherfuckers who did this before I do," he said, and then went back to the gang at the bar.

THE NEXT day, after putting in enough time in the shop to catch up on some projects, I drove back into the Village to call on Esther Ferguson. A young guy in a short-sleeved white shirt and tie was coming out the door as I walked up the steps. I asked him if Esther was in her office and he said he thought so.

"You can knock on her door," he said. "Doesn't mean she's gonna answer."

"She did the last time."

"We all get our share of luck."

Mine held. She didn't answer at first, but on the second try I heard the muffled sound of her saying to come in, if I wanted to that badly.

"Shoulda known," she said from where she sat at her desk. "Nobody round here would knock twice."

I gestured at a chair and she wearily waved for me to sit.

"I still don't know anything about what happened to Mr. Aldergreen, if that's why you're here," she said.

"It's why I'm here, but I have another question."

Esther's desk backed up to a giant window air conditioner, which was under full throttle, chilling the room to about sixty-five degrees. She wore a wool blanket with fringe around her shoulders, in a color that matched her blouse. The fan in the AC was strong enough to ruffle the fringe. I'm sure there was a reason for all this, but I didn't like Esther enough to ask.

"Doesn't mean you're entitled to an answer," she said.

"Did you know a woman named Lilly Fremouth? She was murdered about a week before Alfie."

I'd say that made her scowl if scowling wasn't already a natural part of her face.

"Ben Fremouth is one of my oldest and dearest friends," she said. "I won't hear a word said against him."

"You won't hear any from me. I just saw him the other day. Elegant guy."

She shook her head and looked down as if her thoughts were on display in her lap.

"He told me Lilly was the best and worst thing that ever happened to him. I'd contend the former," she said. "Ben did everything he could. I didn't have the heart to tell him some people are bent on a path of self-destruction."

"I guess you'd know. Did you ever work with her, in your official capacity?"

"You know I can't talk about that."

"Come on, Esther. I'm not asking for her confidential file. I just want to know if she ever came here or got involved with any of your other clients."

The intensity of her suspicion almost heated up her meat-locker office. She leaned in toward the desk, gripping her blanket with both hands.

"If you got something specific on your mind, Mr. Acquillo, just spit it out."

"I want to know if she knew Alfie Aldergreen," I said.

She sat back in her chair with a look of satisfaction.

"Those two would make a pretty strange pair, now wouldn't they?" she said.

"I'm not asking if they dated. Just if they knew each other."

She drummed a syncopated beat on the desk with her long, painted nails.

"You ever heard of an encounter group?" she asked, putting the emphasis on the first syllable of "encounter."

I told her I had.

"Lilly was coming in for hers just when she ran into Alfie on the sidewalk. He started warning her about all the elves that can fool you with their beautiful faces, but then turn on you, seeing how they've been seduced by the dark side. Lilly said she wished she'd known that before dating her husband. Next thing you know he's sitting in the group, all attentive and polite. I didn't have the heart to tell Lilly that group therapy's a waste of time for a brain as disorganized as Alfie's, but then again, I thought, it might do her some good to try."

"So they were friends," I said.

She tilted her head and made a face.

"I wouldn't exactly call it a friendship. But they knew each other, yeah."

"How often did they meet in the group?"

"Half a dozen times, I guess, before Alfie forgot which day we held it on. Lilly asked about him, but it wasn't up to me to get him into the building. 'Cept to ask army boy to bring him around, but as usual, that didn't do a lot of good."

She frowned at me, easily conflating me with her other adversary, Jimmy Watruss.

"Did they ever spend time together, just the two of them, outside the group?"

"How the hell would I know? She left with him a couple times, but I never saw them out on the sidewalk. Lilly lived up in Flanders. She only came down here when she had to."

I tried to pull out more information, but I'd already gone well beyond where Esther wanted to go, so I got up to leave before she had a chance to shoo me away. I was on the way out the door when she coughed at me, which I correctly took as a command to listen to one more thing.

"Even a junkie can have a heart," she said. "Girl like Lilly, scraping along at the bottom of the heap, probably thought she could do some good for somebody even lower down. I've seen it a lot in my line of work."

Knowing Alfie the way I did, I wondered which of the two was the more generous and compassionate, the more eager to rescue a soul so thoroughly damaged by forces of evil incomprehensible even to the dark side.

I STOPPED off at Mad Martha's hoping to catch up with Jimmy Watruss again, but he wasn't there. I went back in the kitchen to ask Jaybo if he might be coming around, and he told me Jimmy was at a vets' meeting up in Riverhead. The guy who was in the truck with Jaybo the day he ran into me was at a chopping block dicing up onions. He kept his head down, as if expecting I'd take a poke at him just for being there. Instead I went back to the bar and ordered a stack of fried flounder, so the visit wasn't a complete waste.

After a slow meal, it was getting late by the time I was on Noyac Road heading back to my cottage on the Little Peconic. I was about to turn into my neighborhood when I heard a siren and saw a Southampton Town patrol car bearing down on me, lights ablaze. I pulled out of the way and the car swooshed by and made the hard left onto Oak Point. I stuck the gearbox in low and roared after him.

Against faint hope, I followed the cop to the end of the peninsula where he turned into the driveway I shared with Amanda. I stopped breathing.

Eddie was in the yard barking his head off, something he rarely did. The patrol car raced down the drive to Amanda's, and I saw Danny Izard leap out of the car, drawing his sidearm in a single, fluid motion.

In the time-compressed moments an experience like this creates, I sent prayers to a god I didn't believe in to spare every life inside that house, noting that those were the lives I loved more than any others in this world.

When I reached the door I almost collided with Danny as he ran back out, now with a flashlight in his other hand.

"In the living room," he yelled as I shoved by.

Amanda was sitting on the floor with her back braced against one of her white, over-stuffed couches. Paul Hodges had his head in her lap, his legs stretched out and feet at cockeyed angles. She had her hands pressed against his temples, as if she were squeezing a cantaloupe. Nathan stood over them, blood running from a gash in his own head, which he ignored. His hands shook like frightened birds. In one of those hands was the old Colt automatic I'd given him.

Amanda looked up, her handsome Italian face a symphony of shock and worry.

"I didn't see them," she said. "Nathan carried him in here."

"I shot over their heads," said Nathan. "I didn't know what else to do."

Hodges opened his eyes and said, "Next time, shoot 'em *in* the head."

"What happened?" I asked him.

He took a while to answer, and I almost felt bad making him talk. His words were closer to a whisper than full speech.

"Eddie was barking like I'd never heard before. I went out the front door and these two jamokes were coming up the path. One of them whacked me with a hammer before I had a chance to ask what the hell they were doing here."

"What'd they look like?"

"Hoodies and scarves. That's all I saw."

Nathan looked over at me.

"They whacked me, too, before I could get the gun out," he said. "I had to shoot while I was flat on my back. I didn't want to hit Hodges."

There was a tremor in his voice, but his words were firm. No apologies.

"Where's that fucking ambulance?" said Amanda.

I looked around at all the big open windows, the bay breeze blasting in around Amanda's pretty tied-back curtains.

"You're too big a target standing there," I said to Nathan. "Sit next to Amanda and keep both hands on the gun."

I snapped off all but one lamp and went outside. I could
see Danny's flashlight whipping across the trees that lined
the backside of our properties. Eddie was in the driveway,
still barking like a mad dog. I whistled and he shut up and
ran over to me. I scrunched around his neck and told him
everything was okay, even though I knew it wasn't.

I got my own flashlight out of the Grand Prix's glove
compartment and walked with Eddie out toward the bay. It
was a heavy Maglite, which I carried more for its double-duty
as an effective club than to light my way. I saw no sense in
giving anyone a nice bright target to shoot at.

When I got to the edge of the breakwater, the only thing
moving was the restless Little Peconic Bay. The moon was
highlighting the tips of the miniature bay waves with white
paint, and off in the distance a motorboat slid silently across
the water. I went back to the house.

Danny met me at the door.

"Long gone," he said. "Can they ID?"

"No," I said, repeating their story.

"What the hell," he said.

"That's what I'm wondering."

"I can run through here every day on patrol, but I can't
park in your driveway."

"I know. Do what you can."

The ambulance, also lit up like a roman candle, finally
wallowed down the driveway. We watched them pack up
Hodges and haul him out of there. I got a chance to squeeze
his shoulder and do a lousy job telling him how grateful I was.

"Just do me a favor," he said, as the paramedics hoisted
him into the ambulance. "When you find those guys? Truly
fuck them up."

Danny Izard sat in his car and called in the report, and I
went back in the house. Amanda was in the kitchen working
on Nathan's wound.

"He refused to go with Hodges," she said.

"I'm fine. No way I'm going anywhere anyhow."

"So nothing at all that could identify them," I said.

He shook his head, causing Amanda to pull back her hands.

"Two men. One tall, one short. Jeans and hoodies, with no logos, or any of that stuff. They both had big, square hammers."

"More like a mallet," I said.

"Yeah. Better to pound on people's heads."

"Did they say anything?"

"No. Not that I could have heard over Hodges's cursing and screaming."

"You'd think that would've scared them away," I said.

I left him with Amanda so she could finish fussing around with the wound and went upstairs. Allison was sitting up in bed, her eyes red and swollen and the bandage on her right cheek soaked with tears.

"Daddy?"

I sat on the bed and let her hug me. Her body shook as she took deep, hoarse breaths. I hugged her back and stroked her long hair where it fell down her back until she wanted to let go.

"Everything's going to be okay," I said.

"No it's not and you know it."

"Yes it is. It's one thing to beat up my daughter, but go after my bartenders, that's taking things too far."

"I don't think you're funny," she said.

"Yes you do. You're actually laughing on the inside."

"How's Nathan?"

"He's downstairs. Refused to leave you."

"I don't deserve him. I treat him like shit and he's being, like, Mr. Impossibly Wonderful."

"He's wonderful because you do, in fact, deserve him."

She looked over my shoulder and made a frightened little yelp. I turned my head toward the door, even though all the muscles in my neck had turned to steel rods. It was Danny Izard, filling the room with his dark blue uniform and the panoply of weapons and electronic devices hanging from his belt.

"How're we doing?" he asked, looking at Allison.

"Peachy, Danny," she said. "Are you coming to stay with me?"

"No, but Joe Sullivan is," he said, now looking at me.

"Really," I said.

"I'm hanging around till he gets here. I'm supposed to tell you he's taking another leave of absence to move in with Amanda and the gang. Say, Sam, that gun the kid fired. I'm sure it's registered, right?"

"If I told you it was, you'd believe me?"

He frowned. Not unlike Sullivan, Danny thought strictly adhering to every dopey law and regulation was something law enforcement officers were put on earth to do.

"I might," he said.

"Well, then there's your answer," I said.

"It's not an answer, but I'll take it for now."

When he left, Allison confessed that she'd had a bit of a thing for Danny ever since they were teenagers hanging out at the surfers' beach off Flying Point. I asked her what a tall, square-jawed, narrow-waisted, broad-shouldered, steely-eyed boy scout like Danny Izard could possibly have on a scrawny nebbish like Nathan Hepner.

"I have a secret lust for boy scouts, though that's not the kind of thing a daughter should discuss with her father."

"Agreed. I have a better subject."

She looked defensive.

"I'm working rehab like a good little girl. They'll tell you."

"It's not that," I said, then took a deep breath and said, "Honey, do you have any idea, whatsoever, of what you might have done to attract this kind of attention? Did you see anything, do anything, say anything to the wrong person, anything at all?"

Her face immediately turned overcast.

"I knew you were going to blame me."

"I knew you were going to say that. I'm not. Do you know how many innocent bystanders are killed every year just because some sick shit wants to eliminate witnesses?"

"No, do you? Do you study crime statistics?"

"Just answer me," I said, as gently as I could.

She looked down at her hands folded in her lap.

"No," she said, softly. "I think about it all the time. I have no idea."

"What about the copywriter, Brandon Weeks? People tell us you and him had a bad falling out."

She cracked a surprisingly broad smile.

"That dickless jerk? More likely I'd kick his ass from here to Cleveland."

"Tough break for Cleveland."

"Brandon is harmless," she said. "Unless you count the damage his lousy copy has done to the consumer psyche."

"Another reason not to watch TV."

"You probably don't remember teaching me how to fight," she said. "All the dirty tricks."

"Not dirty enough, apparently."

"Let's decide that when we see the other guy."

I gripped her knee through the sheet and gave it a little shake.

"We're working on that, Allison. This stuff can take longer than anyone wants it to."

"What about forever? How long does that sound? Joe Sullivan has to go back to his job. I've got to go back to my job. Nathan has to actually get one."

It was times like these that I understood why Abby called my daughter The Apple.

"My faith in you is limitless, my appreciation of your drive and relentless work ethic unsurpassed," I said.

"What are you trying to tell me?"

"You're not the type to give up."

"I'm persistent," she said, "if that's what you mean."

"You're pig-headed."

"Like you."

She let it go at that, and I stood up to leave, which I did after asking one more question.

"How do you know that guy doesn't have a dick?"

CHAPTER EIGHTEEN

J oe Sullivan arrived shortly after with a camo backpack and a grim expression on his face. Danny had briefed him, so we didn't have much more to talk about. He put his stuff in Hodges's bedroom after poking his head in to chat with Allison, then he joined me, Nathan, and Amanda out on the patio. He told us he would be on guard for all but eight hours from early afternoon through the night—two hours for beer, six for sleep. Nathan would take over during his time off, with backup from me. When I asked if that was enough relief, he told us it was better for him to be on all the way, all the time.

Eddie and I spent that night with Amanda in the first-floor bedroom suite, though only Eddie got much sleep, evidenced by the low, but persistent snoring coming from the foot of the bed.

So I was up early enough to make coffee for Nathan when he took over active duty, and sit with Sullivan while he downed a six-pack before lumbering up the stairs to bed. I would have hung with Nathan, but after the night before, the kid deserved to know he had my full confidence. So I went back to my cottage and spent the morning in distracted and inefficient woodcraft.

This was the pattern we settled into over the following few days. The first real interruption came when Jackie called my cell phone and told me she'd finally put together a memorial service for Alfie Aldergreen. It was to be held at the Polish Catholic church in Southampton.

"Aldergreen doesn't sound very Polish," I said.

"It isn't. But it's Father Dent's church and he's the only priest I know. You better show up."

"Wouldn't miss it."

So IT was the next day I was standing outside the front doors of the Polish church with Jackie, Amanda, Joe Sullivan (while Danny Izard spotted him at Amanda's house), Esther Ferguson, Jimmy Watruss, Jaybo Flynn, and Lionel Veckstrom, who had the good sense to come without his campaign flacks. Father Dent asked us to wait outside while he and some laypeople spruced up the altar. It was another lustrous Hamptons summer day, so no one complained.

It wasn't the ideal conversational configuration. Sullivan stood like a statue with his hands in the pockets of a lightweight jacket underneath which was enough firepower to storm a hostile nation. Veckstrom wore an off-white linen suit, which wasn't as well made as the one I was wearing, a long-ago gift from Abby whose sartorial sensibilities I'd pit against all but the most supercilious toff. Jackie was speaking sotto voce to Amanda, holding the tips of her fingers up to her mouth to catch errant syllables. Jimmy and Jaybo were likewise a separate sphere, though I could hear them talking about a fishmonger's impending arrival at the wholesale shed behind the restaurant.

Jimmy wore his staff sergeant dress uniform, with a beret and a chestful of ribbons. I didn't know what any of it meant, but there were too many colorful stripes to be routine commendations. As if to complete the effect, he'd shaved and cut his hair back to regulation length. Jaybo, not a military man, had cleaned up as well, presumably out of respect for Jimmy. It struck me he was actually a decent-looking kid.

By default I was stuck with Esther Ferguson, who must have felt odd surrounded by so many people she would have far preferred to avoid. To make it easier for her, I talked about some of the park bench conversations I'd had with Alfie, on subjects both earthbound and surreal. She had similar recollections, and we managed to find some common ground of loss and affection for the troubled vet. She even talked briefly about her brother, how she often wondered if she would have cared for him as much if he hadn't been mentally ill. It was a surprising admission, which I honored by assuring her she certainly would have.

To everyone's relief, Father Dent finally came out and herded us into the church. He assigned seating in the pews, breaking up the natural pairings, as if to assure a seamless atmosphere of social unease. This time I drew Lionel Veckstrom and Jackie got Esther.

Dent was not a young man, but he wore his years with a clear eye and ramrod posture. I wasn't much for organized religion, though Dent's charm was manifest, made more so for me by a borough accent you could cut with a knife.

Still as soon as he started running through the standard prayers and invocations, my mind did what it always did during church services. Drift off into the clouds. That's why I didn't realize Jimmy Watruss was up at the pulpit until he started to speak.

"I asked the Father if I could say a few words and he told me that's what these things are for, so here goes. I'm not going to tell you that when you serve with other soldiers during wartime, you get to know each other in ways you can never duplicate in any other part of life. You know that already, since you've seen the movies and read the books. What you don't know is that for over a year, Alfie and I spent almost all our time crammed into an armored tin can called a Bradley Fighting Vehicle, which is like a cross between a tank and a personnel carrier, if that makes any sense. Alfie was our driver. I handled the weapons, including the 25-millimeter cannon, TOW missile launcher, and M240G machine gun. Which means you get busy when things heat up, and you can't be worrying about how your driver's going to perform. I never worried about Alfie. Not in training, or out on the gunnery, or in combat. I trusted him to do his job without thinking twice about it, meaning I could concentrate on doing mine."

He paused and looked down at the pulpit, closing, then opening, his eyes again and raising his head.

"So whatever you might have thought about Alfie Alder-green, the nut job cripple with the saxophone, the Looney Tunes going on about elves and wizards, that wasn't the Specialist Alfred P. Aldergreen that I knew in situations I can't really describe here. I won't describe here, because I can never do justice to the bravery and sacrifice people like Alfie demonstrated every day in places so distant and different from a town like Southampton, they might as well be on the planet Mars."

He smiled.

"Maybe that's where Alfie thought he was. I hope so. It might've made it easier to take."

He almost looked like he wanted to say more, but after a brief hesitation, he thanked Jackie and Father Dent for putting on the memorial service, and promised everyone a night of free drinks back at Mad Martha's if we wanted to stop by.

"So they did see combat together," I said to Veckstrom in a soft whisper, since Father Dent was up at the pulpit again wrapping up the ceremonies.

"So what," he said.

"It's interesting."

Veckstrom looked over at me.

"Why interesting?"

"Just interesting," I said. "I'm interested in lots of things."

"Bullshit."

"I'm interested that all three snitches knew each other," I said, in a seeming non sequitur, though he knew what I meant.

"There are often subterranean relationships between people, invisible ties, sometimes quite strong," he said. "But you know that better than anyone, don't you, Acquillo?"

"I know a lot, but I don't know everything," I said. "If we pooled our knowledge, we'd figure this thing out a lot quicker."

He looked at me again, through partially hooded eyes.

"That would be a cold day in hell."

"Okay," I said with a shrug. "Don't say I didn't give you a fair shot."

"Whatever the hell that means."

"You'll know."

Father Dent was still chanting on about something, but I had to get up at that point and go back out for some fresh air. It wasn't all Veckstrom's fault. This usually happened to me whenever I got stuck in a church. I blame it on my mother, who hated pomp and circumstance even more than I, but dragged me to church every Sunday anyway out of some misplaced concern for my everlasting soul.

As TEMPTING as it was, Amanda, Sullivan, and I passed on Jimmy's offer of free drinks at his restaurant and headed back to Oak Point. Amanda drove with Sullivan so I could stop at Hawk Pond Marina on the way and check in on Paul Hodges, who'd been released from the hospital and was recuperating on his boat. Since my boat, the *Carpe Mañana*, was berthed in the next slip, I got to check in on her as well.

I'd bought the boat from my friend Burton Lewis after he decided it was more of a heavy displacement cruiser than he wanted, having succumbed to the questionable allure of club racing, a pursuit I would never understand. The last thing I wanted to do was compete in a sailboat. For me, the point of sailing was to ghost along under a moderate breeze while avoiding drunken idiots in big powerboats who thought spending about one hundred dollars a minute producing deafening noise and spine-crushing vibration was fun.

She seemed shipshape, so I went next door. Hodges was in the cockpit with his two lazy shih tzus lying all over him. He had a bandage around his head, not unlike Allison's, and a drink in his hand, which was encouraging. I'd brought along the reserve supply of Absolut from the *Carpe Mañana*. After digging into Hodges's ice chest and topping off one of his plastic mugs, I made myself at home in his cockpit.

"How's the head?" I asked.

"Better since the two double bourbons."

"Shouldn't mix with the painkillers."

"They *are* the painkillers."

"Sorry I got you into this," I said.

"I'm sorry I fucked it up. Not your fault."

"You didn't fuck it up. They got the drop on you."

"Nah. Wouldn't have happened ten years ago. I'm too old and too slow."

"Like I said, I'm sorry I got you into it. Sullivan's taken over the position. He's on a leave of absence."

"So now you want to hope those knuckleheads try again."

We sat for a few moments in silence, drinking, and relishing the images that notion conjured up.

"We had a memorial service for Alfie Aldergreen today," I said. "Jackie set it up with Father Dent."

"I thought the VA was handling that."

"Just the burial. Though we did get a surprise eulogy from Jimmy Watruss. Showed up in full-dress uniform."

"Good for him he can still wear it. My uniform pants wouldn't get past my knees."

"Turns out he and Alfie were in the same armored vehicle," I said. "I wonder why I never knew that."

"Cause you're a civilian and it's none of your damn business."

Hodges had been on a patrol boat on a river in Vietnam, the result of an enlistment in the coast guard that went terribly wrong.

"I guess you're right," I said. "Even Alfie kept a tight lip when it came to Iraq. He was more focused on the great sack of the Dwarven City of Khazad-dûm."

"Guys stuck in a war together are funny about that," said Hodges. "To this day, I'd give my life for any of my shipmates if it came to that. Provided there weren't any sledgehammers involved."

"Stop talking like that or I'll whack you on the head myself."

We drank in silence for a bit, then Hodges said, "Somebody bought Joey Wentworth's picnic boat. I guess it came with rights to the slip."

"Really. Nice boat."

"Haven't seen the new owner. Just hear those twin power plants firing up. Or feel the vibrations, more like it. That thing must go like snot."

"Joey's commercial interests required fast transit," I said, describing Joey's part in the burgeoning drug flow through the East End.

"Is that how he ended up splattered all over the inside of his pickup?"

"That's my guess, though nobody's saying."

"I'd prefer if the boats around here stuck to hauling fish," he said.

We honored his sentiment with a few more minutes of calm silence, then I said to him, "You know, Hodges, we pay a lot of money to keep up these big boats, we ought to sail them once in a while."

He nodded agreement.

"You got that right. Though the only rhumb line I can follow now is from here to the quarter berth."

"We can take the *Carpe Mañana*," I said. "If you man the helm, I can screw around with the sails."

He thought that was a fine idea and we set a date far enough out to assure his helmsman readiness.

"It'll give me a chance to show you how to sail that thing," he said.

The shih tzus noticed the arrival of a pair of Canada geese out in the channel and burst in a flurry of black and white fur out of the cockpit and over the cabin top to the bow, where they loudly expressed their disapproval until Hodges yelled at them to shut the hell up.

"You'd think they'd get tired of doing that," he said.

"Not as long as God keeps making water fowl."

CHAPTER NINETEEN

I called Jackie the next day and proposed a field trip. I even offered to drive. All she had to do was come along and criticize my car.

"Your allegiance to that antediluvian ark is not my fault," she said.

"At what point does an ark become postdiluvian?"

"Just pick me up. And bring coffee."

Our destination was the headquarters of the New York National Guard Forty-Third Infantry Brigade Combat Team.

One of the distinctions of a national guard force over the regular army in a hostile theater is all the soldiers come from the same state, often the same towns and cities. That's why the unofficial name for Jimmy and Alfie's unit was the Long Island Forty-Third. Likewise, the VA center in Nassau took care of local veterans, so it wasn't surprising that Jimmy had stumbled over Alfie in the psych ward.

I didn't exactly have a reason to go there, other than heightened curiosity about their service together in Iraq. I assumed Jimmy had already said whatever he was going to say, so this seemed the next best way to go. I didn't know if they'd talk to me, which was another reason to bring along

Jackie, who was almost as good as Eddie at getting people to open up.

It wasn't until we were under way that Jackie bothered to look up the address on her smartphone, so we were a little surprised to learn the place was nearly in Queens. I began to wish I'd brought Amanda's Audi, but at least I'd installed a decent modern radio in the Grand Prix and it had a nice riding quality if you didn't mind zero communication with the road surface. Also Jackie was never at a loss for words, so all I had to do was listen and offer trenchant commentary for her to dispute.

An hour out, Jackie had a brainstorm and called the headquarters and asked to speak to the public information officer. It turned out they had one, and after a brief delay, he came on. She told him the truth, that she was a defense attorney investigating the murder of a client who'd served in the Long Island Forty-Third in the Iraq War. She gave him Alfie's name, and we were both relieved to have the guy confirm that Alfie did indeed serve in Iraq, as an E4 specialist trained to operate an M3 Bradley Fighting Vehicle. She said she wanted to learn more about his service, and asked if she and her associate could drop by for a chat. He said sure as long as his commanding officer gave the okay. He said he'd get back to us.

"We could've called before we left," she said, after getting off the phone.

"Yeah, but where's the adventure in that."

While waiting we distracted ourselves talking about Allison's unsteady recovery, and Jackie repeated her firm recommendation that we use the plastic surgeons who worked on her after that concussion from the car bomb turned the left side of her face into a sunken soufflé.

"They work on the Upper East Side," she said. "You see their faces on the street up there every day, and you'd never know it. Which is the point."

I'd already been in touch with them and told her so. She promised me she'd stop by and talk to Allison at the next opportunity, show off her face, and generally run her through the reconstruction process. I told her I appreciated anything she could do. Then she changed the subject to Alfie, asking me if I had any theories I hadn't shared, something she often accused me of doing, probably because I often did.

"No," I said, honestly. "I think the three murders are connected, and that there's something very funky going on with the Southampton Town Police, which may or may not have anything to do with Alfie's murder, his message on your answering machine notwithstanding. I think the killers could be from anywhere, though the motive is local. And I have very little real evidence to support any of this."

She nodded.

"I agree," she said. "I also think you've made yourself a big fat target by agreeing to work with Ross and telling the whole East End that you're after Alfie's killer."

"*We've* made ourselves big fat targets."

"Point taken," she said.

"Just keep your Glock and that man mountain close at hand."

"Always do."

THE HEADQUARTERS for the Long Island Forty-Third wasn't an attractive building, which you'd expect. It had a low profile and was built with white-painted cinder block, though there were lots of flags and the grounds were neatly trimmed. Which you'd also expect.

We hadn't heard back from the PR guy, but that wasn't surprising or much of a deterrent to either of us. I found a big enough parking spot to handle the Grand Prix and we marched through the front doors.

The lobby was guarded by a huge glass case filled with trophies, medals, and other commemorations of the

Forty-Third's storied past. Somewhere behind the case was a receptionist, though it took some time to find him. Jackie leaned over the wide expanse of glass in a vain attempt at invading his space and said we had an appointment with the public information officer. The young soldier looked unsettled, but picked up the phone anyway. After a brief discussion, he told us to make ourselves comfortable in the waiting area, an impossible assignment given the remarkably uncomfortable furniture.

About fifteen minutes later, a blocky woman strode into the lobby and approached us with an awkward gait that was nevertheless brisk and forthright. We both stood up in time to shake her outreached hand.

"Captain Jane Aubrey," she said. "Brigade judge advocate."

As we introduced ourselves, Jackie told me she was a military lawyer, which I already knew, but acted freshly informed.

"I'm not sure if we can help with your inquiry, but I'll hear you out," she said, addressing Jackie and ignoring me.

Jackie went through the same explanation she'd given the PR guy, which Captain Aubrey listened to intently. Then she asked us to follow her and brought us to a small conference room just inside the inner door. It reminded me of the interrogation room back at Southampton Town Police HQ, without the one-way mirror, cigarette burns on the tabletop, or other pleasant amenities.

We all sat.

"Let me be clear about one thing," she said, without preamble. "Military records are maintained by the Federal Records Centers and are only accessible by the veteran personally, in this case not an option, or immediate family members."

"Since Specialist Aldergreen was an orphan, that's not an option either," said Jackie, in a soothingly quiet way. "Though we're not looking to get his records. We just want to find someone who can talk to us about his experience in Iraq. Someone willing to talk."

"No one here is authorized to provide that sort of information."

"Does anyone here care that one of your own was brutally murdered?" I asked.

"Is that a question or an accusation?" said Captain Aubrey, with no change of tone.

Jackie gave me a look I knew to be the equivalent of a swift kick under the table.

"This matter is being treated strictly as a civilian homicide," said Jackie. "I'm only here to fill in some background on the decedent. Just doing my job as an officer of the court, and an advocate for my client, who deserves a full and thorough investigation of his death. What you would be doing if you were in my shoes."

"I would never be in your shoes," she said. "Very bad for your feet."

"You're right," said Jackie. "I keep telling myself to be more age appropriate."

That's when I really knew I wasn't actually part of the conversation.

"Tell me what you want," said the captain.

"As I see it, there're a few ways we can go about this," said Jackie. "We can go through all the official channels, fill out applications, mount appeals, start pulling political strings, and make a general nuisance of ourselves, which we both know will mean you and I will be playing canasta in the old folks home before we learn anything of substance. Or we could go to the media with cries of bureaucratic intransigence, and implications of a cover-up. I've got the phone number of Roger Angstrom of the *New York Times* on speed dial."

She pulled out her smartphone, pushed a few buttons, and slid it across the table before continuing.

"Or we can track down the men who served with Specialist Aldergreen through the public records that do exist, though who knows what they'll say. Or my favorite option,

you can direct us toward those most likely to have a credible and responsible recollection of the young man's combat
experience, giving us a clear and accurate picture that we
can fold into our background profile, which might have some
bearing on this investigation, unlikely as that seems at the
moment."

Then she sat back in her chair to give the captain some
room to return the volley, which didn't take long.

"You're aware that Alfred Aldergreen was severely mentally ill," said Captain Aubrey.

"He thought Elrond of Rivendell should run for president,
if that's what you mean," I said.

"Alfie was a friend of ours," said Jackie, back in her temperate mode.

"Then you're also aware that he was being treated at the
VA center in Nassau County," said Captain Aubrey.

"We are," said Jackie.

"So you must also know that Colonel David Cardozo of
the New York National Guard, retired from the military and
his practice in psychiatry, is a regular volunteer at the VA
center. Such a fact could not have escaped the notice of a
diligent advocate such as yourself."

"Of course not," said Jackie.

"So there is no reason for this office to provide any information beyond what you already know."

"None that I can see," said Jackie.

Captain Aubrey put both hands flat on the table.

"Very well," she said. "Then this meeting has reached an
appropriate conclusion."

"I believe it has," said Jackie.

With that the captain escorted us back out to the lobby
and all the way to the walkway outside the building, where
she told us to have a nice day, and then disappeared back
inside. Jackie led the way to the Grand Prix, which we used
to execute a strategic retreat.

"That went well," I said.

"It would've gone better if you'd waited in the car."

As I drove, Jackie did some digging around on her smartphone before placing a call to the VA center. She told the person on the other end of the line that the New York National Guard asked her to get in touch with Retired Colonel Cardozo, a frequent volunteer at the center. The person was unable to confirm or deny the colonel's whereabouts, but would gladly pass along a message. So we ended up riding around Nassau County for a while hoping to hear back. Which we did, right before throwing in the towel and heading for home.

"Hello, Colonel Cardozo, or is it doctor?" said Jackie, then after a pause, "Okay, David."

Then she gave him the same story we gave the judge advocate. From her animated tone, the conversation was going well. It ended with an agreement to meet at a bar in Center Moriches, a shore town well on the way back to the Hamptons, which to me meant it couldn't have gone any better.

Once you took away the art galleries, mansions, and stock brokerages, Center Moriches, like most places on the East End, was basically a small town, with a main street, firehouses, schools, public library, and locals' favorite seafood restaurant, this one you got to by walking through the gaping jaws of a shark. Jackie said that, given her line of work, the entrance felt right at home. We found places at the bar, already well patronized, including by a tall, bony guy with a long, hooked nose. His eyebrows and temples were grey where the hair tufted out from under a Mets cap. It wasn't hard to figure him for Cardozo, especially after he caught sight of Jackie and stood up from the bar.

"The lawyer, I presume," he said, offering his hand.

"You presume well," she said. "This is my associate, Sam Acquillo."

"Thanks for meeting me here," he said. "It's close to home and if I don't stop by every night they call missing persons."

"It's the least we could do," I said, scanning the shelves behind the bar for regular, non-flavored Absolut.

We arranged the bar stools so all three could easily share in the conversation. As the drinks arrived, Cardozo told us he'd been a widower in good standing for more than ten years and never learned to cook, another reason to be a restaurant regular, a situation Jackie and I had little trouble relating to. As he spoke, I noticed a gentle accent, which I asked him about.

"I grew up in Lisbon," he said. "Portuguese father and English mother. And how did I end up here, you're going to ask next?"

"I was."

"Medical school and a US military in desperate need of psychiatrists, even ones with big noses and funny accents."

"Not that big," said Jackie, looking appraisingly.

"You should meet my friend Rosaline Arnold," I said. "Make you look like a pug."

We all shared some more personal information, which surprised me given we'd just met, until I realized the guy was a shrink trained to pull that kind of stuff out of people. Even though my track record with folks in that line of work was a bit checkered, I liked him. You got the feeling he was genuinely interested in you, so if it was just part of the act, he was pretty good at it.

Eventually we got down to talking about Alfie. He'd heard through the veteran grapevine that Alfie had been killed, and how, which brought him a great deal of pain and sorrow. He said if you knew Alfie, which we clearly did, you'd know a violent death would have been particularly horrifying for him, not that any are easy.

"That he expected something like that to happen to him is no consolation," he said.

"We just learned a little about his time in Iraq," said Jackie. "So he did see combat."

Cardozo gave a sad nod.

"Oh, yes," he said. "Of the most serious kind."

"So I guess his mental state was no big surprise," she said.

This time he shook his head.

"It's very important to understand that what Specialist Aldergreen suffered from was not post-traumatic stress disorder. There could have been some comorbidity there, and I think the stress of his environment might have triggered his first psychotic break, but Aldergreen was a person with paranoid schizophrenia. It's a condition inherent to a diseased mind, not something you acquire from your environment, no matter how ugly the experience."

For some reason, I always thought that was the case, though it was good to hear it from someone who knew something about that stuff. Not that it would help Alfie much now.

Jackie encouraged him to go into more detail about the clinical aspects of the psychopathology, which he took to eagerly. You're not the only one good at pulling information out of people, doc, I thought to myself.

She asked how much of it related to Alfie specifically, conceding that we might have traveled into confidential territory. He was unfazed.

"Who's going to complain?" he asked. "The man's dead with no next of kin."

Then he went on to call Alfie's a textbook case, presenting classic symptoms in his early twenties. He was born to a single mother, who committed suicide before Alfie turned two. Cardozo felt strongly that she suffered the same condition, since "there's a strong hereditary correlation with first-degree relatives."

He then reversed course a little by admitting that no symptoms for any mental illness were classic, since every person's
brain was a unique vessel. For example, he noted, Alfie was
generally a happy sort.

"Not all his hallucinations were threatening," he said. "I
think he had a rich inner life, complex and engaging, albeit
entirely delusional. Who wouldn't like a lot of imaginary
friends?"

I had to agree with him, realizing for the first time that
Alfie might have thought I was no different from some guy
with long robes and a staff sitting there with us. It prompted
me to ask a gnawing question.

"Before he died, Alfie told Jackie the cops were after
him," I said. "He'd complained about them before, but it
wasn't his regular thing. Is it possible to separate his real
experience from his hallucinations?"

Cardozo seemed amused by that.

"You know the old joke, 'Just because you're paranoid,
doesn't mean people aren't out to get you.' So no, you can't
separate those things. Though let me put it another way.
Aldergreen could have absolutely perceived a genuine threat
and responded to it in a completely appropriate way. Don't
forget he'd been in real battles with real enemies shooting
at him."

Cardozo slid his Mets cap back on his head, revealing a
full head of hair, mostly white, but thick and long. His fingers were long and slender, though his hands looked strong
enough to crack cue balls.

"You said it was bad over there," said Jackie, giving the
conversational course another gentle shove.

Cardozo took a big pull from his drink and then looked
down at the barroom floor. We waited.

"He was in one of the nastiest actions of the war," he
said. "You probably read about it, then forgot, because it's
impossible to really keep track of these things much less

absorb them from afar. It's impossible for me, and I hear it every day directly from the mouths of these young, devastated men and women."

He paused again, organizing the memory.

"Aldergreen and Watruss were in their Bradley Fighting Vehicle. They were about an hour from base when they got ambushed by a well-armed bunch of insurgents who obviously had some intel on the platoon's activities. It gets really messy, and half the platoon is hit with RPGs—rocket propelled grenades. Including our boys Aldergreen and Watruss. But it's worse than that. They also have the company commander on board their vehicle, Captain Herschel Bergeron. The three of them had been together since training days and it's a tribute to Watruss and Aldergreen that they were trusted by the highest ranking officer in their unit."

"This is where Jimmy Watruss gets shot up," I said.

"It is. Aldergreen is knocked out by the initial concussive force of the grenade, but is otherwise intact. Watruss, on the other hand, is pretty mangled. Bergeron isn't in great shape himself, but he's the one who drags the other two clear of the burning Bradley, which subsequently gets blown entirely to shit by another RPG."

"Presumably with no one else on board," I said.

"Yeah, thank God. It could have been filled with troops. According to the official report, Bergeron continued to lead the platoon, mounting a counterattack, pulling wounded to safety, even manning a machine gun in a disabled vehicle, laying down covering fire that allowed another of his team to get in position and basically mow down the bulk of the insurgents. It was a bad day for the Forty-Third, but most of the people who ambushed them never made it back home. So who knows."

"That captain is quite a hero," said Jackie.

Cardozo again looked amused, though I began to realize there was more than an element of irony in his every smile.

"Was. You can only get shot so many times before all the blood drains out. I hear rumors of a posthumous Medal of Honor, though they've been stingy with those things."

Cardozo's voice was so precisely moderated that I was as much hypnotized by the style as the content of his story. He partially broke the trance with an uptick in volume.

"What else does a guy have to do to win one of those goddamned things?" he asked the whole barroom, rhetorically of course.

"So that ended Alfie's and Jimmy's combat careers?" Jackie asked, pulling him back.

"Careers? Yes. Jimmy was evacuated to the Green Zone, then after a stop in Germany, shipped back to the Nassau County VA Center in the good old US of A. My favorite garden spot."

Those last words were slightly slurred, and I realized that the retired colonel had downed about a half-dozen bourbons on the rocks, delivered with military precision by the young lady bartender who hovered nearby seemingly for that purpose alone.

"What about Alfie?" Jackie asked.

"He came later. After we released Sergeant Watruss, whom I didn't know very well at the time. Never seemed to have need of my services. Sturdy young man. Centered. Later we became colleagues when he joined the VA center's volunteer corps. He's made quite a contribution, I have to tell you, especially with our substance abusers, who are plentiful."

He dropped his head again, though not quite in the way he'd done before. More as a person starting to pass out than collecting his thoughts. Jackie reached over and held his cheek, which caused him to open his eyes and perk up a bit.

"Jesus, I'm not the drinker I used to be."

We spent the next half hour gently discouraging Cardozo from having another few rounds, aided by the bartender, who told us one of the guys back in the kitchen was already assigned to drive him home, this being a more or less nightly occurrence. We didn't press Cardozo for any more information, out of kindness and concern for his waning acuity.

When the time came, we followed the kitchen guy who drove Cardozo to his house and helped the diminutive Latino haul the big old Anglo-Portuguese into his house and onto his sofa, where we all thought our obligation ended.

I was the last one out and about to shut the door when Cardozo said, "They didn't just trust Captain Bergeron with their lives, they would have trusted their children's lives, and their children's children. They loved their captain in a way unimagined by mortals who've never known the intimacy of war."

I walked back in the house, but that was the last thing he got out before falling into a deep and, I hoped, as untormented a sleep as possible.

CHAPTER TWENTY

I have this little screen on the outside of my cell phone that displays the phone number of the person trying to call me. I don't know if you have one of these, too, but it's an extremely handy feature. That morning in my shop, the number that came up was nothing I'd seen before, so I did my usual thing and ignored it.

Then it showed up again. After the third time, I swore and flipped open the phone.

"What."

"I need to talk to you," said a deep male voice, accented.

"Who's talking?"

"No names. But the last time we met, you wrecked my nice silk suit."

Mustafa Karadeniz.

"What are we going to talk about?" I asked him.

"Not on the phone. Man, you know nothing about electronic monitoring? What country you living in anyway?"

"The Oak Point part of the country. The only monitoring we do is through a screen window."

"Go to the location of our last happy encounter and you'll find out where to go from there. Come alone and leave your hot head at home."

"Sorry. My head goes where I go," I said. "Can you at least give me a headline?"

"You asked me some questions. Maybe I got some answers."

"When."

"Two hours," he said.

"Time enough to get into my nice suit."

I ACTUALLY wore a pair of new blue jeans, T-shirt, and Yankees cap, accessorized with a piece of oak sawed off a broken market umbrella. I wrapped one end in duct tape for grip and cut it short enough to fit comfortably into the back waistband of the blue jeans.

I checked up on my grumpy daughter, her angst-ridden boyfriend, and stoic bodyguard. Allison said they were all great, just great. Amanda, still out working on her houses, wasn't there to comment, so I took her at her word.

Eddie was in the yard happily chewing on something I couldn't see, so his opinion went unrecorded.

I decided not to tell Jackie about the upcoming meeting with Mustafa, feeling she'd only complicate things with excessive fretting, and as much as I liked her and her Glock along for the ride, I wanted the extra elbow room.

I took Amanda's Audi, believing with some justification that the Grand Prix lacked discretion, which seemed called for in this situation. I'd never failed to ask her permission before, so I was a little worried she'd report it stolen, bringing on more ruckus than either of us wanted. But you take your chances in life.

I thought maybe giving her free use of the Grand Prix might make it up to her. Wouldn't actually require a captain's license, as she once intimated.

I spent the time driving up to Riverhead listening to jazz, drinking coffee, and pretending I didn't want a cigarette. To compensate, I gnawed on a fat carpenter's pencil until I realized it might have the greater carcinogen content. I tossed it out the window.

A few blocks from Mustafa's warehouse, I got out of the car and walked the rest of the way. It was early afternoon, and the sun was warmer than it had been in recent weeks. The Yankees cap kept my face in the shade but did nothing to block the solar blast off the cracked, exhausted sidewalk.

As before, the warehouse parking lot was empty. The old stone building was shut tight and there was no sign of life anywhere. I walked up to the sliding door, on which was pinned a note written with a Sharpie on a small piece of paper.

It said, "Duck."

A ragged hole suddenly opened up in the door and I felt a spray of splinters wash over my face. I dropped to the pavement, reaching as I fell for the oak club stuffed in my pants. I lay there immobile for a second, then went to push myself back up, when I saw another note taped to the ground.

"Run."

I stood back up and looked around. Hopelessly exposed. The best bet was an alley around the closest corner of the stone warehouse, twenty feet away.

Another bullet hit the warehouse wall. This time stone dust pelted my face and upper body. I bolted for the alley as fast as my fifty-nine-year-old legs would run, but before I got to the corner, another bullet hit the wall in front of me. I turned and ran in the other direction, knowing it was fruitless, but unwilling to just stand there and get shot.

This time the bullet hit behind me, and I made it to the corner of the building, but not much farther, since it was a blind alley walled off with brick. On the brick was another sign.

"Call me."

I pulled out my cell phone and hit his number. He answered by saying, "How do you feel about oysters?"

"I don't like them that much," I said, as I tried to catch my breath. "Prefer clams. On the half shell. With bacon."

"I don't know why you're running away. I'm only trying to ask you to lunch."

"The gunfire. It's a distraction."

"Oh, of course. Wait there."

I peered around the corner and saw Mustafa striding over the pavement wearing another precisely tailored suit, this time set off with a large, complicated-looking pistol equipped with a muzzle suppressor and a laser sight mounted above the barrel. He stopped midway and spoke into his phone.

"If I wanted to kill you, you'd already be dead," he said.

"So what else do you have in mind?"

"Only talk."

"I can do that," I said.

"I just want you to know I'm serious and not to fuck with me."

"I will not fuck with you. Trust me on that."

"I don't trust anyone who doesn't like oysters," he said, continuing across the parking lot with the pistol pointed at the ground. When he was within ten feet, he stopped, dropped the ammunition clip out of the handgrip, carefully set it down on the pavement, and stepped away.

I stuffed the club back in my pants and walked over to the gun. I picked it up, and having no idea how to check for a round in the chamber, aimed it at the ground and pulled the trigger. Nothing.

"You scared the shit out of me," I said.

"Good. You embarrassed me. Now we're even."

"I hope so."

"Can I have my gun back?" he asked.

"I'll trade you for the clip."

He tossed it to me.

"Of course I could have another one in my pocket," he said.

I walked over and handed him the gun.

"Just don't shoot me till after lunch."

WE WENT to The Benevolent Oyster Bar a few blocks from his warehouse. The place had opened sometime in the early fifties and they wisely allowed wear and tear to establish the ambience over the decades. Even the wooden stools at the raw bar had the worn-down feel of an old pair of leather shoes.

We waited until the seafood in various states of preparation was arrayed on the bar before getting into the heart of our discussion.

"I know what Joey meant when he said beware of Greeks," said Mustafa.

"I think I do, too, but let me hear your theory."

"Not a theory. He was talking about Bennie Gardella. They call him the Greek, because that's actually what he is. A Greek with an Italian name."

"So who was he to Joey?"

"You probably know that, too. Back in the early nineties, the Greek brought down more guys involved with a certain illicit trade than any other cop in the city. He's a fucking legend."

"This is what I hear, too," I said. "Not much good as an undercover now that he's uncovered. They tell me he's in Southampton straightening out the PD's paperwork."

"That's right. And I'm 100 percent focused on importing coffee tables and oriental rugs."

A small pack of summer people came into the Benevolent looking wary but expectant. They chose to sit next to us at the raw bar, so after paying our tab, we gathered up our meals and went to a distant table in the outdoor seating area. The day was getting hot, but it was bearable under the umbrella.

An optimistic seagull stood on the top of a phony pier several feet away, but otherwise the conversation stayed private.

"Okay," I said, "so an experienced narco cop shows up in town to help the local police with a recent increase in drug trafficking, and a person involved in that traffic tips off one of his colleagues, what's the big surprise?"

Mustafa winced a little at such an unlacquered characterization, but didn't quibble.

"A big increase for who?" he asked. "Sure things were getting active for a while, but ever since Joey departed from this world, it's very different."

"Different how?"

"Different as in not so good anymore."

I waited for him to elaborate, but he looked like a man who really wanted to talk about something he was afraid to talk about. I tried to help him along.

"Look, Mustafa," I said, "you're talking to me because I'm not the cops, but I know the cops. My only interest is finding out who killed my friend Alfie Aldergreen. I think there's a connection with your guy Joey Wentworth, but I don't really know. If you can help me, and that helps you, so what."

He took that in, then said, "I told you there were a million Joey Wentworths ready to take his place, but apparently not so. In fact I hear his whole deal has moved over to people who are cutting links out of the chain, and anyone who tries to push back on that is sure to follow Joey to wherever that shotgun sent him to."

Now I knew why Mustafa was feeding me clams on a half shell and Absolut.

"You're one of the links," I said. "They're cutting you out."

"Trying," he said. "I'm not one to go so easy. But I'm getting signals from upstream that sticking with the rugs and coffee tables might be better for my long-term health."

"Do you know who these new people are?" I asked.

He shook his head.

"No, but I think Joey did," he said. "And lately I've been getting the feeling that he wasn't afraid of the Greek as law enforcement."

"Then what?"
"Competition."

I WAITED until the next day to tell Jackie about my visit with Mustafa. I withheld the substance of the meeting as an inducement for her to ride into the city with me. When she was finished with the verbal equivalent of gnashing teeth, I proposed that she drive, since the Grand Prix had a wider beam than many of Manhattan's cross streets. She took that about as well as expected, though she did show up at my cottage an hour later, giving me time to make the rounds over at Amanda's, feed Eddie, and rustle up a full thermos of French Vanilla.

I kept her distracted with my Mustafa story, overemphasizing the incoming bullets with words like "hail storm" and "barrage," hoping that would mitigate my leaving her out of the mission. It didn't.

"You could have gone in first," she said. "I hold back, take a secure position, then take him out at the first shot."

"Destroying any chance of obtaining crucial intel, Annie Oakley," I said. "And tying you up in police actions and legal proceedings, including suspension from the bar, thus making you worthless to me and all your worthy, albeit probably guilty, indigent clients."

When she quieted down, I distracted her by talking about my attitude toward cops, which was complicated. I mostly stayed out of trouble as a kid, so it wasn't until my father was beaten to death in the back of that bar that I even talked to a cop, much less formed an opinion on their net contribution to society.

I decided early on it was mixed. As with any subculture, there's an even distribution among police of honest, decent, well-meaning people, neutral schlubs, and venal sociopaths. Though I'd say with cops you get more extremes at the extreme, both heroic and reprehensible. It's the environment they live in—the constant exposure to people at their worst, the stiffened postures at their approach, the daily pressure to stay within thin legal lines their opponents feel no reason to honor.

When I spent time with my father at his apartment in the Bronx, many of the sidewalk cops lived in the neighborhood. They hung out at the same bars, stuffed heart-choking food into their mouths at the same breakfast joints, played in the same softball league. It was one reason kids like me stayed out of trouble. The uniformed guy grabbing you by the scruff of the neck likely got drunk with your old man on Saturday night, or sat next to him at Mass on Sunday morning. You were wary of the cops, but every kid I knew was far more terrified of his father.

In my case, that was a realistic fear.

But when he was killed, I didn't get much help from all those backslapping buddies on the force. What I got was mostly tight-lipped silence and the subtle implication that I was better off letting it go and moving on with my life.

I never learned if that was to protect me, or them, or people I didn't know. I was too young, too weary from the pressure of working my way through MIT in the boxing ring, too burdened with a mother who'd given up all hope in life, a sister who wanted nothing but to get the hell out of town, and a girlfriend from a loftier social caste whose principal goal in life was to redefine the boundaries of sexual endurance.

It wasn't until I exchanged my marriage, suburban house, and corporate career for full-time drunkenness that I was reacquainted with rank-and-file law enforcement. Luckily much of what I did went unreported, and thus unpunished, though I'm not sure how. Maybe that's why there's such a thing as luck.

And after that, I'd more or less lived around people like Ross Semple, Joe Sullivan, Danny Izard, Janet Orlovsky, and Lionel Veckstrom, and the rest of the Southampton Town Police Department, who more or less proved my theory of the universal ratio of regular humans to significant assholes within any subset of the population.

Though like Mustafa, I felt like things had changed. There was a warp in the continuum. A distortion in the fabric of the cop universe I'd never felt before. I said as much to Jackie, who agreed.

"When I was a kid, I wrote a short story called 'The Day Everything Was Different,'" she said. "You walked on the ceiling, your parents told you to eat candy for dinner, the cat barked, the dog meowed, and the fish in the aquarium played Bach concertos."

"Not Haydn?"

"That's how it feels to me. Everything is different. But I don't know why."

"How did the story turn out?" I asked.

"I don't remember. Maybe I should go back and look."

"Let me know, because I don't know why either."

On the way I put in a call to Detective Fenton, who actually sounded happy to hear from me, even though he had nothing to report on Allison's assault case. I told him I was bringing Jackie along and wondered if he could take some time out to talk to us. I offered beer and burgers as recompense, and he was quick to agree. Which probably explained why he was happy to hear from me.

It would be a lot cheaper than fresh oysters from the Benevolent, so I still felt ahead of the game.

Jackie was lucky enough to squeeze into a parking space on the street in SoHo a few blocks from Fenton's chosen destination. He said they had the best burgers in the city, and we had to believe him, since it probably took him a half hour to get down there from his precinct in Midtown.

We met him out on the sidewalk and he had his usual look of a man who'd just rolled out of bed after sleeping a few days in his clothes. His happiness, already foretold, was enhanced considerably when he laid eyes on Jackie. She gave him her custom cop handshake—a straight-arm and finger-snapping grip, which only served to increase the allure. I'd been through this a lot, so I knew to maneuver him into a seat on the opposite side of the table before we sat down.

They played the usual game of Who-Do-You-Know, which was important for Jackie to establish her bona fides as a native in the legal establishment. He seemed satisfied, and she seemed genuinely charmed by his attitudes and perspective. We were off to a good start.

For about a half hour, Fenton went through Allison's case, mostly for Jackie's benefit. So I was barely listening, and nearly missed it when he said they'd found someone else's DNA in the blood samples lifted off the walls of her apartment.

"You did?" I asked.

"Yeah. I don't know how they missed it the first time, or why they went back for a second look," he said. "I think you got to that CSI. Probably the daughter thing. She's working it."

"Any matches?"

"No. Though what's interesting are the two Xs."

"Female chromosomes," said Jackie. "It's a woman's blood."

Fenton grabbed a waitress who was passing by, alert to the diminishing state of his beer glass. We focused on another round before he told us more.

"It makes me a lot more interested in the fifty-foot-tall woman," he said.

"He means Althea Weeks," I told her. "Allison's former employer, and regular provider of freelance work. She's tall."

"Fucking enormous," said Fenton. "She could take me down. Probably not Sam, but you don't know."

"What's the motive?" I asked.

Fenton made a "who knows" gesture.

"No motive. I'm just talking here."

With that conversational path at an end, we reverted to regular small talk, which Jackie diverted into the area we'd come there to explore.

"Bill," she said, as if they'd known each other forever, "you knew Ross Semple and Bennie Gardella pretty well back in the day, right?"

Fenton caught the switch in tone, but looked ready for it.

"I did. I transferred out of the Bronx before all the legendary stuff happened, but we more or less came up together."

That was news to me, but I acted like I knew it already.

"Is it all true?" she asked. "You know, the legendary stuff."

He nodded, reminiscence lighting up his face.

"Oh, yeah. The legends don't do it justice. Those guys were totally gonzo. It's hard to imagine today. But things were different back then. Everybody thought the whole big fucking city was going down the tubes. Extraordinary times, extraordinary measures, if you know what I mean."

"I think I do," said Jackie.

You could see that Fenton wanted to say more, but was constrained by tethers of the past.

"So they stepped over the line," I said. "Occasionally."

His ambivalence seemed to deepen, but he said, "Depends on what line you're talking about."

"Legal versus illegal," said Jackie.

That got a rise out of him.

"If you mean, did they stretch the definition of proper investigative procedure, yeah. Or engage in a certain amount of operational flexibility, not entirely authorized, yes again. Did they violate the Constitution, or profit personally from any of the activities they engaged in? Absolutely not. I wasn't there, but this I don't believe to be true."

I got the feeling these words had been recited before, in a very different venue.

"Honest cops," I said.

"Honest cops," he repeated. "Too honest for their own good."

"Sorry, Bill," said Jackie, "but how can you be so sure?"

He looked at her as if realizing for the first time she was a defense attorney.

"Their captain in those days is my cousin," he said. "We grew up in the same house. There's nothing he knows that I don't know. Which I'll deny under oath till the end of time. And if you're wearing a wire, may God preserve you."

His face, usually on the reddish side, had turned near purple. Jackie reached across the table and gently placed her hand on his forearm. The one holding the beer glass, and thus unlikely to pull away.

"Nothing like that, Bill," she said. "We don't know Gardella, but the only thing twisted about Ross Semple is his sense of humor."

Fenton studied our faces, each in turn, a fresh flood of questions crossing his.

"What the hell is this all about?" he asked.

It was time to let it all the way out.

"There have been accusations. Some vague, some explicit, that something's rotten in the Southampton Town Police. Corruption tied to a surge in the drug traffic flowing through the East End. We think it's tied to the murders of our three confidential informants. We don't know how, but there's too much of a buzz around the idea to ignore it."

Fenton's mood swung from indignant to confused. I couldn't blame him.

"Not Ross," he said. "No way, no how."

"That's what we think," said Jackie. "But circumstantial evidence is starting to pile up."

"Jesus Christ," he said, picking up his beer, then putting it down again without taking a sip. "You're supposed to move out to the Hamptons to get away from this shit."

There was no point in bursting that bubble by telling him that shit follows you no matter where you go. No one wants to hear that human nature transcends location, that, in fact, venality flourishes in a place where the haves have so much more than the have-nots that you begin to wonder if we come from the same species.

"Your cousin, the one who supervised Ross and Gardella, is he still on the job?" Jackie asked.

"Sure," said Fenton. "They made him deputy inspector. Runs a precinct on the Upper East Side. I still call him Officer Gilliam so he doesn't forget where he came from."

"Can we talk to him?" she asked.

"Sure. How about right now?"

Like any good detective, Fenton knew how to read people, and he obviously read Jackie pretty well.

WE LEFT the Volvo in SoHo after Fenton told the traffic cops to let the meter run out and took a cab Uptown. Jackie grabbed the front seat to avoid getting squeezed between us, which unsettled the cabbie, but he acquiesced. Thus configured, it was hard to talk, so after Fenton called ahead to his cousin, everybody rode along with his and her private thoughts. Mine were back on Oak Point in Southampton, where like Ross Semple, I'd once fooled myself into thinking I'd find some sort of refuge from the ugly turmoil I'd made of my life. I didn't try to draw any conclusions, since they were self-evident.

The precinct station was off Second Avenue and made obvious by the blue and white patrol cars crammed along both sides of the street. Fenton paid for the cab and led us into the building. He chatted up the desk sergeant who then put in the call upstairs to his boss. We didn't wait long.

Fenton's cousin was named Joshua Fenton Gilliam. Though there wasn't much of a family resemblance. Gilliam had a slight, fit frame and a face like a tropical bird, accentuated by a pair of silver wire-rimmed glasses. He looked more like a newspaper editor than a precinct commander, though after Ross Semple, I'd long ago shed cop stereotypes.

They hugged in an unabashed way as Bill asked Gilliam if he'd lately busted any french poodles or heiresses for having nonregulation manicures. Gilliam took it like he probably always did, with easy humor. We got introduced and Gilliam took us upstairs to his office.

If Semple's office was a toxic waste dump, Gilliam's was a Buddhist shrine. It was a nice departure for me, though I guessed Jackie would feel out of place. We sat at a round steel and glass conference table and Gilliam had his adjutant bring in coffees.

"How is Ross these days?" Gilliam asked us. "Still quoting Cicero?"

Jackie did a good job of describing the chief, how he ran his department and what everybody thought of him. Gilliam said that's how he remembered him, though they hadn't been in touch for many years. He asked about Mrs. Semple and I admitted I'd never seen the woman, much less spoken to her.

"Too bad," said Gilliam. "Talk about idiosyncratic."

Detective Fenton, likely mindful of his cousin's time pressure, got to the point of our visit. As he set up the situation, Jackie filled in the details, adding some of our experience with prior cases, tactfully leaving out the time I'd been charged with murder. Gilliam listened with a focused intensity that reminded me of Father Dent. When we got to Ross asking Jackie and me to help out, ex-officio, with the investigation into Alfie Aldergreen's death, he made us repeat the story, pressing us for nuances and opinions of Ross's behavior.

"Odd," he said, when we finished the briefing.

"That's what we thought."

"More than odd," he said. "Entirely nonstandard, even for Ross."

Given his reaction, I went ahead and told him we had a similar deal with Edith Madison, the Suffolk County DA. At that, he jerked his head back and his eyes went wide, as if startled by a sudden loud noise.

"You're sure about that," he said. "She actually asked you to inform on the police?"

"There was no ambiguity in the request," said Jackie.

"Mother of God," said Gilliam, which seemed fairly nonstandard for him.

"That's what I'm thinking," said the other Fenton.

"We felt similar things," said Jackie, "though you seem particularly stunned. Are we missing something?"

The cousins looked at each other, exchanging unspoken thoughts. As the silence grew, Jackie scowled, like me, feeling our candor deserved freer reciprocity.

"Come on," she said. "Give it up."

Gilliam looked at her, more like a bird of prey than a parakeet.

"You probably wouldn't know this," he said. "But Edith Madison is one of my best friends. She took me to the Metropolitan. I went to Yankees games with her husband. Their apartment is about two blocks from here."

"What are you sayin', Josh?" said Fenton, doing Jackie and me a big favor.

Gilliam tried to get more comfortable in his chair, a tactic I'd seen before used by people stalling for time. Jackie started to breathe in a way you could hear. I knew what was coming.

"You better just share with us now, sir," she said. "It won't get any easier."

Gilliam moved his head from side to side, another familiar tic of people under pressure.

"It would be preferable if that particular can of worms stayed closed," he said. "I'm talking about Edith's husband's death. Given her political situation, the last thing she needs is that sad story dredged up and plastered all over the reprehensible press."

Everyone thinks large-scale engineering is only about dynamic systems adhering to inviolate natural laws. And it is, mostly. Though sometimes something goes wrong, even though all the instruments, tolerances, and specifications say it shouldn't. Back when I had my corporate job, figuring that stuff out was my specialty. Since everyone I worked with had a near religious faith in the infallibility of quantitative analysis, I didn't admit my approach had much more to do with gut instinct and decidedly nonanalytical reasoning.

Einstein said that imagination was more important than knowledge, but he was Einstein and could get away with saying things like that.

He also knew that even intuitive leaps had their own logic, a certain symmetry that you felt even before you could describe how all the component parts fit together.

I knew the feeling, which often resembled an attack of vertigo.

"He jumped," I said, the words escaping before I had a chance to stop them.

And Edith's great, good friend Gilliam just stared at me.

CHAPTER TWENTY-ONE

The only one in the room who didn't immediately grasp the full implication was Detective Fenton, who scanned all our faces and said, "What? What?"

His cousin chose his words carefully.

"Our investigators determined that Mr. Madison's death was an accident, based on the testimony of Mrs. Madison, who stated that the family's cat had a habit of walking out on the ledge, and that her husband frequently retrieved the cat. On this occasion, he overreached and fell to his death."

Jackie shook her head as if to dislodge the rush of thoughts crowding her mind.

"Of course," she said. "If that was Edith's statement, then your conclusions were well founded. Obviously there's no evidence that would contradict her testimony," she added, looking at me.

"Not as far as I know," I said. "I'm just thinking hypothetically."

Gilliam looked equal parts annoyed and relieved.

"So what if he did jump?" said Fenton, catching up with the conversation. "If she can survive getting grief counseling, she can survive a little change in the cause of death."

"You're not thinking this through," said Jackie.

"I'm not?"

"While some may feel Edith should have revealed seeing a psychiatrist, the reason was understandable, and even laudable, and easily excused under the category of personal privacy. The difference that Sam is suggesting is that Edith made a sworn statement that her husband's fall was an accident. If he committed suicide, she's filed a false police report that was material in a police investigation, which is a crime. At least a misdemeanor, possibly a felony. It would at the very least end her candidacy."

"Isn't it wonderful to have an attorney present to advise us on matters of the law," said Gilliam.

"I missed it, Josh," said Fenton. "Don't go bustin' on the lady."

Gilliam looked unhappy with the reprimand, but let it go.

"To get back to our reason for being here," said Jackie, "I don't think Edith would be pleased that we revealed her request for our help. We'd appreciate that staying between us."

"Of course," said Gilliam, though I wasn't sure what he actually meant. "And meanwhile, if you do uncover malfeasance within the Southampton Town Police force, with evidence that would stand up in court, I can aid in alerting the proper people."

"We appreciate that," said Jackie.

"I don't care where it goes, how far up the food chain," he said. "Personal relationships have to be incidental when upholding the law."

The words had the gloss of a sound bite for the press, but I felt like he meant it. And he wasn't only talking about Ross and Bennie Gardella.

"We understand," said Jackie, again using the first person plural to signal me this would be our shared position. Which she did a lot, not always successfully.

We sat through some more family talk between the cousins, with Fenton thanking Gilliam for letting us barge in on him. Gilliam assured him he was glad we did.

"Good discussion," he said. "Help us be prepared if the shit hits the fan."

You mean "when," I thought, but kept my mouth shut to maintain solidarity with Jackie Swaitkowski.

"IF YOU'RE right about Edith's husband, she's sunk and Veckstrom's got the job," she said, when we were back in the Volvo and heading east.

"I had a professor at MIT who said, 'If you think it's true, it probably is.'"

"What did he teach?"

"Zen Buddhism."

"You do have a reason why you think her husband jumped," she said.

"I do, but it's part of a bigger idea that isn't fully formed."

"I knew it. You have a theory you're not sharing with me."

"Not a theory, just a guess. Of very recent vintage. Give me a chance to think about it."

Luckily the day had worn her out and she didn't have the energy to press me. Instead she let me divert her with an assessment of the year's baseball season, a subject about which she had neither knowledge nor interest, so it was safe territory for both of us.

I CONVINCED Jackie to stick around when we reached Oak Point. Allison, Amanda, Nathan, and Joe Sullivan were out on Amanda's patio enjoying the north-northeast breeze that often delivered perfect summer evenings to the Little Peconic Bay.

Allison was in her wheelchair looking pale and shrunken, but as we walked up to the patio I saw her smile at something Nathan was saying. I was pleased to see Amanda's outdoor dry bar had been rolled out onto the paving stones, and even more delighted to see the Penguin ice bucket covered in condensation. Eddie barely stirred from his spot next to Amanda, who he could safely assume would slip him treats off the cheese and cracker tray. At least he wagged his tail at me, acknowledging that the serious food was only delivered next door.

The sun was where it was supposed to be over Robbins Island, getting ready to turn red and ignite a row of clouds on the horizon put there to make a flashy production out of the sunset.

The surface of the Little Peconic Bay was rippling, but the breeze had yet to push up respectable waves. Out of habit, I located a sailboat and tried to judge sea conditions by the angle of heel and the amount of sail the captain was putting into the wind. With a twinge, I decided conditions were likely perfect. Dry air, decent wind, moderate wave action, magic-hour light. I asked myself why I wasn't out there, and the answer was the same as always. Too much happening on shore. This time that was indisputable, which made the other times seem foolish. I made a mental note. If I get out of this situation intact, I'm getting out on the water.

Jackie poured her requisite tall white wine. Then she brushed her big ball of strawberry blonde hair away from her face before pulling a chair up next to Allison, a not-so-subtle display of the wonders of reconstructive surgery.

"It went okay," I said. "Do you know a deputy inspector named Josh Gilliam?" I asked Sullivan. "Runs a precinct on the Upper East Side. He's Bill Fenton's cousin."

Sullivan said he'd heard of Gilliam from his time with Ross and Gardella, but never met him.

"Edith Madison's apartment is in his jurisdiction," said Jackie. "His detectives handled her husband's death. Determined it accidental."

"Was it?" Sullivan asked.

"No reason to think otherwise," she said. "Unless you're Sam, who also has no reason to think otherwise."

"Contrarian suits him," said Amanda.

"How 'bout that sunset?" I asked.

We lapsed into a frequently repeated appreciation for the rosy sparkle of late afternoon on the Little Peconic Bay. It gave me a chance to down half my tumbler, which did the job of settling the agitation that crackled like background static through my nervous system. A pack of cigarettes would have helped that, too, I thought, for the millionth time.

"Speaking of Edith Madison," said Amanda, spoiling my diversion strategy, "she's down in the polls. Not so much because of Veckstrom. Some people are questioning whether she really wants to win."

"I'm one of those people," said Jackie. "You can't blame her. After all the years in the job, her reward is listening to Veckstrom and his party dump all over her performance."

"And having her personal life dragged through the media," said Amanda.

"If she quits now, she hands the job to Veckstrom," said Jackie. "It's too late for another contender."

"That'd be a big disappointment to Oksana Quan," I said.

"The Snow Queen," said Allison. "That's what we called her at RISD."

"So you knew her," said Amanda.

"A little. I don't think anyone actually knew her, like, as friends. She just walked around campus looking gorgeous and then disappeared on breaks and weekends. The word was a guy at Brown. That happened. Not everybody liked the freaky, deaky social life at RISD."

"She said they were all jealous of your talent," said Amanda.

Allison looked surprised.

"They did? News to me."

"I bet the guy was prelaw," I said.

"Might explain it," said Jackie.

Allison disagreed.

"There were a lot of brainy kids at RISD who ended up there through some romantic notion about the life of the artist," she said, "or because they got accepted and didn't know what else to do. You could take courses at Brown, and we'd see some of them drift away. By senior year, the hard core was still there spending all night in the studio and experimenting with their hair. I should have bought a tattoo franchise."

"So Oksana bailed," I said.

"I guess. She wasn't at graduation. I assumed she finished over at Brown, though who knows. We didn't exactly care what happened to the HPSS types."

"HPSS?" Jackie asked.

"History, philosophy, and social sciences," said Allison. "You could actually major in that if you didn't like getting oil paint all over your clothes."

"Sounds like prelaw," said Jackie.

"Closest thing we had," said Allison.

As they talked I imagined Oksana drifting like a wraith through the crowded, narrow streets of academic Providence, aloof from the burning passions of the confused creatives, yet possessing a passion of her own, finally realized as the fierce defender of another Snow Queen, this one doomed to fade back into the shadow world.

I managed to finish off my tumbler, and a second, by which time all I wanted was to fade back into my cottage next door, where with any luck I would get through to morning with the spirits that haunted my inner consciousness bludgeoned into submission.

PERHAPS INSPIRED by the word bludgeon, I found myself the next morning on the way to Sonny's boxing gym with my workout clothes and a tankard of dense coffee. Mostly on autopilot, I didn't fully realize my actual motivation until I was pulling into the parking lot right behind Bennie Gardella. He gave me a blank look as we got out of our cars, but said nothing as I followed him into the gym.

And that was how it stood as we both went through warm-up exercises at opposite ends of the room. I'd always known the value of stretching, which at this point had nearly existential importance. So it was over a half hour before I put on my gloves and started working on the speed bag.

I rarely allowed my ego to infect any of my life's pursuits, feeling that a wary humility was a safer posture, having seen hubris bring down any number of aspiring boxers, carpenters, and corporate executives. But I had a secret pride in my ability with the speed bag, and even at this stage of waning reflexes, I knew how to keep the thing chattering away without looking like I was much trying.

I often got a little grudging validation for this from the kids who hung around the gym, leading to more than one impromptu boxing lesson for the ones who also knew how to keep their own egos from cluttering up their progress.

So I wasn't completely surprised to realize Gardella was standing there watching me, though it did disturb my rhythm. So as not to completely flub the performance, I stopped the bag with both gloves.

"Anything I can do for you?" I asked.

"Just watching the circus act," he said.

He wore a set of gloves himself. They were well broken in and of an expensive type the pros used for sparring. He was shaking out his arms as if getting ready for just that.

"Want to see how that fancy shit works out in the ring?" he asked me.

I said I already knew.

"And I don't do that anymore. Doctor's orders."

"Old age?"

"Concussions," I said. "Three at least. You're only allowed so many."

He didn't exactly jeer at me, but I could feel waves of menace coming off his face. I let go of the bag and adjusted my stance.

"So not just because you're a pussy?" he said.

A blanket of weariness settled over me.

"Jesus Christ, Gardella, what's with the hostility?"

He didn't hesitate to answer.

"I don't like you," he said. "I don't like amateurs with their noses stuck up the asses of professional cops. People who never had to actually live with the responsibility for containing the lowlifes of the world while the world treats us like we're even lower. Self-righteous suck-ups like you who hang around cops like a groupie trying to fuck some brainless rock star."

As with many contact sports, boxing is in great part a head game, and not just as a punching bag. You need to have as much control over your emotions as your body. Muhammad Ali demonstrated that with poetry and precision. Gardella would have to do better than insult to goad me.

"You won't believe me," I said, "but I admire what you did back in your undercover days. From what I hear, you did a lot. So maybe that explains the bad attitude. I don't know, but I'm not risking dementia just to help out with your anger management therapy."

He stood and processed that for a few moments, though it didn't seem to quell the animus.

"I know what you're up to, Acquillo," he said, pointing at me with his glove. "I've been on you every step of the way. You want to drag Ross and the Southampton cops into some trumped-up corruption charge. Some snitches get wasted and everybody's first thought is dirty cops are in on it. That's bullshit. Nobody's going down for this other than the bastards who actually did it. I'm here to make sure that's what happens."

One of the most important benefits of keeping your head in these situations is it allows the thinking part of your brain to keep working while the more animal parts are picking out targets.

"Who have you been talking to?" I asked him. "I thought Ross brought you out here to help him look inside his department. And not just their filing system."

"Is that what he told you?"

I admitted he didn't.

"No. I inferred."

"Well, you can stick your inferring up your ass. That's bullshit."

"Inferences. I think that's what you meant to say," I said.

He dropped his right shoulder and took a step toward me, his face shifting from seething rage to something a lot more businesslike. I knew what was coming.

So I sat down on a bench and put my gloves over my ears.

"What the hell are you doing," he said.

"Protecting my head. It's the only one I have."

"Chicken shit."

"Fear is sometimes a useful thing," I said. "Do you know it's physiologically akin to anger? The old fight-flight."

"Crazy fucker."

I took my gloves away.

"You get the same basic adrenal response," I said. "Good for clubbing a predator to death with a stone ax or running like hell. In either case, the things you need the least are your higher-level cognitive functions. So they essentially switch off so your animal brain can take over and do its job. In other words, nothing makes you stupider than fear and anger."

His own cognitive functions were grappling pretty hard with some of these concepts, which at least caused him to hesitate long enough for a couple of my unofficial boxing students to wander into that part of the gym. Neither one of them would be much use against Gardella, but there were plenty more where they came from.

I pointed that out, causing his hesitation to turn toward uncertainty.

"I'm not going to fight you, Bennie. I'm not that angry, or afraid."

I waved over the two kids. Gardella took a step back.

"Hey, Lewis," I said to the bigger one. "Do you think I'm stupid?"

He looked disturbed by the question.

"Shit no, Sam. You be more of a smart motherfucker."

His friend agreed.

"That's right," he said. "Sam's in possession of some serious knowledge."

"The rest of your posse here?" I asked him.

Lewis gestured toward the far end of the gym.

"Five, six of 'em if they can get they asses out of the locker room."

"Do any of them think I'm stupid?" I asked him.

Lewis got even more upset.

"Nobody thinkin' you do stupid shit, Sam. Exceptin' that dumb ass ride of yours."

"I think that settles it," I said to Bennie, and pushed past him on the way to the locker room. I could hear the two kids saying things like, "Maybe that old fucker gez got hit too many times," but I didn't much care, still in possession of all my higher-level cognitive functions, to say nothing of my serious knowledge.

Chapter Twenty-Two

I drove directly to Southampton Town Police HQ to save Ross the trouble of demanding my presence. Orlovsky was back at her post behind the glassed-in desk, so that saved me the need to be nice to the new adjutant. She was thinner and darker, as if she'd tried to bake off her sorrow in the sun. She showed little affect as I approached the window.

"Tell him I'm here," I said, and sat down to wait. She made the call then, a moment later, buzzed me in. I walked back to Ross's office.

Sergeant Lausanne looked up as I passed her desk without saying anything. Her face was still sprightly, though the effervescence had lost some of its froth.

I didn't bother to knock. Ross was in his chair, seat pulled back and feet on top of a pile of papers. Cigarette smoke clogged the room.

"Ronny called me," he said. "So spare me the commentary."

"What the hell is going on, Ross? You bring this head case out here from Up Island to help you investigate your own police force and he thinks he's on a crusade to defend it from me. I'm getting the feeling he's got a point. Something's very fucked up around here."

He took his feet off the desk with some effort to avoid spilling the papers off onto the floor, with partial success. He lit a fresh cigarette with the half-smoked one still in his mouth.

"It's interesting how so many people in and out of the police department think I have some sort of control over Bennie Gardella," he said.

"You don't?"

"I didn't bring him out here. I just requested an administrative officer to clean up the mess we've made out of our paperwork. I want to go digital. Stick everything in the computer. A false hope, some may say, but we need to keep up with the times."

He gathered up the remainder of his footrest and dropped it on the floor.

"That doesn't make any sense."

"I'm sending Bennie back to Nassau County. They need to give me somebody who actually *wants* to sit in front of a computer screen all day. Lucille's pretty good, but she can't do it all herself."

"You really didn't bring him out here."

"I really didn't. I'm the one who pulled him out of undercover, before he got so buggy that the bad guys shot him out of sheer self-preservation. I'm the one who sent him into rehab as a condition of his continued employment in law enforcement, though I almost regretted that he took us up on it. I was hoping I'd seen the last of him when I took the job out here."

I couldn't tell if it was all the smoke in the air or my state of anxious confusion that made me want to leap across the desk and grab the pack of Winstons out of his shirt pocket and stuff the whole thing in my mouth.

"You like reminding me that you owe no explanation for anything you do," I said, "but at this point, it would sure help."

He leaned forward and put both elbows on the desk so he could use his hands to roughly illustrate his narrative.

"Do you know how they find new subatomic particles?" he asked. "They first have to theorize their existence. What makes a good theory? Things are happening that make no sense. Even in the weird world of quantum mechanics, reality has to operate within certain constructs, even if they're only explainable mathematically."

I told him they mentioned something about that in physics class at MIT.

"Really? I barely got past Aristotle," he said. "Anyway whenever there's anomalous behavior by various forces and objects in the universe, scientists start thinking, well, if this thing is doing this, and that thing is doing that, ergo, there must be some unseen agent, whether made of energy or mass, that causes these things to happen."

"Alfie might have suggested the Nazgûl."

"Trouble is, theorists can't just say, 'there's this thing we've never seen nor heard from that is causing all this nutty behavior by all these other things.' They have to prove its existence. So what do they do?"

"Break for lunch?"

"They call in the experimental boys, the ones with the colliders, the particle accelerators, who basically smash things together until the thing they're looking for zings out of the ether."

"Which one are you?" I asked him. "Theorist or collider?"

He seemed pleased with the question.

"I tend to the empirical, the demonstrable truth. But when it comes to collisions, no one's better than you, Sam. I admit it."

"Not sure if I should say thanks."

"What's more, you're good on the theoretical side. It's no wonder your company let you run R&D. You were a double threat. Until you fucked it up, of course."

I learned from the professor who taught Zen at MIT the importance the masters put in humility. A lesson Ross seemed particularly suited to reinforce.

"You're the one who told Gardella I was out to screw the Southampton Town Police," I said. "At the same time you had me out there chasing the snitch killers."

"God, that'd be devious."

"You wanted to smash some things together to see what popped up."

"Some metaphors are a little too close to home," he said.

"So what did you learn?"

"Inconclusive, though I don't think you're done colliding."

There wasn't a lot of lightness in the way he said that, and I took it accurately as a dismissal. I wanted to stay in that sulfurous atmosphere as long as it took to wrench more information out of the chief's byzantine mind, but I knew I had all I was going to get. I also understood, as exasperating as the situation was, that Ross had told me the truth.

Just not the whole truth, so help me God.

ON THE way back to Oak Point I called Jackie before she had a chance to call and accuse me of holding out on her. I made her listen to the whole story, despite several attempts to interrupt me. When I got it all out, she said, "Oksana called. Edith wants to see us ASAP."

"Really."

"She was very insistent."

"You don't refuse a Snow Queen."

"I'm heading over to pick you up. Please don't disappear on me."

I moved a little faster to beat her to the cottage so I had time to check on Allison and crew, but not to fill anyone in on the latest events. It was just as well. They had plenty of their own concerns to worry about.

I even took a few moments to empty out my mailbox, which I usually let fill up until the mail carrier couldn't close the little door. There was never anything good in there, so I didn't feel the urgency. This time there was the usual stack of bills, junk mail, and useless catalogs, and one big manila envelope.

There was no return address, but the postmark was New York City, New York. Inside was a single piece of 8½" × 11" paper, a photocopy of an invoice prepared by the office of Jules Weinberg, DVM. A vet bill.

I folded up the paper and stuck it in the rear pocket of my blue jeans.

Eᴅɪᴛʜ ᴀɴᴅ Oksana were waiting in a conference room featuring a level of discomfort and sterility unachievable by all but the Civil Service. Neither of the women offered to shake hands, though Edith did say, "Thank you for coming on such short notice."

"Certainly," said Jackie, whatever that meant.

Edith seemed to shrink under the burden of what she had to say, maybe because she had to say it to members of such a tiresome social class.

"I had a lengthy conversation with Deputy Inspector Joshua Gilliam," she said. Oh boy, I thought. "He detailed the conversation he had with you. I found it disturbing, to say the least."

"Was this at the opera or the bridge table?" I asked.

"You were under explicit instructions to keep our," she paused, "arrangement, entirely confidential. I couldn't be more disappointed."

"Don't sell yourself short," I said.

"It's worse than that," said Oksana, the stare of her pale blue eyes through their wintry eyelashes enough to freeze the air.

"The allegation you made regarding my husband," said Edith. "How loathsome."

"Wait a minute, Mrs. Madison," said Jackie. "It was in the service of your request of us that we were consulting with Mr. Gilliam. And he, in fact, provided some valuable information, along with an offer to help in any way he could. I'm offended, frankly, that he felt compelled to report this to you. Secondly, there were no allegations made. It was a free-flowing conversation in which many thoughts were raised, some entirely speculative and raised merely to salt the discussion. I'm not privy to what the deputy inspector told you, but I assure you, the only thing loathsome here is your insult to our integrity and good intention."

Edith waited to hear if there was more, then said, "My."

Oksana said, "We order you to cease and desist any and all activities relating to police behavior in the matter of the confidential informant homicides, or any other police action, from this moment forward. Any violation of this order will be treated as an obstruction of justice, and interference in a police investigation, and will result in a recommendation that charges be brought by the appropriate legal authorities."

Jackie actually guffawed, which surprised them but I took as a good sign.

"What, you're giving us a formal, official order to stop performing an informal, inappropriate, and entirely extralegal duty?" she asked. "I'd like to see the statutes underlying that legal logic."

Neither of them seemed to have such a thing handy, so they took another tack.

"You're right," said Oksana, while Edith listened mutely. It was getting more obvious why the Snow Queen sat at Edith's right arm. "There was no formal agreement between us. No record even of our conversation. So any such characterization on your part we deny. It is the Office of the District Attorney's word against yours. An accused felon and his unpaid attorney."

"I actually paid her a dollar," I said.

Edith sat back in her chair and rapped the tabletop with a bony knuckle. It got our attention.

"I knew this was a terrible idea," she said. "Trusted advisor or not."

Then she stood up and for the second time that day I was dismissed. I told myself to get better at seeing it coming so I could walk out before the dismissers got the chance.

Oksana stood as well and so we were marched out of the conference room. On the way to the exit, Oksana asked to speak to me in private. Jackie's face, already scarlet, got even redder. I followed Oksana into another bland, window-less room. She shut the door behind us.

"If you aren't actually working for this office, however informally, it will make it easier," she said.

"To do what?"

"See you."

Perplexity morphed into something more like bewilder-ment. I'd chalked up that coziness on the park bench to the self-delusion of deepening middle age. This time I clarified.

"You mean, like in, man and woman?"

"Of course that's what I mean," she said. "You're an attractive man. And still quite vibrant, proven by all three assault charges you've managed to avoid."

"I already have somebody."

"I don't see any rings on any fingers."

She moved in closer, as before, close enough for me to appreciate a complexion like fresh-fallen snow and a natural aroma you'd bottle under the label "Unfair Advantage."

I stepped back, but not that far.

"Okay, Oksana, sure. Pick a time and place. Somewhere in the city where we'll get lost in the crowd."

Her smile was wry, mixed with touches of triumph and eager anticipation.

"I told you surprising things can happen," she said. "If you have an imagination. Apparently you do."

I ignored Jackie's withering stare all the way out of the building, across the parking lot, and into the Volvo. When the doors were shut, she said, "What did she want?" with most of the emphasis on the word "what."

"Not what you think," I said.

"Then what?"

"A date."

Jackie held the steering wheel with both hands as if to steady herself.

"You are shitting me."

"I'm not. She thinks I'm attractive. And vibrant."

Jackie put her head on the steering wheel between her two clenched hands.

"Unfuckingbelievable."

"You don't think I'm vibrant and attractive?"

"No. But Amanda does."

"I'm not going to do it," I said.

"What?"

"Go out with her. Though I did ask her to throw out a time and place."

"Why?" she asked.

"Might help us with Edith."

"So you are going out with her."

"Maybe technically. Let's see what she comes back with."

Jackie and Amanda had always understood you didn't need to be good friends to play on the same team, though there were times in the past when it was hard to tell if they were playing the same game. So even if I offended Jackie's feminist predilections, I knew she'd keep it to herself, loyalty in this case trumping principle.

CHAPTER TWENTY-THREE

The first thing I did when Amanda came home from her construction site was to tell her about Oksana making a pass at me.

"Really. Did you pass it back?"

"Not exactly," I said.

"You could be more specific."

"I can only love one woman at a time."

"How many so far?"

"Abby and you. In that order. I'm working my way down the alphabet."

"Oksana doesn't even start with an A."

I told her about our meeting with Oksana and Edith, with all the resulting consequences and implications. Then I backed up and told her about my run-in with Bennie Gardella and subsequent chat with Chief Ross Semple.

"You've been busy," she said. "All I did was irritate my finish carpenters with a change in the kitchen design."

"Tell 'em they can be changed out just as fast."

"So you really did work in corporate America."

"I didn't turn Oksana down outright because there're too many things in flux," I said. "I can't afford to alienate Edith any more than I already have, and as time goes by, Oksana is looking more and more like Edith's interface with the world."

"Very well. Just don't sleep with her. I'd feel foolish."

I STAYED with Amanda that night to illustrate the depths of my devotion and she seemed pleased with the results. So that's where Jackie found me when she barged into our sanctuary at three o'clock in the morning.

Sullivan was all apologies when I opened the door, but I absolved him of responsibility.

"You know how she is," I said, nodding toward Jackie.

"I do," he said.

"Jesus Christ, Jackie," I told her as Sullivan went back to his post. "You're lucky he didn't shoot you."

"I'd shoot him back."

"What's going on?"

"We need to talk."

"Okay. Let me stick my face in a bucket of water and meet me out on the patio."

Eddie was there when I came out, fussing over Jackie in a way that always irritated me. No treats, no toss of the ball, just a little scrunch on the top of the head and sweet nothings in his ear.

Jackie was in flip-flops and a silky summer dress that was working overtime to contain all her feminine parts. I was glad to have Amanda blessedly passed out upstairs.

"I've been doing some digging," she said.

"There's a surprise."

"I was struck by Allison's description of Oksana at RISD."

"How so?"

"No good reason," she said. "I'm just nosy. And I don't like Oksana."

"Fair enough."

"So I pretended to be a potential employer and asked for her transcript."

"You can do that?"

"Not without the student's permission. So I had Randall Dodge pretend he was her."

"Online of course," I said. "Not many ten-foot-tall Indians look like the Snow Queen."

"She didn't graduate from RISD, just like Allison said. She transferred to Brown for her senior year."

"So what did Brown say?"

"They didn't," she said. "Or rather, wouldn't, without convincing ID. I think I ran into a registrar with scruples."

"Inconvenient."

"I have a plan."

"You often do," I said.

"It means a trip to Providence, Rhode Island."

"It's a small state. Easy to miss."

"I'll drive, of course. You have three hours to sleep before we leave. I'll stay on your sunporch with Eddie."

"Okay, not a problem. But why the urgency?" I said, looking around at the moonless night to reinforce the point.

She leaned into her words, which nearly caused the balance of her unrevealed breasts to spill out of the top of her dress. I wasn't all that interested, but in these things reflexes rule. She gathered up the wayward fabric before answering.

"The woman at RISD sent Randall everything she had. Included was an impressive stack of recommendation letters. All glowing, of course. Though one stood out."

She took her time telling me, the usual game we played. I was probably too sleepy to pry it out of her, so she just gave it up.

"It was written by Brown University Assistant Dean of Students Herschel Bergeron, future captain in the Long Island Forty-Third. Jimmy Watruss and Alfie Aldergreen's commanding officer. The guy who gave his life saving theirs."

I looked at an imaginary watch on my wrist.

"If we catch the seven A.M. ferry we can be in Providence by ten," I said.

THE TRIP was one of my favorites. Up through the North Fork of the East End of Long Island to Orient Point, where you took a big ferry over to Connecticut. Whenever I went this way, I was nearly cudgeled with gratitude for being born and raised in such a place. I didn't know if all the anxious drivers around me felt the same way, but I forgave them.

On the way to the ferry dock, I opened the window to let some North Fork air into the car. Jackie was unsure about this, though she didn't complain. She just held back her wad of curly hair with one hand and drove the Volvo with the other.

I kept the radio on a scratchy jazz station, turned up to barely tolerable levels, another thing for Jackie to endure. I sat back with my head on the car seat, seemingly passed out, which likely only added insult to injury. Still I made it all the way to Orient Point without getting heaved out of the car.

We were early enough to walk around the staging area before boarding the first ferry out in the morning—time I spent skipping stones across the choppy bay water and petting the dogs of ferry-goers inclined to let their dogs breach my personal space. A few suggested that I had a dog of my own, and I copped to it.

Jackie busied herself tapping on her smartphone, a sorry way to treat the glorious day.

The ferry ride itself lived up to its promise. The air was clean and the wind a steady blow out of the north. I stood on the upper deck and spotted sailboats, getting a sense of their progress by the tilt of the sails and the wave heights passing by the ferry's towering hull. Jackie eventually joined me up there, probably worried I'd gone overboard, which likely explained why she held me around the waist with both hands and stuck her face into my shoulder. I put my arm around her as well, to let her know all was safe, and thus secured, as we made our way into New London, Connecticut.

F ROM N EW L ONDON , you take Interstate 95 north to Providence. It was a better trip for me than Jackie, who had to avoid getting us mowed down by tractor trailers. I got to look out the window at New England woodlands, occasionally interrupted by ugly industrial buildings and retail glitz that could be wreaking the same aesthetic carnage anywhere in the country.

Rush hour was all wrapped up by the time we saw the modest skyline of Providence, so we quickly made it over the river and into the area of the city that contained Rhode Island School of Design and Brown University. It had been several years since I'd been there, on one of my rare visits to Allison's tiny jumble of a student apartment. She never seemed all that crazy to have me there, and I used that as an excuse to pay less attention to her than I should have. It's lamentable that parents often don't realize their children's behavior signals the opposite desire until it's too late to do anything about it.

Though I liked the feel of the place. Hilly and cramped, with ancient buildings sharing space with modern architectural experiments, the rolling sidewalks filled with kids both prematurely wise and hopelessly puerile.

As we homed in on the registrar's office at Brown, Jackie revealed her plan by handing me her driver's license. Or a version thereof. It was her face, but the name on the license said Oksana Quan.

"How did you get this?" I asked.

"Randall Dodge. The guy's amazing. I don't know what I'd do without him."

"You'll learn when he's wearing an orange jumpsuit."

"Never happen. He's got a great lawyer."

The registrar's office was down a story from street level. Campus security was through the same door, which added to the experience. Jackie told me Randall's alteration would never get by official scrutiny, but it was plenty good enough to fool an admin at a university registrar's office.

So we hoped, as a large man in a navy blue police uniform with a radio transceiver clipped to his shoulder passed us on the way through the double doors.

The woman who approached the counter to meet us looked young enough to be Allison's daughter. Her eyes seemed to fill half her head and they spoke of her sheer pleasure in satisfying our request.

Jackie gave her Oksana's name and graduation date and slid the phony license across the counter. The girl looked at it for a second before handing it back. Then she disappeared for about ten minutes, which seemed longer than necessary. I stole looks through the glass door behind me at the entrance to the security office.

"I'm sorry for the wait," she said, returning with a manila folder. "I had to cross reference with admissions to find the file."

"How so?" Jackie asked.

The girl looked pained at what she had to say.

"You gave the graduation year. I'm sure you meant the year you planned to graduate," she said, in a voice just loud enough to hear.

"Can I see?" Jackie asked.

The girl let go of the file as if it were about to spontaneously combust. Jackie opened it up and read. I smiled what I thought was a kind and avuncular smile at the young admin, and it seemed to take. She smiled back.

"Yes, of course," said Jackie, handing back the folder. "I should have been more specific. Can you copy everything in there?"

The girl looked relieved. The copier was in plain sight so we could watch her perform the task. A few minutes after that we were back on the street. Jackie stood on the sidewalk and looked up at the sky through a pair of cat-eye sunglasses.

"She didn't graduate," said Jackie.

"Never?"

"Not from RISD and not from Brown. Would have been hard after flunking two requirement courses in what should have been her last semester." She looked struck by a thought. "Wait here."

I didn't wait long. When she came back out she headed off down the sidewalk with her usual authority. I followed.

"Where're we going?" I asked.

"Dean of students."

It wasn't a short walk, but the day was still young enough to be cool and breezy. I took in the slightly denser atmosphere than we get on the East End and the slightly deeper green of the trees. I wanted to see what was in Oksana's records, but it's hard to walk and read, and anyway, it was easier to surf behind Jackie's wake.

At the dean of students' office she dropped the false identity and set a different course, handing a woman at the first desk her business card and stating that she was on official business as a representative of the New York State judicial system. The woman, this one thoroughly middle-aged, took that seriously enough to move briskly down the hall to retrieve her boss.

The guy who came out was about my age, with a fringe of grey hair clinging below a balding crown, thick plastic-rimmed glasses, narrow shoulders, and ballooning midriff. His tie was loosened and his light blue dress shirt showed sweat around the armpits.

He introduced himself as Dean Chaplin. Not to be confused with Chaplain Dean, he noted with a vague smile, as he probably had a few thousand times before.

"We're collecting background information on the victim of a homicide on Long Island," said Jackie. "We just need to ask a few questions."

"Should I get university counsel?" he asked.

"Why don't you hear the questions first, then you decide," she said.

He agreed with that and took us into an office that resembled the middle-management caves I was used to back in my corporate job—signed football jerseys mounted like paintings, executive games on the desk, Hirschfeld-style caricatures, signed photos of Chaplin shaking hands with a second-tier golf pro, out-of-date photos of the family.

"You've been dean for how long?" Jackie asked, getting right to it.

"Close to twenty years, believe it or not."

"So you knew Assistant Dean Bergeron."

His face took on a sterner set.

"I hired him. And gave him his good-bye party. You know he passed away."

"We do," said Jackie. "Was the party before he joined the service?"

"Before he took another position. At NYU. In admissions."

"You don't mind these questions?" Jackie asked.

"No. It's all public knowledge. He'd just mustered out of the army before I brought him in as a clerical assistant. Served in Korea. He worked his way up to assistant dean, but wanted to go back to Long Island where he had a lot of family. I'd heard he'd joined the National Guard to get into the Iraq War. I wouldn't say exactly gung-ho, but he was patriotic. Sort of the classic All-American, square-jawed type who believed in serving his country. Sounds like a stereotype, but thank God they're out there."

"Was his family military?" I asked.

"On Long Island? Not his family. His wife's. Big mob of Italians that lived in Queens. Poor choice of words. You know what I mean."

"We do," said Jackie. "So he was married during his tenure here."

"Married while still in the army. Nice girl, if you could get past the accent. You could cut it with a knife."

Jackie looked over at me, a person she often accused of torturing vowels to telegraph my Long Island roots.

"Hard to judge a person by the way they talk," I said, making sure the accent showed through.

"Right," said Chaplin. "Anyway Herschel lived in Queens and commuted into the city and trained with the guard until he shipped out to Iraq, and it sounds like you know what happened after that."

"We think we do, but why don't you tell it," said Jackie.

So he did, with little deviation from Cardozo's version, without the military nomenclature. The effort made Chaplin noticeably sadder, something describing Bergeron's ultimate heroism did little to allay.

"I'm sorry," said Jackie.

"Don't get me started on that idiot war," said Chaplin.

"I think we already did," said Jackie. "So I'm doubly sorry."

He grinned a sad little grin.

"Do you know if he knew an RISD transfer named Oksana Quan? Good-looking platinum blonde?" I asked, giving him the year she would have been on campus.

The sad face abruptly turned angry, and suspicious.

"What does that have to do with a homicide investigation?" he asked.

"As we said, background," said Jackie. "Mr. Bergeron served in Iraq with the victim."

"Herschel was a devoted family man. Loved his wife, loved his kids. A real square, as we once said. It wasn't his fault the girl developed a crush. Nothing ever came of it, that I assure you."

"Though you knew her," I said.

"She'd visit him here at the office, and I'd see them around campus," said Chaplin. "I know it sounds bad, but you didn't know him as I did. He was eager to mentor, and the students loved him. Not in that way," he added, frustrated with fumbling the defense of his dead assistant.

"We believe you," said Jackie.

She must have meant herself and somebody else in the room, because I sure as hell didn't.

"Everyone thought they were doing it," I said.

That pained him further, but he nodded his head.

"Is that why he left for NYU?" Jackie asked.

He nodded again.

"His wife wanted to move back to Long Island, but not just to be close to family," he said quietly into his desk. Then he looked up. "It's hard to exaggerate Oksana's beauty. I don't know why she didn't go into modeling. Maybe she did. I don't know."

"So you don't know what happened to her," I said.

"I don't. Never tried to find out. Herschel never mentioned her after he left. We eventually stopped writing each other, and then he was dead. The whole thing was so awful I suppose I just wanted to forget about it. That's all I can tell you, which is a lot more than I probably should have."

Jackie assured him his candor was welcomed and well within the limits of propriety, and he would never have to revisit the subject again. That seemed to relieve him and he was gracious when he showed us out the door.

Jackie was quiet as we walked across the campus, and it seemed wise not to talk about our chat with the dean until we were safely back in the car. As the doors closed I asked her the one question stuck at the front of my mind.

"Say, Jackie, where did Oksana go to law school?"

She dug out her smartphone and tapped around the screen for a few moments, then handed it to me.

"It's in her official New York DOJ biography," she said. "Look near the bottom."

After zooming in to raise the type size, and moving the text around with my index finger, I finally found it.

"NYU," I said.

Jackie didn't bother to respond, since she knew that already.

CHAPTER TWENTY-FOUR

J ackie had me drive the Volvo back to Long Island so she could make calls, text, and send e-mails from her smartphone. It made me glad I didn't own one of those things, though I was a little curious about how they worked.

She claimed to know people at NYU law school, people who would freely tell her things and not force her into unethical deception, much less outright fraud. She wrote them as we drove, and I occupied myself piloting the heavy station wagon through New England traffic down to the ferry landing in New London.

Among the many fine amenities on the big ferry was a full-scale bar with a real live bartender. I took the drink out on deck to watch for sailboats and allow the stiff sea breeze to ventilate the pondering part of my brain. Jackie was mostly quiet, tangled in deep deliberations of her own. She didn't share her thoughts, nor press me on mine. I had the feeling we were following similar mental paths, and maybe she did, too, so there was no need at that point to expend conversational energy.

When she dropped me off at the cottage I changed my clothes and went down to the shop after calling Nathan and getting the message that all was status quo. So neither good nor bad.

After achieving enough progress to satisfy my schedule with Entwhistle, I cleaned up and took the Grand Prix into Southampton Village.

Mad Martha's was filling up fast, but I found a spot at the bar in one of the darkened corners. I knew a lot of the people in there, but didn't see Jimmy Watruss, the person I was looking for. I asked the bartender if Jaybo was in the back orchestrating things like he usually did. The bartender said he'd go get him.

"Say, Sam, wazup?" Jaybo asked, walking down the bar wiping his hands on a bloody apron. "How're you feeling?"

"A lot better," I said. "Ribs only hurt when I get out of bed. Makes you want to sleep in more."

"I hear you," he said. "I'm really sorry."

I shooed the thought away.

"Knock it off about that. Do you know if Jimmy is coming in?"

"I don't think so. Some tenants moved out of a shop on Jobs Lane without telling him. Or paying all the rent. Left a mess. He's been over there cleaning up and yelling about lawsuits."

I thanked him after getting the address and took my time leaving the bar and walking down Main Street into the Village and hooking a right onto Jobs Lane. Night had settled in by then and the air was warm with a dash of damp Atlantic breeze. The wind was out of the southwest, which brought along the sound of the ocean waves, faint but undeniable.

The sign above the place said, "Totally Hip, Totally Now," which explained why it flopped faster than a suicidal mayfly. Someone had taped brown paper over the insides of the windows, but light was seeping through around the edges. I pounded on the front door and Jimmy answered.

"Shit, Sam, I thought it was my disappeared tenants," said Jimmy.

"That'd make them bad at disappearing."

The store was brightly lit by ceiling lamps, and a few work lights mounted on floor stands. The white walls reflected it all into a blinding glare. Chrome clothing racks stood empty, or lay on the floor as if tossed there by the escaping retailers. Jimmy was featuring his usual rangy cowboy look, complete with chewing tobacco, that made him seem more like a squatter than the owner of the place.

"Fuckin' asshole Romanians," he said.

"Romanians?"

"That's what they told me anyway. The rental agent thought they were actually Bulgarian, like, what the fuck's the difference? All I got was the two months upfront and a security deposit, and these racks. What do you think they're worth?"

"Nothing to me," I said.

He looked at me as if suddenly realizing I was in his abandoned store.

"What's up, anyway?" he asked.

"I want to talk. When you're not busy."

"Nothing busy about this. I'm just standing around getting pissed."

"So let's sit," I said, and sat on the dirty industrial carpet and leaned against the wall. He sat and leaned against the opposite wall.

"How'd you know I was here?" he asked.

"Jaybo told me."

He took off his baseball cap and scratched his head, as if still getting used to the recent crew cut.

"Kid works too hard," he said. "There day and night. Almost makes me want to get back in the kitchen and help him out. Almost."

"I never told you what a nice job you did at Alfie's funeral," I said. "Probably not easy dragging all that stuff up, even for a good cause."

He didn't seem entirely pleased with the compliment.

"I didn't say anything special. Just talked about what was."

"And it was pretty bad," I said. "I got the story from Colonel Cardozo."

He looked even less pleased.

"Freaking, drunk-ass head shrinker. How would he know? He wasn't there."

"He thinks a lot of you."

He closed his eyes and rolled his head around, stretching his neck muscles.

"He's all right. Means well."

"I'm wondering why you didn't mention Herschel Bergeron. From what I hear, he saved both your lives."

"Saved? You mean by keeping us from getting killed? Oh, that. He did that. You weren't in the service were you."

"No," I said.

"Too bad. They could've used you."

"Thanks, Jimmy."

"Bergeron was a good man. I mean like in a good person. You run into a lot of asshole officers in a situation like that. Not all actually did the job they were supposed to while acting like a human being."

"I'm sorry he didn't make it," I said.

I noticed his eyes were wet with tears, though he did nothing to hide it.

"You know, this isn't my favorite topic of conversation," he said. "I like you, Sam, but I'm wondering why we're having it."

"You spent a lot of time with Alfie and Bergeron in that Bradley Fighting Vehicle," I said. "From what I understand, it could be pretty boring, when it wasn't extremely intense. Or terrifying. It's the sort of situation where you get to learn a lot about each other."

"You understand correctly," he said, "though I still don't know why we're talking about it."

"I need to know what he said about Oksana Quan."

Those wet eyes turned into narrow slits.

"You are one nosy bastard, you know that Sam?"

"I know that," I said. "I'm also a persistent bastard. Not an easy combination, I admit it. Once I know something, I can't shake it loose. And I know that you were a lot closer to Alfie than you ever let on. And that Herschel Bergeron was a lot closer to Oksana Quan than he should have been. So what does all that mean? I don't know. But I think you do."

He pulled away from the wall and did the stretching thing with his neck again, then shook out his shoulders.

"You wouldn't know it, but Alfie scored top marks in close quarters combat training. Skinny fucker, but fast. Like a mongoose. The only way to beat him was to get him in a clutch and hold on. Muscle him to the ground and squeeze till his eyeballs popped out."

"I knew guys like that when I was boxing. Easy to underestimate."

"He grew up an orphan, living in all sorts of shitholes and foster homes. That'll toughen you up plenty. Not like me. Had it made. It was too easy. Probably why I joined the army. Prove to myself I had what it takes. Turns out I did. Didn't matter. An RPG doesn't care how tough you are."

"What did Bergeron tell you about Oksana Quan?" I asked.

He shook his head, grinning.

"You're right. You are a persistent bastard. Who cares what he told us?"

"I'm going to find out anyway, whether you tell me or not. I want to hear it from you."

The tears had stopped, but now he was breathing hard. There was stored energy in his posture and rampant indecision on his face.

"Let me ask you something," he said. "How would you like getting your ass kicked? Coming onto my property. Threatening me. I'd be justified."

I rolled up from a sitting position into a squat. He stayed seated, still leaning against the wall.

"Others have tried."

"I know you're good with your fists, Sam, but they won't do much good on a guy who knows a hundred ways to kill you before you know you're dead."

"I know that. I'm not here to fight. I just want information. And if you don't give it to me, there'll be other people after me asking the same things. It won't go away."

He settled back deeper into the wall.

"Jesus Christ, I hate this shit."

"What shit?"

"Civilian shit. No honor. No loyalty. Just civilian bullshit." Not knowing what to say to that, I just waited him out. "The guy was a boy scout, what can I say. But not stuck on himself, not some holier-than-thou. You're right. You live with somebody day in and day out in those circumstances, you talk about things you'd never talk about with anyone else. Fine for me. I was a general fuck-up and didn't care one way or the other what anybody thought. But the captain had this one thing eating his guts out.

"The only dumb thing he ever does and he's like burning up with guilt. You're Catholic, right? They tell us we have to confess shit like that to keep our ass out of hell. The captain didn't have a priest handy so me and Alfie were the next best thing."

"Oksana," I said.

"What guy doesn't catch a little extracurricular tail, especially when it's served up by a drop-dead babe like that? I've only seen her a couple times, but oh my Lord."

I didn't tell him I never caught the opportunities flung my way when I was in a miserable marriage, nor in any situation where the only restraint was a matter of honor and loyalty.

"I hope it made him feel better," I said. "Telling you guys."

His sadness reminded me of Dean Chaplin's. The type expressed by men who've lost other men in ways they have trouble fully understanding.

"I guess," said Jimmy. "Only it wasn't the fooling around part that had him so tied up in knots."

"It wasn't?"

"I'll make it easy for you. Oksana had this crazy thing for the captain so he tried to shake her by changing jobs. Got a gig with NYU in the city, but she tracks him down. That's when the serious shit kicks in. She tells him she'll put a billboard up in Times Square about the two of them if he doesn't get her into law school. So he does, somehow, even though she's no way qualified. That's what ripped the poor bastard apart. Not boffing the beauty queen, but for cheating to get her into NYU. I'm thinking, that's it? But everybody's got their own demons."

I should have been feeling sympathy for Herschel Bergeron's moral burden and for Jimmy Watruss, having carried it around for his friend all these years, but there were more important things for me to focus on right then, God forgive me.

"Who else did you tell this story to?" I asked, leaning forward from my squat, far enough to upset my balance and render me even more vulnerable to attack.

Jimmy seemed confused by that.

"Nobody. You're the only one."

"But Alfie knew it, too. He was there when Bergeron spilled his guts."

"He was," said Watruss. "He was indeed."

ON THE way home, I tried Jackie a few times on her cell phone and got nothing. So I spent a few hours with the family and crew, then went to bed.

Hodges called me up as the sun was rising. He reminded me of our plan to sail the *Carpe Mañana* around the Little Peconic Bay. I asked about the tender hour and he told me it had to be an early sail to hit the tides. The channel leading in and out of Hawk Pond had its share of shallow water, and the *Carpe Mañana* came with a seven-foot keel. Meaning a low enough tide would stick us in the sandy bottom for a few hours, resulting in potential harm to the boat and certain damage to my standing as a worthy seaman.

I told him to get her ready while I regained conscious-ness and put together a vat of coffee. It was early enough to catch Amanda as she drove out in her little red pickup. Her pleasure in the plan to sail with Paul Hodges was tempered only by regret that she couldn't go herself.

"I'll be looking for that rain check, buddy," she said, as she rolled away.

I fed Eddie his breakfast and watched him lope over to Amanda's house where he'd been hanging out during the day. It'd be nice to think he was part of the protective unit, but the actual allure was Allison's fawning attention and Amanda's ready supply of Big Dog biscuits.

When I got to Hawk Pond, Hodges had all but two restraining lines off my boat and the inboard diesel burbling in anticipation. The day was a fair representation of the good weather we'd been having, with a steady northwesterly spinning the anemometer at the top of the mast and flap-ping the American Ensign I'd rigged on the backstay.

In a few minutes we were under way.

I let Hodges pilot the boat along the twisty channel while I put a dent in my oversized mug of coffee. Now that I was heading out to the bay, any sluggishness was replaced by the usual semieuphoria the experience provided, no matter how often it happened.

An osprey glided overhead, ignored by the cormorants diving for breakfast or drying their wings on the rigging of the half-dozen sailboats moored in the wider reaches of Hawk Pond. The gulls were out as well, though we couldn't hear their indignant kvetching over the rumble of the motor beneath our feet. ·

There wasn't any particular reason to converse until we left the channel for the open water and it was time to raise the mainsail. Hodges kept the bow in the wind while I did all the hard work, glad for the cleansing effects. When the mainsail was aloft, we killed the engine and unfurled the big genoa, and in moments the *Carpe Mañana* was shooting off across the Little Peconic at about six knots with a gentle heel and the barest rise and fall over the comely bay waves.

"That's what I'm talking about," said Hodges, and I knew what he was talking about.

The wind dictated our course, which it always did, sending us well to the northwest of the bay, where we decided to come about and head back toward Hawk Pond, though we had just enough angle to cut through to the Great Peconic Bay, a bigger body of water affording more sailing time before any bothersome tacking. With both of us slightly banged up and more than slightly lazy, this seemed an excellent strategy.

By then I'd relieved Hodges at the wheel and he occupied himself sprawling like a dead frog on the comfy cockpit cushion. It wasn't until I felt the soothing balm of a sturdy sailboat engaged with wind and sea that I realized how much stress had built up over the events of recent weeks, beginning with Alfie Aldergreen's ugly death, and most prominently, the attack on my daughter. Perhaps knowingly, Hodges avoided the subject, focusing instead on the Yankees' chances of securing the pennant, if not actually winning the World Series. I'd missed most of the baseball season so the commentary was an ideal distraction.

When my cell phone rang, and the screen said it was Jackie Swaitkowski, I almost didn't answer, so disappointed was I by the unwelcomed intrusion.

"What are you, in a wind tunnel?" she asked, when I hit the answer button.

"On the boat," I said, handing the wheel off to Hodges and heading below to the cabin. "I tried to call you last night."

"I know. I was with Harry. He said he'd only go out with me if I turned off my phone."

"I have things to tell you," I said.

"Oksana got into NYU under false pretenses."

"That's what I had to tell you."

"Everything was fabricated," she said. "Including her LSAT scores and transcripts from RISD and Brown."

"Herschel Bergeron," I said.

"Exactly. He worked in admissions. Quite a nice bit of forgery. He must have been motivated."

"I'll bet," I said, remembering the soft caress of Oksana's calf against mine. "What does this mean? Legally."

"Legally, she's a fraud. It doesn't matter how well she did in law school, she cheated getting in. That wipes everything out. Disbarment for starters."

I sat on the settee in the main cabin as if driven there by the jolt of revelation.

"Call Ross," I said. "I know what's going on."

"You're out on a boat."

"I can be at Southampton HQ in less than two hours."

"He'll want a headline," she said.

"Tell him he's a good, honest man and scratch his tummy."

"What?"

That was when Hodges yelled at me from topside.

"Sam, what the fuck."

CHAPTER TWENTY-FIVE

I ran up the companionway and followed where he was pointing. A powerboat, low on the water but with a broad bow planing above the waves, was heading straight for us.

"What do I do?" Hodges yelled.

Sailors know it's all too common for powerboats to wait until they were nearly upon you before turning to the side, leaving you to knock around in their wake. Though not intentionally malicious, they had little appreciation for the speed difference between a boat under power and one under sail.

"He'll turn," I said.

"I'm not so sure," said Hodges.

As the boat continued to bear down on us, shifting course as we shifted, I had the bad feeling he was right. Six knots was a relatively decent speed for a sailboat. For a fast powerboat that was barely idling. It was an impossible contest for us to win, so all we could do was wait for the impact and hope for the best.

I asked Hodges for the wheel and turned the boat so our bow faced the speeding vessel, hoping to reduce the size of the exposure. The maneuver sent the *Carpe Mañana* directly into the wind, where it immediately stalled.

"He's going to hit us," said Hodges. "What do we do?"

"Prepare to jump," I said.

As the big sails luffed crazily overhead, I held the boat into the wind and tried to judge if we should leap to starboard or port. It didn't seem possible that anyone would deliberately ram us at high speed, though I'd often mused over the possibility of a helmsman asleep, or dead, at the wheel, with bad luck guiding his course.

Remembering a distant safety instruction, I threw the cockpit seat cushions overboard and was about to shove Hodges in the same direction when the bow of the powerboat shot up as it suddenly throttled down from planing speed. It banked hard, coming within a few feet of our starboard side and throwing up a wave that nearly knocked me off my feet.

Close in, I could see it was Joey Wentworth's picnic boat. With Jaybo Flynn standing in the stern section holding a shotgun pointing at our heads. So instead of throwing Hodges overboard, I pulled him down the companionway and into the cabin.

The sound of gunshot ripping through the mainsail accompanied the muffled boom. Hodges was cursing like the old sea dog he was, so I had to yell at him to shut up and get in the head that served the quarter berth directly behind the companionway stairs.

He didn't like the idea, but did it anyway. I dropped to my knees and dug a flare gun out of the bottom drawer below the nav table, along with a portable horn, powered by a can of pressurized air, and a roll of duct tape.

The *Carpe Mañana* shuddered as the picnic boat banged into the starboard side once, twice, three times. I heard Jaybo yell to his helmsman to ease back on the throttle. In my mind's eye I saw lines being tossed over the gunnels and secured to our cleats.

I moved to the V berth at the front of my boat and peered out the open hatch overhead. The guy who'd been with Jaybo when he hit me with the fish van was trying to lasso a line to our midship cleat with one hand while steering the picnic boat with the other. Jaybo leaped from his stern to ours, shotgun in hand. He also had a line, which he presumably tied off, though I couldn't see around the raised hatch.

As Jaybo's man managed to snag the cleat, the squeal of our rub rail against the hull of the other boat took the place of the jarring thuds. I dropped down from the hatch and sat on the bed, trying to think through a series of complicated maneuvers a few moments before they had to be accomplished.

I ripped off a length of duct tape and kept my eyes on the companionway, gifted with a clear view from the V berth's open door. Two legs and a shotgun started down the stairs. I waited until he was all the way below, then stuck the horn out the hatch, taped the button open and tossed the blaring thing through the standing rigging and into the cockpit.

Jaybo spun the shotgun back up the companionway and fired off a blast. I stepped out of the V berth, and when he spun back in my direction, shot him in the face with the flare gun.

He screamed and got off another shot that punched a hole in the cabin top above my head, but I was able to rush forward and grab the barrel with my left hand and get my right fist into the game.

They weren't elegant punches, more like a brawler's, but they managed to stagger Jaybo back against the companionway stairs. Smoke and blinding light from the flare filled the salon. The burning ball, after bouncing off Jaybo's face, was busy drilling a hole in the galley's Corian counter.

The hard right jabs finally weakened Jaybo enough for me to wrench the shotgun out of his hands, and I used the stock to plant the deciding blow into his forehead.

Hodges picked that moment to burst out of the head. In the cramped quarters he nearly bowled me over trying to get his hands around Jaybo's neck.

"Don't kill him," I said, gripping Hodges's jacket at the shoulders and dragging him with Jaybo in tow back into the salon.

I was happy to see Hodges let go of Jaybo's neck until I realized he just wanted his hands free to pummel the kid's mangled face. I tried to hold his right arm back, but he just dragged me along with the punch.

"Hodges, knock it off," I yelled at him. "We need this guy alive."

What got him to stop wasn't my entreaties, but the sight of Jaybo's buddy jumping into the cockpit. Hodges shoved past Jaybo and clambered up the companionway stairs with the speed and agility of an orangutan.

I followed with the shotgun, but when I got topsides Hodges had already slammed the guy across the cockpit and was in the process of wrestling him into a headlock. The guy managed to squirt out of Hodges's arms, but before he could get his footing, Hodges landed a cowboy-style haymaker that nearly sent the guy over the safety lines.

"Don't kill him either," I yelled, this time managing to drag Hodges off the guy's limp body after only a few earnest socks to the head.

"Motherfuckers," Hodges shouted, his face toward the heavens, as if blaming the divine.

"Agreed. But right now we need to get them into shore. I've got to go check on Jaybo. Can I trust you not to heave this one overboard?"

He said I could, though reluctantly.

I went below and doused the flare with the faucet from the galley sink. Then I tugged Jaybo's dead weight up onto the salon settee. I checked his pulse and felt a faint patter. I rolled him over onto his stomach and secured his hands and feet with heavy-duty zip ties. Then I went up to the cockpit and repeated the procedure with Jaybo's sidekick while explaining my plan to Hodges.

"Help me toss these assholes onto the picnic boat," I said. "I'll take it to Hawk Pond while you follow in the *Carpe Mañana*. Can you handle that?"

He looked disdainful.

"I've handled boats twice this size, not even drunk at the time," he said.

"Good," I said, then added, "Glad we fucked them up?"

He grinned his homely, too-wide grin.

"Yeah. We fucked them up good."

JOE SULLIVAN, two patrol cops, and an ambulance met me at the dock. I'd called him on the way in, and assured him he could leave his post long enough to make the collars. It was hard to tell him much more than the basics, but there'd be time for that.

I also placed a call to Ross Semple, with whom I had a more detailed conversation. He told me he could fulfill my request, provided the players were available on such short notice. I thanked him and ended the call without further conversation. I had other calls to make.

Jackie told me she could get to Southampton Town Police Headquarters well ahead of me. I asked her to hold her fire until I got there, and she agreed, difficult as that was for her. Then I called Amanda and told her I was feeling overwhelming love for her and my daughter, Allison, though I didn't have time to explain how having a shotgun fired at you can ignite this sort of sentimental response. She was happy to hear the words anyway, and even conceded similar feelings, something it wasn't in Amanda's nature to easily do. So we got off the phone abruptly after that, though not unhappily.

Ross met me in the reception area, so I didn't have to go through Officer Orlovsky. I felt like royalty. He walked me through the squad room, and no one looked up, so radio silence had been honored. We went into the interrogation room and sat at the table after he scrounged up an ashtray and immediately started stinking up the place with nearly irresistible cigarette smoke.

"Are they coming?" I asked him.

"They are. Edith and Oksana. Veckstrom's off today, out there firing up the masses, so we'll have to wait for that."

"You knew all along," I said.

He pointed at me with the end of his burning cigarette.

"Suspected. Big difference."

He tilted back in his chair and rubbed his blossoming gut.

"You were in a tight spot," I said. "You trusted Sullivan and could have used his help, but he was in a bad way after his wife left him, and didn't need extra trouble. Better to get him out of the way, which explains why he so easily got the leave to help me in New York and on Oak Point. There was no one else on the force you could trust the same way, not here and not in the city, so you thought, what the hell, get Sam and Jackie involved. Can't hurt, and they might turn up something."

Everyone has little tics and petty habits that you barely notice, though often recall when describing the person, which become more prominent the longer you know them, and if you're their spouse, are usually featured in divorce proceedings.

These things are often most apparent when stress is building, and Ross had a larger than average repertoire. Which probably explained why the cigarette twirling, face rubbing, ear probing, perilous chair leaning, and eye twitching seemed far more conspicuous than usual.

"I've made worse decisions," he said, his grin not completely devoid of humor.

"You suggested Edith Madison do the same. You're the trusted advisor."

"Is that what she called me?" he asked.

"She had suspicions of her own. But both of you were constrained by the politics. You were vulnerable to accusations of using police and prosecutorial powers to further her agenda. A resolution had to come from outside the usual channels, the standard process."

As usual, Ross kept his thoughts close to his vest as I spoke. It might have come naturally, though years investigating homicides and running a police department had undoubtedly honed the skill.

"Don't forget about your friend Aldergreen," he said. "You were motivated."

Sergeant Lausanne opened the door and told Ross that Attorney Swaitkowski was still waiting in another interrogation room. Ross said she could join the party.

"What did I miss," she asked, dumping her flour-sack purse on the table, "and why did I miss it?"

I brought her up to date as well as I could without giving advantage over to Ross in the cat-and-mouse game we were playing, still not knowing if I was the cat or the mouse.

"Can we be in the interview?" Jackie asked.

Ross put out both hands in an exaggerated display of equanimity.

"Why the hell not," he said.

So we sat killing time, which for me and Ross involved allusions in half-forgotten Latin, and for Jackie nervous pecking on her smartphone, until Miss Lausanne poked her head in again to announce the arrival of Edith Madison and Oksana Quan. Ross left and Jackie and I waited in silence for about ten minutes, after which the door opened again and Oksana walked in, escorted by Ross Semple, whose hand on her back looked less tender than assertive.

Oksana dropped her leather briefcase on the table and sat across from Jackie and me. She let out a bored huff, ignoring Jackie, but looking at me through half-lidded eyes. Even in the unfriendly fluorescent light, they looked like brilliant, tiny blue worlds.

Ross sat at the head of the table, giving him distance and perspective on all three of us. He took the pack of cigarettes out of his pocket, then seemed to have second thoughts, and put them back.

"Miss Quan," he said, "we know you were admitted to New York University law school based on a manufactured undergraduate record. As soon as we provide the New York State Justice Department with incontrovertible evidence of this fraud, you will be relieved of your responsibilities as assistant district attorney. You understand that."

Her eyes let go of mine and drifted over in his direction.

"Bully for you," she said, and started to stand up.

"There's more," said Ross, his voice a low rumble. "Sit down."

She sat back down, a tinge of alarm breaking through the icy cast of her face.

"This is your one opportunity to avoid the most serious charges by showing a willingness to cooperate," he said. "You've had plenty of these conversations yourself, so you know where we're going."

"Does Edith know about this?" she asked.

"I guess she does," said Ross. "She brought it to me in the first place."

Oksana shrank a few inches into her chair after gathering up her briefcase and squeezing it to her chest.

"I'm saying nothing without counsel present," she said.

"Fine," said Ross. "Then I'll do all the talking." He decided in favor of lighting up the cigarette, ignoring Oksana's disgust. "About a year ago, Jaybo Flynn was approached by the Southampton Town Police on suspicion of drug trafficking. Mad Martha's wholesale seafood business had provided the ideal distribution point for heroin coming in off the fast boats, like Joey Wentworth's, to be sliced up and packed inside bags of frozen shrimp and local bluefish for shipment Up Island and parts west.

"Flynn revealed to the investigating officer that he had knowledge that would seriously compromise the standing of a certain Suffolk County assistant district attorney. Fatally compromise, from the standpoint of her career. Flynn was desperate for any leverage he could use to avoid arrest, or at least mitigate the subsequent charges. He had no idea just how fortuitous his gambit was. Because, rather than bring this knowledge to the appropriate authorities, the officer approached the ADA in question. He had in mind a deal of his own."

"You have quite an imagination," said Oksana.

"Actually, I don't," said Ross. "I find it gets in the way of logic and reason."

It didn't seem like a good time to bring Einstein into the discussion, so I kept my mouth shut.

"Veckstrom," said Jackie.

I thought the chief would tell her to keep her mouth zipped as well, but instead he said, "Go ahead, counselor. We're listening."

"It wasn't for the money," she said. "He had all he'd ever need courtesy of his wife. What he needed was a way to keep that wife happy. He needed status, a position in life commensurate with her place in society. For that, your boss's job would do just fine. His qualifications were thin, but his rich wife was more than willing to fund a serious campaign against an opponent who hated campaigning, and could be easily portrayed as used up and out of touch."

"It was still a long shot," said Ross. "Edith wouldn't just wilt away in the face of a fight. But maybe she could be taken out some other way. Maybe there was something damaging in her performance as DA, or in her private life, that only her most trusted colleague would know. And as it turned out, like Jaybo Flynn, he hit pay dirt."

Oksana's face stayed set in stone, though a touch of pink started to show on her cheeks and on the small bit of skin exposed by her modest silk blouse.

"It was a tidy quid pro quo," said Jackie. "Jaybo Flynn stayed out of jail, Lionel Veckstrom had a way to eliminate Edith from the race when it was too late for another candidate to take the field, and you got to keep your career. Enhanced when the grateful new DA took the helm. Each of you had something on the other, but that would just strengthen the bond."

Since Jackie was allowed to blather away, I decided to weigh in.

"Things weren't quite tidy enough, though, from your point of view," I said to Oksana. "There was still some cleaning up to do. A few loose ends, in particular Alfie Aldergreen, who set things in motion by spilling your secret to Jaybo while eating a free meal out of the back of Mad Martha's. With access to the police files on confidential informants, you knew he was Sullivan's snitch. That was too big a vulnerability. So you circled around to Jaybo, gave him his options, and the son of a bitch took it from there. Eliminating the other two CIs was an extra precaution, and for Jaybo, a nice bonus, since it allowed him to take over Joey Wentworth's leg of the drug run. Lilly Fremouth was just an innocent bystander."

"Like Allison," said Jackie.

I let that sink in before continuing.

"She rang you in," I said. "You and Jaybo. It was my fault. I told you she went to RISD. I was already another loose end that Jaybo tried to deal with by smashing in my rear windshield with a meat mallet from the restaurant. And running me down with the fish van. And you tried to sic Bennie Gardella on me with some nutso story that I was out to take down the Southampton cops. It was clear that Allison had no memory of the attack, but Jaybo and his partner were committed by now, and gave it another try out on Oak Point, knowing I was gorging myself on fried flounder back at their restaurant. But like Sullivan said, the Acquillos aren't that easy to dispense with."

I didn't share another of Oksana's strategies for dealing with me, though I'm sure the thought crossed Jackie's mind.

"I don't need to sit here and listen to this," said Oksana.

"I'll bet we'll find your DNA in Allison's apartment," said Ross. "And Jaybo's. So yes, you do have to sit here, because in a few minutes you're going down to processing where we'll take a sample of your blood, after we snap your picture and get a set of prints. You are familiar with that little ritual, am I right?"

The pink on her cheeks bloomed into red.

"I need an attorney," she said.

"You do," said Ross. "Maybe Miss Swaitkowski's available."

"Not on your life," said Jackie.

Ross let Oksana make her call from the interrogation room while the two uniformed officers waited outside. The rest of us walked down the hall to the conference room next to Ross's office where he met with people he'd rather not have stepping over his stacks of paper.

Edith Madison was already there, holding a Styrofoam cup of coffee between two hands. She looked up at us as we settled in around the table, her face notably thinner and more wrinkled than when I'd seen her last. She was in casual clothes, and her white hair, never fully tamed by the tight bun, was pulled back with a felt-covered headband.

"I owe you all an apology," she said, without preamble.

"No you don't," said Ross.

"Oh, but I do," she said, in a quiet voice. "Especially for the rough treatment I gave these two."

"You had no choice," said Ross. "Oksana had to believe you were appalled by your decision to ask for their help."

"Apology accepted," said Jackie, "though I agree it isn't necessary. I'm used to rough treatment from the DA."

She didn't bother including me in all that.

"When did you suspect Oksana?" I asked.

Apologies aside, she didn't seem to relish speaking with me.

"Veckstrom seemed to know too much about the DA's office. Nothing that couldn't leak out one way or the other, but he was too knowledgeable, too in command of our day-to-day challenges and issues. He's a smart fellow, and I expected

him to be good on the stump, but not that good. I didn't
know anything about his relationship with Mr. Flynn or any
of that. It wasn't until I spoke with Ross, who'd heard rumors
of police on the take, that the greater suspicions arose."

I wanted to get more out of her, but Ross got extra fidgety
and moved to shoo us out of the room. Before that could
happen, I pulled the folded piece of paper out of my back
pocket, unfolded it, and put it down in front of her. She took
awhile reading it, then looked up at me.

"Where did you get this?" she asked.

"It showed up in my mailbox," I said. "Don't know who
sent it."

I told her I'd kept it to myself, so she could stop looking at Jackie and Ross Semple as if we were all in on some
conspiracy.

"What do you intend to do now?" she asked.

I shrugged.

"Nothing," I said. "It's your decision. I'm not dumb enough
to stick my nose into something like that."

She folded the paper up again and slipped it into her purse.

"Don't sell yourself short," she said, and let Ross usher
us out the door.

I could hear Jackie sputtering something like "What the
hell was that all about?" quietly enough that I could pretend
not to hear it.

When we got to reception I asked Ross about Veckstrom.
He told me two uniforms had been dispatched to wait for him
at his big house on the ocean. They'd pick him up there,
presumably away from the eyes and ears of the media.

"I want him to myself before the shit entirely hits the fan,"
he said. "That boy's got some explaining to do."

"He's not the only one," said Jackie.

Back in the fresh air, she didn't waste a lot of time before
saying, "Out with it."

"It was for your own good," I said.

"I doubt that."

I waited until we were safely away from anyone coming in or out of the HQ to tell her.

"After we paid that visit to Fenton's cousin Mike Gilliam, an envelope showed up in my mailbox, and like I told Edith, nothing inside but a single page."

She didn't bother asking the next question, so I didn't insult her by holding back the answer.

"It was a copy of a bill from Edith's veterinarian," I said. "It covered the three days her cat was being treated for some intestinal blockage."

"On one of those days her husband went out the window," she said.

"Gilliam probably figured I'd get there eventually, so he did what he could and hoped for the best. If I'd showed you that invoice, you'd be obligated to bring it forward. Not an ideal way for a defense lawyer to build rapport with the district attorney's office. Anyway, like I said, I want Edith to make the decision herself, either way."

"This is what Veckstrom and Oksana had waiting as an October surprise," she said. "Leaking Edith's grief counseling was just a shot across the bow."

"I'm guessing Oksana was the only person outside Gilliam's squad who knew the truth. When Veckstrom approached her, she knew she held the ticket to paradise."

Jackie absorbed all that for a moment, then asked, "How do these sociopaths manage to find each other?"

"Secret handshake?"

CHAPTER TWENTY-SIX

Edith Madison wasn't the only one moved to issue an apology. At least mine was more sincerely felt, consumed as I was by self-reproach. On the way back to Oak Point, I ran through the usual string of what-ifs, beginning with my full-out quest to uncover Alfie Aldergreen's killers. The way I made myself a conspicuous target, hoping to draw fire, to force an error by the opposing team.

Instead I managed to get my beautiful daughter beaten up and nearly killed, the person whose safety and well-being was to me the most cherished in the world.

I'd piled up a pretty big mountain of regret and remorse over the years, but this time it felt like the thing had grown big enough to topple over and bury me forever.

Allison would have none of it. Neither would anyone else after I'd gathered the Oak Point crowd out on Amanda's patio to break the latest news. I had to listen to my daughter and Amanda, well supported by Joe Sullivan, beat me nearly senseless with claims of my good intentions and admirable tenacity, until I had to concede a few points to get them to knock it off.

After that the vodka, wine, and wet, early autumn breeze off the Little Peconic worked their sorcery and all talk turned to the happily inconsequential.

This worked out well until I got a call from Jackie Swait-kowski, who'd heard from Ross Semple moments before. Apparently when Lionel Veckstrom failed to show up as scheduled at his house, the uniforms went to look for him, an easy job since he'd never left the hotel room his people had booked Up Island to plot his ongoing campaign strategy.

They found him in the bathtub with a bullet in his head, delivered by his service weapon through the soft tissue under his jaw, which an experienced cop like Veckstrom would know was the surest way to commit a successful suicide.

It turned out that Oksana used her phone call in the interrogation room to alert him that disaster was on its way, rather than contact her attorney, which in hindsight was the better choice. There was plenty of time to secure representation, but only that moment to effectively claw her partner in venality into the abyss that awaited her.

What should have been a triumph for Edith Madison turned out to be a crisis for the New York State Board of Elections, after Edith withdrew from the race stating that the grief caused by her husband's death had, in fact, affected her more than she realized, and thus she no longer felt confident in her ability to fulfill her duties as Suffolk County district attorney

So the governor appointed an interim DA, and the board scheduled a special election on a date agreed upon by the two parties, who had a bitch of a time scrounging up viable candidates.

None of whom I knew, which I hoped was a good thing.

I only heard this on the radio, having no interest in the proceedings, preoccupied as I was with my healing daughter, goofy dog, self-contained girlfriend, and the capricious acts of nature enacted daily over the sacred Little Peconic Bay.

ACKNOWLEDGMENTS

I'm deeply grateful to my military counsel, who not only provided technical verisimilitude but had a material impact on the story itself, and the development of several key characters. My brother, Lieutenant Colonel Whit Knopf, US Army Reserve, Retired, helped me with various details and nomenclature, and importantly, put me in touch with Colonel Christopher Carney, also of the USAR, who saw active duty in Bosnia-Herzegovina and Afghanistan; and his son, Captain Shannon Carney, a 1994 West Point graduate, who served five years in command of a platoon of Bradley Fighting Vehicles in the Republic of Korea.

Invaluable help with crime scenes and the people who inhabit them (dead and alive) was provided by Michelle Clark, Medicolegal Death Investigator with the Connecticut Medical Examiners Office, and an inspiration to crime writers across New England. Other insights into police practice and procedure came courtesy of Connie Dial, mystery novelist and former journalist, undercover narcotics investigator, and commanding officer of LAPD's Hollywood Division, and Lieutenant Art Weisgerber, of the Norwalk Police Department Crime Scene Unit.

In the colorful English-accent department, thanks to Matt Hilton, mystery writer and Cumbrian lad in good standing with the Geordies. And for all-out translation, thanks to adman Erkan Kurt, adviser on all matters involving Turkish tough-guy expletives.

Back stateside, legal adviser (strictly fictional) Rich Orr again helped quite a bit on what you can and cannot do within the law, as well as what you can and cannot get away with in the political realm.

Psychologist Dr. Mark Braunsdorf informed the passages relating to mental illness—behaviors, attitudes, and the professional world that surrounds it all.

Food and beverage maven, and former stinkpot operator, Tim Hannon, gave some excellent insights into illicit transport behaviors among the marine trade, as well as alternative applications of certain kitchen implements.

Additional nautical support was provided by Kip Wiley and Chick Michaud, service managers at Brewer Pilots Point Marina in Westbrook, CT.

Thanks for the briefing on student life at Rhode Island School of Design by graduates Jane Cleary, graphic designer at the Chrysler Museum, and Shana Aldrich Ready, of the "Ropes of Maine" nautical bracelets.

Any errors or misrepresentations anywhere in the book are the author's responsibility alone.

Special thanks to my esteemed presubmission readers Jill Fletcher, Sean Cronin, Randy Costello, Leigh Knopf, Mary Jack Wald, and Bob Willemin, who work hard to keep me out of editorial trouble. And of course Marty and Judy Shepard and their exemplary Permanent Press team, notably copy editor Barbara Anderson, cover designer Lon Kirschner, and production artist Susan Ahlquist.

And as always, thanks to my wife, Mary Farrell, whose brace of Lakeland Terriers does so much to focus a writer's concentration.